Georgia Le Carre

ALSO BY GEORGIA

The Billionaire Banker Series

Owned
42 Days
Besotted
Seduce Me
Love's Sacrifice

Masquerade

Pretty Wicked (novella)

Disfigured Love

Hypnotized

Crystal Jake

Sexy Beast

Wounded Beast

Beautiful Beast

Click on the link below to receive news of my latest releases and exclusive content.
http://bit.ly/1Oe9WdE

Cover Designer:
http://www.bookcoverbydesign.co.uk/
Editors: Caryl Milton, Elizabeth Burns & IS Creations
Proofreader: http:// http://nicolarheadediting.com/

Dirty Aristocrat

Published by Georgia Le Carre

Copyright © 2015 by Georgia Le Carre

The right of Georgia Le Carre to be identified as the Author of the Work has been asserted by her in accordance with the copyright, designs and patent act 1988.

ISBN: 978-1-910575-26-0

Dedication

To all my readers who like it hot and hotter!

'A secret's worth depends on the people from it must be kept.'

—Carlos Ruiz Zafón, The Shadow of the Wind

CHAPTER 1

Ivan de Greystoke
The Dirty Aristocrat club, London

'**L**ord Greystoke? You wouldn't be related to Tarzan, would you? You sure look a lot like him,' she said with a brainless little giggle.

'I could be, if you're into that sort of thing,' I drawled lazily.

'I am,' she said eagerly, her hands greedily skimming the muscles of my upper-arms.

So I pulled her, I think her name might have been Kitty, into the dark shadows of the club, and slammed her up against the wall.

'Oooo,' she cooed, her breath reeking of peppermint and alcohol, and her eyes wide and begging me to fuck her. Against the thin material of her outfit her nipples were straining.

I grabbed her dress—well it could have been a dress if it had not had such a drastic hemline: the poor girl had to fight all night to keep it down—and pulled it right up to her waist, exposing a black satin thong. The material had crept into her pussy and sliced her lips into two juicy pieces of luscious flesh.

Nice.

I got down on my haunches, and with her pussy at eye level, curled my fingers around her sweaty waistband and pulled the ridiculous scrap of cloth down. The lips had been shaved bald, but she'd left a small triangle of curly dark hair above them.

Awww ... fuck. Not another fake blonde.

Still she was plenty sexy with a big red mouth that looked like it loved being stretched over a cock, real boobs, a round ass, and extra long legs, but her golden hair was the thing that had pulled me to her like a magnet.

It would just have to be doggy style.

She stepped out of her thong. It was still warm from her body heat. I brought it to my nose and inhaled. The wonderful musk from a night spent rubbing up to a lusty, moist vagina filled my nostrils. I became hard immediately.

'Oh kinky,' she squealed. It occurred to me then that her voice was too high and a tiny bit irritating.

Honey, you don't know the half. I stood up and pulled her dress down over her ass cheeks and gave one of the round globes a good slap. 'Now, get back on the dance floor, you dirty little slut,' I growled.

'Pervert,' she accused.

'I like to think so,' I said and stepped aside.

She giggled and pushing herself off the wall, began her bottom-wriggling walk towards the dance floor. Already her dress

was beginning to ride up her ass, and I could see a glimpse of one smooth ass cheek peaking out from under the material. She made no effort to pull her dress back down. Instead she looked back over her shoulder at me, sultry as a summer night in Istanbul.

I smiled slowly, approvingly.

She pretended to drop her purse and with her legs apart and bottom pushed up and out, bent down from the waist to pick it up. Yup, both her pussy and asshole were on full display. The flash of so much pink drove my cock crazy.

She made it to the edge of the dance floor and turned to face me, pushed her breasts out, and started rubbing her nipples as she gyrated her hips. With every movement she made, her skirt was creeping higher and higher. There was something animalistic and raw about the way she stood, her thighs spread apart and glistening with sweat, utterly unashamed of the fact that she was making a spectacle of herself.

Looking intently at me, she deliberately lifted her hands over her head so her pussy lips poked out from under her dress. She was giving every man in that club a show. I looked around. Hundreds of eyes were crawling all over her body. Who doesn't recognize wet pussy? A man dancing next to her accidentally/purposely rubbed his hand along her bare ass cheek.

Crude drunk.

That ass was made for this dick.

 3

I gave him the stink eye as I prowled towards her, hornets in my blood. He jumped out of the way as if he had come across a rabid dog. It was hot and crowded on the dance floor and the beat of the music was as relentless as jungle drums. I stuck my leg between her spread thighs and she ground her hungry pussy onto the leather of my trousers. Her tits were bouncing and shaking with excitement.

She wanted a show.

And fuck was she going to get one.

Picking up her left leg, I curled it around my waist. Her naked pussy splayed open. With one smooth movement my hand slipped down her stomach. Here kitty, kitty. I cupped her pussy.

Fuck she was wet! I ran my middle finger down her slick slit and slipped it into her. I had planned to be subtle, but she grasped my hand with both of hers and shoved my finger deeper into her hot, hungry hole. I pushed another two digits in and she groaned in ecstasy and frenziedly ground herself on me.

The other dancers stopped their pathetic little moves and stood in a circle to cheer me on. It was that kind of club, seedy. And this was her thing. Exhibitionism. Letting people watch while strangers finger fucked her. This was what she whispered into my ear at the bar earlier.

Music crashed and lights flashed around us while she rode my hand. She didn't last long. The heat. The music. The audience. She

climaxed all over my hand. Her juices squirting on the dance floor.

I pulled my fingers out of her and looked down at the hot, sticky mess I had made between her open thighs. Her legs were still trembling and her pussy lips were red and swollen from the vigorous finger fucking I had just given her.

Yeah, she'll do nicely.

I released her leg, and with a satisfied smirk she pulled her dress over her dripping bits. She'd had her fun and now it was my turn. I dragged her off the dance floor towards the men's toilets. Unlike her I like a bit of privacy when I get my rocks off.

Here I wasn't Lord Ivan De Greystoke. Here I was Ivan the Terrible.

Tawny Maxwell
Barrington Manor, Bedfordshire

'Whatever you do, don't *ever* trust them. Not one of them,' Robert whispered. His voice was so faint I had to strain to catch it.

'I won't,' I said softly.

'They are my own flesh and blood so they are dangerous in a way you will never understand. Never let your guard down.'

'OK,' I agreed immediately. I just wanted him to stop talking about his children. These last precious minutes I didn't want to waste on them.

He shook his head unhappily. 'No, you don't understand. You can never let your guard down for even an instant. Never.'

'All right I won't,' I said in a placating voice.

'I will be a very sad spirit if you do.'

'I won't,' I cried passionately and reached for his hand. The contrast between our hands couldn't be greater. Mine was smooth and soft and his was gnarled and full of green veins, the skin waxy and liver spotted. His nails were the color of polished ivory. The hand of a sixty-year old dying man. I lifted it to my lips and kissed it tenderly.

His eyes glowed briefly in his wasted, sunken face. 'How I love you, my darling Tawny,' he murmured.

'I love you. I love you. I love you,' I cried desperately. I felt frightened. I didn't want to lose him. The world stretched out as a cruel and lonely place without him.

'Keep our secret and they cannot touch you,' he said calmly.

'I won't tell anyone,' I promised.

'No one,' he insisted.

'No one,' I agreed, shaking my head.

He sighed. 'It's nearly time.'

'Don't say that,' I urged even though I knew he was right.

His eyes moved to the window. 'Ah,' he sighed softly. 'You've come.'

My gaze swung to the window. It was closed. The heavy drapes pulled shut. Goose pimples ran up my arms. 'Don't go yet. Please,' I begged.

He dragged his gaze reluctantly from the window. His thin pale lips rose at the edges as he drew in a rattling breath. 'I've got to go. I've got to pay my dues. I haven't been a good man.'

'Just wait a while.'

'You have your whole life ahead of you.'

He turned his unnaturally bright eyes away from me. Looking straight ahead, and with a violent shudder, he left this world.

For a few seconds I simply stared at him. Appropriately, outside the January wind howled and dashed itself into the shutters. I knew the servants were waiting downstairs. Everyone was waiting for me to go down and give them the bad news. Then I leaned forward and put my cheek on his still, bony chest. He smelled strongly of medicine. I closed my eyes tightly. Why did you have to die and leave me to the wolves?

In that moment I felt so close to him I wished this time would not end. I wished I could lie on his chest, safe and closeted away from the real world. I heard the clock ticking. The fire in the massive hearth cracked and spat. Somewhere a pipe creaked.

I placed my chin on his chest and turned to look at him one last time. He appeared to

be sleeping. Peaceful, at any rate. I stroked the thin strands of white hair lying across his pinkish white scalp. I let my finger run down his prominent nose and it shocked me how quickly the tip of his nose had lost warmth. Soon all of him will be stone cold.

I wondered whom he had seen at the window. Who had come to take him to his reckoning?

My sorrow was so complete I could put my fingertips into it and feel the edges. Smooth. Without corners. Without sharpness. I had no tears. I knew he was dying two hours before. Strange because it had seemed as if he had taken a turn for the better. He seemed stronger, his cheeks pink, his eyes brilliant bright and when he smiled it seemed as if he was lit from within. He seemed so much stronger. I asked him if he wanted to eat.

'Milk. I'll have a glass of milk,' he said decisively.

But after I called for milk and it was brought to him he smiled and refused it. 'Isn't this wonderful?' he asked. 'I feel so good.'

At that moment I knew. Even so it was incomprehensible that he was really gone. I never wanted to believe it.

'In the end you wanted to go, didn't you?'

There was no answer.

'It's OK. I know you were tired. It was only me holding you back. You go on ahead. Find a place for me.'

He lay as still as a corpse. Oh god! I already missed him so much.

'I understand you can't talk. But you can hear me. When it is my turn I want you to come and get me. I'll be expecting you to come in through the window. Go in peace now. All will be well. They will never know the truth. I will never tell them. To the day you come back to collect me.'

I opened up my nail kit and began to do his nails. With gentle care I filed and polished the yellowed nails.

'There you go. That will last you forever. No one will ever be able to say I did not do a good job.'

Then I began to cry, not loud ugly sobs, but a quiet weeping. I didn't want the servants to hear. To come rushing in or call the doctor waiting downstairs to come in and pronounce him dead. I knew what waited for me outside this room. Another hour ... or two won't make a difference. This was my time. My final hour with my husband.

The time before I became the hated gold digger.

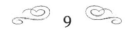

Ivan De Greystoke
Mayfair, London

I closed the door and turned to her. She was looking up at me with a secret little smile. As if she knew something I didn't. Quite frankly, I profoundly disliked girls who played these kinds of mind games.

'Can I take your coat?' I offered, shrugging out of my leather jacket and throwing it onto a chair nearby.

She turned away and stood quietly with her back to me. Her accent and her manner were all reminiscent of someone from a much higher class than the people who frequented The Dirty Aristocrat. Perhaps it was that disconnect, that thread hanging loose from the sweater that made me bring her home with me. I helped her out of her coat and tossed it on top of mine.

'Want a drink?' I asked walking into the hallway.

'Screwdriver, heavy on the screw.'

I turned to face her. Her expression was bland and yet there was something about her. Something I couldn't place my finger on. She was sexually aggressive in a fake way. I understood Kitty. You got what you saw. I didn't understand this one. 'What did you say your name was again?'

She smiled. 'Chloe.'

'Right,' I said and carried on walking towards the bar. I poured myself a large cognac.

'Did you fuck the slut in the red dress in the toilets?'

I let the fiery liquid run down my throat. 'Yup.'

'Was she any good?'

I looked at her curiously. 'Why did you come back with me?'

'I liked what you did to her on the dance floor.'

Somehow that was not the end of the story. 'And?'

She bit her bottom lip. 'My mother knows yours.'

My mouth tightened. Ah, the loose thread waiting to ruin the entire sweater. 'Look, I went to The Dirty Aristocrat for a mindless fuck and I brought you back here for more of the same. If you're looking for a relationship I'm not the guy for you.'

'You're exactly the guy for me. Wouldn't you like a hot little cocksucker to finish the night with?'

I smiled, my cock twitching. 'Yes, I could do with a hot little cocksucker.'

'Then you won't find a better one this side of the Atlantic,' she said huskily.

I threw my drink down my throat and said, 'What are you waiting for then?'

The hot little cocksucker got on all fours and fucking *crawled* towards me. When she reached me she rose to her knees, unzipped my jeans, and with her mouth stretched wide around my cock she began to swallow it like she was starving.

Tawny Maxwell
Barrington Manor, Bedfordshire

It must have been hours before I finally raised my head from his body and looked around me. The fire had become embers, and there was no warmth left in him. A light pinkish-brown mucous was coming from his nose. I scrunched a bit of tissue and gently inserted it into his nostrils.

'You're free now,' I whispered.

There was no answer.

Time to go find the good doctor. Time to start the whole merry-go-round. I straightened my back and walked down the great staircase with its blue runner carpet. On the walls were priceless paintings. I found the doctor sitting in the Yellow Room reading a book. It was a grand room with several sets of superb hand-painted Oriental wallpaper depicting stunning artwork of idyllic scenes from everyday life in ancient China.

'He's gone,' I said, and it surprised me how perfectly calm my voice was. Inside I felt as brittle as glass.

Dr. Jensen's eyes flashed dislike. He had always distrusted me. His absolute loyalty to Robert meant I would always be the enemy. He would never allow me to administer any medicine. Always it was him or the nurse who did it. Everything was kept in a locked cupboard. As if they were afraid I would hurry him to his death. They had no idea.

If only they knew my secret. But they will never know. I will never tell.

Wordlessly, he ground his cigar into the side of the ashtray and, snapping up his little black bag, left the room. I hugged myself and thought of him entering the room, checking for signs of life in Robert's still form. The room felt cold. I looked at the goblet of brandy he had left half-drunk and I wished for a drink, but I needed all my wits about me.

I stood by the window staring out at the darkness until Dr. Jensen's image appeared on the glass beside me.

'He's stone cold,' he accused.

The cold hostility was like a slap in my face. He would never have spoken to me like that while Robert was alive. I reacted in the only way I knew how. Aggressively. Not the way Robert had taught me, but how my mother had fought all her wars.

'What do you expect? He *is* dead,' I said.

His eyes were narrowed and suspicious. 'How long ago since he died?'

'He went ages ago.'

 13

He shook his head disapprovingly. 'You don't do yourself any favors.'

I turned around and looked at him challengingly. 'Would you pity me if I cried?'

'I wouldn't waste my pity on you. You got exactly what you wanted. It's all yours now. Congratulations,' he sneered.

A bead of cold sweat raced down my spine. I never wanted it. My dream was completely different. It was small and sweet and wonderfully ordinary. 'It's not all mine. Robert had three children.'

His smile was cold and his voice stabbed. 'Come, come, Mrs. Maxwell, let's not play childish games. I think we both know how this cookie will crumble. You worked bloody hard for it and now you get the lion's share.'

I took a deep breath. This was just the beginning. Everyone was going to say this and if they did not, they were going to think it. I might as well get used to it. 'Robert was no one's fool. He did exactly what he wanted at all times.'

'I'll have to put it into my report that you did not come down to report his passing earlier.'

'Go ahead,' I challenged. I had nothing to fear. There was nothing anybody could do to me now.

He stared at me. 'Why didn't you? I might have been able to do something for him.'

'What for, Doctor? So he could suffer the bedpan for a few more hours or days? He had enough. He *wanted* to go.'

'Careful, Mrs. Maxwell, you're revealing your true self and it's not a pretty sight. I suggest a little more subterfuge,' he said scornfully.

It was at the tip of my tongue to rage at him, but what would be the point? Robert was gone, and I was alone in a poisonous environment.

'Perhaps it would be better if you left,' I told him.

We stared at each other. I couldn't understand why he was suddenly so openly hostile.

His lip curled. 'What an excellent suggestion.'

With my insides churning and my heart troubled, I watched him stalk out of the room. When I could no longer hear the tread of his shoes, I turned around and carried on staring at the night. It had begun to snow. Soft, beautiful, big flakes. If it carried on it would be a winter wonderland tomorrow.

The butler, James, came in.

I saw his reflection in the glass and turned around to face him. He had been with Robert for twenty years. His bearing, as always, was erect and stiff.

He coughed politely.

'What is it, James?' I asked. My voice sounded tired and listless.

'I'm sorry, Ma'am, but I couldn't help overhearing. It used to break his heart to think of you alone in this den of vipers. You have to find a way to be nice to them. You can't carry on like this.' His voice was grave.

I hugged myself. The quiet strength of James seemed to cross the room and calm down my chaotic thoughts and feelings. 'I know, James. I know I'm not doing myself any favors. Why can't they see how much I loved him?'

'It doesn't matter what they think, Mam. The master always knew.'

I smiled sadly. 'Yes, he knew.'

He nodded. 'Can I get you something to drink, Mam? A pot of tea perhaps?'

'A pot of tea sounds lovely. Thank you, James.'

'Very good, Mam.' He bowed in that old-fashioned way of his. I never thought man-servants like him existed outside of books. In fact, when I first came to this house, it shocked me to learn that he carefully ironed any little creases out of the morning newspapers before he brought it up to Robert. He was already at the door when I opened my mouth and called to him.

He turned around, his expression polite and helpful. 'Yes, Mam.'

'Thank you. Thank you for everything you did for Robert,' I said.

His expression softened. 'It was an honor to serve Mr. Maxwell.'

I bit my lip. 'You will stay on, won't you, James?'

He allowed himself a small smile. 'I'd be delighted to, Mam.'

 16

'Thank you.' I almost cried out with relief. I needed people around me I could trust. The last time I felt this vulnerable was when my mom died and I was all alone in a trailer and medical bills I could not pay. At that time, I had run away from my past, my debts, my pain. I had come to England and found Robert.

'If you are agreeable I will take upon myself the task of informing the staff of Mr. Maxwell's passing.'

I exhaled. 'Yes, thank you. That would be very helpful,' I said in acceptance of his kind offer.

He paused.

'What?' I prompted.

'It would be prudent for you to inform Lord Greystoke as soon as possible,' he said quietly.

I felt every cell in my body shrink at the thought.

'It is what Mr. Maxwell would have expected.'

I nodded slowly. 'Yes, you are right. Of course I will. I'll call him right now.'

'I'll go and see about your tea.'

When his footsteps died away I walked up to the phone. I knew Ivan De Greystoke's number by heart. Robert had forced me to memorize it.

'He is the only one you can trust. No one else is to be trusted. No matter how nice they seem to be,' he said again and again.

I dialed Ivan's number and waited nervously. Some part of me hoped he was asleep and I could just leave a message on his answer phone, but he picked up my call on the third ring.

'Is he gone?' His voice was business-like and abrupt. It was so late, I must have pulled him out of bed, and yet he sounded so wide-awake, so unyieldingly hard.

'Yes,' I whispered, my hands gripping the telephone hard.

'I'd like a word with the doctor. Put him on,' he instructed. No sorry for your loss, or any kind of platitude for the grieving widow.

I closed my eyes. 'Dr. Jensen left a little while ago.'

Even across the distance I felt his displeasure and irritation. I could imagine exactly the forbidding expression on the most arrogant, aristocratically chiseled, granite-like face I ever had the misfortune to meet. The only redeeming feature in his firmly set, hard face were the surprisingly full and sensuous lips.

Although I had assumed he must have been in bed, in my imagination he was still dressed in a suit or a dinner jacket. I had never seen him in anything else. Each one splendidly cut and terribly civilized, but unable to hide the raw, animal power of the lean, powerful body beneath. At six feet five inches and wide shoulders rippling with muscles he towered over most men.

I heard a woman's voice, glamorous and trailing, ask, 'Who is it, Ivan darling?'

His reply was brisk and left no doubt as to exactly what he thought of me, a pain in his neck. 'No one. This will only take a few minutes. Get back in bed.'

Stung, I said the first thing that came into my head. 'I'll start making the funeral arrangements tomorrow.'

There was a second, pregnant with disbelief before he spoke again, his voice strangely quiet. 'Everything has already been taken care of. My secretary, Theresa, will liaise with you so you know where and when to present yourself.'

'Oh,' I said, at loss for words.

Of course, how silly of me. Obviously, everything had been done. It was not how it was when my stepfather died, when we ran around trying to arrange everything while he lay in the mortuary. Robert's funeral would be a well-attended affair requiring much planning ahead.

'I'll see you at the funeral,' he said, and the line went dead.

I replaced the receiver back on its hook and slowly walking to the window stared at the coating of snow on the edges of the windowpane. Ivan De Greystoke had eyes the color of sunlight falling on gray tinsel, but the moment Robert introduced me as his wife, they became glacial.

Expressionlessly, he extended his hand and took mine in a warm, strong clasp. I had not wanted to shake hands with him, not wanted any part of his body to touch mine, but when our skin met, I was overcome with the strangest sensation of wanting to prolong the contact.

The same was not true for him. He had pulled his hand away almost immediately as if he was touching something dirty or repulsive.

'May I say, Robert,' he had mocked dryly, 'you are the envy of every man tonight.'

Robert glowed with pride and happiness, but I blushed, because I knew he did not mean it. He detested me. He thought I was a gold digger and nothing I said or did subsequently made him change his mind. His dislike was eventually obvious even to Robert, so I never understood why he made Ivan the executor of my trust. At first I begged him not to let Ivan be in charge.

'Why for god's sake? You know he doesn't even like me,' I pleaded.

'He's the only one I can trust,' Robert replied sadly.

Ivan De Greystoke
Mayfair, London

I killed the connection and stared out of the window. So: he was dead.

The man who had the thing I wanted for so long was dead. I tried to imagine her at Barrington Manor. She must be in the Yellow Room. That would have been where the doctor had waited. He must have insulted her as he had been instructed to do. And yet her voice had been cool as if she was fucking giving me the weather forecast. I could almost picture her. Jeans. Blouse. Her long blonde hair in a thick plait down her back. Her mouth: as if butter wouldn't melt in it.

Little gold digging bitch.

I had a raging hard-on.

'Ivan,' Chloe called from the bedroom. Her voice lilting. She had not lied. She really was the hottest cocksucker this side of the Atlantic and I've had enough to know. I walked to the bedroom.

She was lying on the bed with her legs spread open. She was the kind of girl that you could have done anything to. I walked up to her. She began to play with herself, slowly inserting her finger into her hole.

Very nice.

'Sit up,' I told her.

She obeyed immediately.

'Plait your hair into a rope down your back.'

'I don't have a tie, you dirty aristocrat you,' she said flirtatiously.

I went to my wardrobe, extracted a random tie and threw it at her.

She began to plait her hair. She tied it as best she could with the tie.

'On your hands and knees.'

She couldn't wait to comply. The tight star of her ass was just begging to be filled. I grabbed the golden plait and pulled it hard. Her head jerked back. She moaned and wriggled her ass invitingly.

Fucking gold digger you. Then I fucking raped her, Tawny. I mean Chloe.

Tawny Maxwell
Barrington Manor, Bedfordshire

I turned away from the phone and a bright shiny glint caught my eye.

The simple gold band on my finger.

I looked down at it and a distant memory tugged. I was only eighteen. Robert and I had flown to Vegas. We stayed in the most expensive hotels. We behaved like kids. Everybody - waiters, people in shops, random people we met, all of them thought he was my father. Again and again we had to

correct them. Then he produced this ring and we got married.

It was the most awful wedding you could imagine.

The only people in that chapel were the man officiating the wedding, a heavily made-up, relentlessly smiling woman who was supposed to be helping, and a sad looking man Robert had dragged off the street and paid a hundred dollars to witness the ceremony. Even the kiss he gave me had been chaste.

Then we had both run out laughing.

Robert drove us in a brand new, baby blue Cadillac to the desert to see the sun setting. I had never seen such a blazingly red sun before. It was so beautiful I began to cry.

He put his finger under my chin. 'I have a plan, Tawny. It's a great plan. A long-term plan. But you must trust me. Even when it seems as if everything is nose-diving into the deep blue sea you must trust that I know what I am doing.'

I didn't know it then, but he was already very ill and he knew it.

'All right,' I whispered, and I meant it.

Even now, when it looked as if his plan had already nosedived into the deep blue sea, I still cling to the idea that his plan would work. That in the end my life would not be completely ruined and the things we had done become all for nothing.

I touched the gold circle. It had become so loose it spun around my finger, only my

knuckle kept it from falling away. I slid it off and let my fist close around it. I clutched it so tightly the metal dug into my flesh.

The ring was warm, but he was gone. Irrevocably. Forever. I would never see him again. See his bright eyes and hear his cackling hyena laughter. I unclenched my fingers and looked at metal lying in the middle of my palm.

In my head a voice taunted. 'Lies, lies all of it.'

I put the ring back on my finger and closed my eyes with terrible pain in my heart.

The Funeral

CHAPTER 2

Lord Greystoke
In My Apartment

I stood in front of the mirror, pulled the knot on my black tie up towards my throat and ran a brush through my hair. It was Robert's funeral today and I guessed I'd be rubbing shoulders with his little widow.

I'm not a religious man, never have been, but when I first looked into Tawny Sinclair's bottomless blue eyes I started praying.

Praying for my fun loving, whore of a dick.

She was wearing a lime green dress. It wasn't tight, or short, or revealing, but it made me actually crave her body. The desire to have her, open her silky legs, and get my dick inside her was so strong I wanted to pick her up like a Neanderthal, throw her over my shoulder and carry her off to my cave. In fact, I hadn't had a hard-on like that since I was a teenager.

Then Robert looked at me with shining eyes and proudly introduced me to her. She was his fucking wife! My stepmother.

The revelation was a punch in the gut. I had to fight not to let my jealously show. Fuck, I was insanely jealous. I thought of his frail body over hers, and I wanted to throw up.

I turned to her and ... oh, butter wouldn't melt in her mouth. She smiled innocently at me with those wide blue eyes and I knew then.

This one's not figuring to leave your ass and take half.

This one's gonna stick around until you fall on your ass and take it all.

A year later he asked me if I would take care of her after he was gone.

'Just protect her until she's twenty-one,' he pleaded.

I said, 'No. Ask some other fool,' and walked out.

But you know what? I was fucking dying to do it. Even the idea of him asking someone else made me feel sick to my stomach. But I couldn't just give in. I had to prove to myself and him that I wasn't soft on her.

I wanted the old man to beg me. And I wanted to agree reluctantly. Let her understand that she was *never* going to twist me around her little finger like she had done to him. I guess Robert knew me very well. He was a crafty old bugger after all. He played my little game and eventually I did the right thing.

I promised to take care of her after he was gone. The responsibility sat on my chest for a while, then without me realizing it seeped into my heart. I had taken her under my wing and though I hated to admit it, I liked it. I wanted to be her protector.

I put the brush back on the dresser and the doorbell rang. I went to answer it.

'Wow! You're pretty unrecognizable in a suit,' Chloe drawled.

I let my eyes wander down her body. She definitely looked the part. Perfectly cut black dress, skin-tone court shoes, black pearls and scarlet lips. 'And you look like you buy your tampons from Gucci,' I replied.

'What makes you think I don't?' she countered.

I looked her in the eye. 'You won't think because I asked you to a funeral that we've got something going, will you?'

'Of course not. Actually, I thought you had a funerals fetish and I might come in handy.'

I smiled and she smiled back.

'Do we have time for a quickie?' she asked, cupping my crotch.

'Does a dog need to be taught to fuck?' I asked, and pulling her in, tore her panties off, slung on a condom, and fucked her right there in the corridor.

'What, I wonder, would all the proper Lords and Ladies say if they ever met Ivan the Terrible?' Chloe purred.

I didn't bother to respond. I just leaned my forearms against the wall, my dick still deep inside her, and felt glad I was taking her with me. Anytime I felt like my dick was growing hard for Tawny Maxwell, I would just drag Chloe into the nearest closet and fuck the shit out of her. Besides, it would tell Tawny Maxwell not to bother going ahead

28

with any poor-little-rich-widow act she might have planned.

In time I'll fuck Tawny, of course. That was always the grand plan, but it would have to be on my terms. She would be nothing but a toy. My toy. One of my many toys. Eventually when I got tired of her, I would walk away.

I was not making the mistake Robert made.

I was not falling for her.

No. No. Fucking no.

Never.

No woman would ever make me stay.

Tawny Maxwell

The day dawned, freezing cold and white.

I stood in front of the mirror in full black: felt hat; knee length, two-piece suit; tights and shoes. My nearly waist-length, straight hair neatly knotted at the nape of my neck.

Yet, I did not look very funereal.

Black simply accentuated the smooth alabaster of my skin, and made not only the blue of my eyes dazzle like the brightest sapphires, but my blonde hair shine like spun gold.

I went back into the walk-in closet and stood looking around it. At the white carpet, the lovely French oil painting of a young ballet dancer, the velour tailor's dummy, the pure white doors and drawers that moved or swiveled noiselessly to expose the expensive designer clothes, bags, shoes, belts, scarves, hats, and accessories.

This was my favorite place in that whole house. Sometimes I came in here and sat for hours. No matter what problems I had, just being in here on my own calmed me. This was my zen space. Maybe it was because I still couldn't believe that this closet was almost as big as our entire trailer back home in Tennessee. I looked around longingly. How I wished I could simply hide in here amongst my sweet smelling clothes for the next few days.

But it was not to be.

Today had to be faced.

I keyed in the safe's code, opened the heavy door, and selected a slim velvet box from inside. I lifted the lid and held up the large teardrop sapphire pendant necklace lying inside. I looked at it and felt no emotion. I could still remember gasping with shock when I first saw it. I had never seen anything so fabulously beautiful. Even my untrained eye could tell that it must have cost Robert a small fortune.

Two point five million pounds, actually.

I could still remember that day like it happened yesterday. It was my eighteenth

birthday. The weather was bad and we had decided to stay in. Just the two of us. In those days he was still well enough to come downstairs so we sat in the blue drawing room by the big fire. Him in his big armchair and me curled up at his feet on the carpet.

Oh, we had so much to talk about then. He had so much knowledge and I was like a sponge. Soaking everything up. I was his Eliza Dolittle. I arrived at this house a teenager bringing with me all my trailer trash talk. Patiently, slowly, day by day, he had polished away all the rough edges.

On that day he had leaned back in his chair and watched me with indulgent eyes as if I was a particularly exuberant puppy.

'Oh my little Tawny, if only you had come into my life sooner,' he whispered.

'I'm here now,' I told him.

That was when he pulled the box out of his dressing gown pocket. I started crying with joy and sadness. Even then we already knew his time was short. Then he cried and, later, when we were both drunk on champagne vodkas, he insisted I must wear it at his funeral.

With a sigh I fixed the necklace around my neck. The metal was cold. I turned around and looked at the mirror. Against the pallor of my skin it glowed like blue fire. I stared at my reflection and heard his raspy voice again.

'It's going to be all old money, so venerable, so impeccable, so I want you to blow their silly socks off. Don't hold a dreary wake for me. Throw a party. Serve the most expensive champagne. Hire musicians, dancers and fire-eaters. Make an inappropriate toast to me. Celebrate. But whatever you do don't try to please those painted peacocks. They'll despise you for it.' His eyes twinkled. 'You will be richer than most of them. Let them bloody well try to please you.'

'Won't they just hate me all the more?' I asked.

'So be it,' he said cryptically.

I frowned, confused. 'Why? Why make them hate me more?'

His eyes gleamed with unholy light and I got a glimpse of the cutthroat businessman he must have been before he became sick and weak.

'Because a greater prize than my money waits for you, my darling.'

No matter how much I asked he would not explain what he meant. 'Trust this old man,' he said.

As I stood in front of the mirror, the memory of that night was so clear I could almost smell the burning logs, see the wicked gleam that shone in his cunning eyes, and hear the rich timbre of his voice. I touched my hat and his voice filled my head.

'A good hat is a thing of beauty, but worn at the right angle it is a work of art.'

Of their own accord my hands moved to tilt the hat to a rakish angle.

I smiled at the effect. 'You were right, Robert. A small tilt makes all the difference.'

Without warning, pain like a stone wedged in my chest. Oh, Robert. I will never see your kind, clever face again. Suddenly the cocoon of protective numbness was ripped from around me and I felt as if my world was spinning out of control. Oh my God! All those people waiting for me and every single one of them bearing hostility and envy in their hearts. I felt as nervous as a long-tail cat in a room full of rocking chairs. I placed my palm on my midriff and took deep breaths.

You need to be one hundred percent, Tawny. It's an elite club you've wandered into. You can't let our side down.

I looked into the mirror, my eyes were wide and panicked. *No, this won't do.* I forced myself to think of my mother.

'Oh, Mama. I'm afraid,' I whispered.

The last thing she told me before she died floated into my head. '*Ain't nothing to be afraid of, honey. Take a deep breath and count to what you are. A ten.*'

I started to count. There was a discreet knock on the door and I whirled around and walked quickly into my bedroom. 'Come in,' I called.

The housekeeper stood holding the door handle. 'The car is here. Are you ready, Mam?' she asked.

Oh, how I miss being back in warmth of the Southern states again. Everyone here was just so damn polite and so hidden. There

were layers and layers of mannerisms to trip on and show yourself up as the foreigner, the person who did not belong.

'Yes,' I told her nervously.

'Good. It's getting late and the car is waiting downstairs.'

'Thank you, Mary.'

She nodded and closed the door softly.

I went to the dresser and picked up a framed photograph of Robert and me. My arms were thrown around him. The sun was shining and we were both laughing. It was taken during my first summer in Barrington Manor. I didn't know he was ill then. He did though. My heart felt like it was in a vise. I put the photograph down, slipped into a thick woolen coat, and pulled on my black gloves. *Deep breath,* I told myself and went down the curving stairs and out through the great doors.

Outside it had stopped snowing, and there was neither wind nor cloud. Just sub-zero temperatures and everything covered in a pristine layer of white. Even the leaf stems were white and sharp. Winter was always my favorite time at Barrington Manor. I looked around at the still wonderland with a kind of dull pleasure. I recognized its beauty even though I was too heavy hearted to actually appreciate it.

Still, how bizarre! All this now belonged to *me*.

The chauffeur opened the back door of the black Rolls Royce. I walked up to the car and

with a grateful smile in his direction, slipped into it. It was warm inside the car. I breathed in the apple scented air-freshener and arranged my skirt over my legs. Then I leaned back and calmly stared out of the window at the passing scenery. My mind was mercifully blank. I would make it through this ordeal. I would wear my brave face. No one would ever know what I was really feeling.

Let them think I was a cold bitch.

CHAPTER 3

Tawny Maxwell

As soon as we reached the church I spotted my stepchildren.

Robert's oldest child, Rosalind, looked at me. Her eyes were shining with malice and hatred. She was the most dangerous and most vindictive of his children. At twenty-nine she was a tall, dark-haired, plain woman who had unfortunately inherited Robert's big nose and strong jaw. She was married to a spineless man who hardly spoke at all and had two young children I had never met.

The middle child, Bianca, was much prettier since most of her genetic identity came from her mother. Unfortunately, or perhaps fortunately for me she was not the sharpest pencil. She was engaged to a well-known footballer who was standing beside her looking rather ill at ease. She was what my grandma would have called an undercover hater. She flashed me a fake smile before turning back to her fiancé and leaning her fair head dramatically on his shoulder.

The youngest was Robert's only son, Dorian. He was the best looking of the three.

He had a full head of straight, dirty blond hair, smoldering blue eyes, and dimples when he smiled. He had charm and confidence, but underneath it lurked something dark. Much darker. In truth I was very wary of him. Slowly, he winked at me.

It was so insolent, so inappropriate, and so disrespectful, I felt something crumple up and die inside me. Robert was wrong. I couldn't handle these people. Not in a million years. Not alone, anyway. They were a totally different species than me. They were devious and cunning and false.

My shocked gaze ricocheted away from Dorian and fell upon Ivan. He stood head and shoulders above everyone else. He was wearing a dark coat and his hair was slightly disheveled from the wind.

Still, it was his face that made me freeze.

Against the whiteness of the snowy landscape it was as if it was hewn from stone. His eyes were almost silver and shone out of his face like lights directly into my eyes. Through the distance something passed between us. Something electric that made the hairs on my body stand. I couldn't look away. It was the strangest feeling. As if I had been walking for a long time in the wilderness and I was finally home. I had come home. As if even the life that I had lived was not my own. My life was with him.

Then he nodded at me and I inclined my head before my eyes slid away to the woman with him. The obligatory blonde. Beautiful, spoilt and from the same class as him. How many times I have seen them, and yet this time I knew a moment of piercing pain. Where I come from we just call it jealousy.

The jealousy surprised and confused me.

Must be the grief, I told myself. *He is not for you, but he will be there for you.*

No matter how cold and distant he was to me I could trust him. He was the only one I must trust. Robert had said so and I trusted Robert. That man will fight your corner, he said.

I turned my eyes towards the church entrance. Yes, I could do this. I would die before I let Robert down.

Ivan's secretary hurried up to me.

'Good morning, Mrs. Maxwell.'

'Hello, Mrs. Macdonald,' I said. All of a sudden I felt a jolt of panic. I clutched her hand. 'The flowers on the top of the casket. They are dusky pink roses, aren't they?'

She smiled faintly. 'Yes, they are.'

'Oh good. For a moment there I thought I forgot to tell Janice.' Janice was Robert's secretary and she had liaised everything with Mrs. Macdonald.

'You didn't,' she said gently.

'They were his mother's favorite flowers,' I explained.

'I see.' Her voice was polite.

Mrs. Macdonald's gaze slipped down to my pendant. I understood. She could not help herself. It was so special. In a rush her

eyes came up again, her expression almost guilty.

'Come this way,' she said and led me inside the cold, damp cathedral filled with hundreds of people. A sudden hush fell upon the gathered mourners. We walked up to the front pew silently, our shoes loud on the limestone floor. I could feel all their heads turn to watch me. Some were curious, others were openly envious or resentful. I am the American girl who appeared from nowhere, married a multimillionaire, and in two years was the heiress of a sizeable fortune. They don't know I loved him entirely, the good, bad, the ugly. I loved all of it. They could not see my silent grief.

They just saw the gold digger.

All I could see was the rosewood coffin. Pale morning light streamed in through the stained glass of the cathedral's windows and fell on his fine casket with its gilt handles and a lush arrangement of dusky pink roses on it. Inside I knew it was silk-lined and perfumed with sandalwood oil.

Robert was lying inside.

I took my seat on the hard bench and listened to the minister's words and the well-spoken words of all those people who had not come to see him in his last months. They waxed lyrical about what a wonderful man he was. Then Rosalind took the pulpit for her tribute. I kept my eyes to the grey flagstones while dry-eyed, she told the world about her great love for her father.

'I sat on his knees. I loved him. Before he lost his mind he knew I loved him. But the sickness, it turned his brain to mush and he could no longer tell the difference between true love and the lies of strangers. People who were only there for what they could get. Daddy, I love you. Always. Wherever you are.'

Then it was Ivan's turn. I looked up and his gaze met mine. I dragged my eyes away in confusion.

I sat staring at the floor and listened to old stories about Robert. Things I never knew. He loved to hunt. I never knew. He could out drink any man. I never knew. There was so much I didn't know. I only knew him when he was sick and diminished.

My eyes became wet, but I did not even realize that I was crying until my ribs began to heave as if they were suddenly too full of sorrow. I put my head down and closed my eyes. It was good that he was gone. He was in pain. It was a good thing.

Of course, I did not take the stand. I told him I wouldn't. 'Please, Robert, don't make me do it.' And he had smiled. 'No, your love is pure. What is pure must never be examined. It will hurt the impure.'

So I didn't speak at his funeral service. Instead there would always be a part of me still dressed in full black, sitting on the front pew at his funeral, listening to 'The Lord Is My Shepherd.'

CHAPTER 4

Tawny Maxwell

https://www.youtube.com/watch?v=1EUgORVsECs

There were six pallbearers dressed in black suits and white gloves. The gold handles glinted in the sunlight as they lifted the casket onto their shoulders. I saw Ivan go up to the man in front, tap him on the shoulder, and take his position. I stared at him. Why, he must have loved Robert too. I stood at the bottom of the church steps and watched them carefully load Robert into the back of the hearse.

I tried to imagine him, lying in there as if sleeping. Finally peaceful.

They closed the doors and I turned away and walked towards the convoy of stationary black cars. My car was at the head of the long line. As I was about to get into it I felt a hand on the sleeve of my coat. I turned around, startled.

Rosalind smiled at me. Her dry-eyed crying had not smudged her make-up at all. Everything was perfectly in place.

'Would you mind terribly if I rode in the car with you? Seeing that you are alone and ours is overcrowded with my obnoxious brother.'

I didn't want her in the car with me, but there were people all around us avidly watching the stepmother and daughter's interaction, and I could hardly turn her down. Mercifully, the ride to the cemetery was a short one.

'Of course,' I said.

With a triumphant smile she stepped in front of me and slid into the car. She did not close the door as if she expected me to close it for her and go on over to the other side. I stood bemused, the color rising into my cheeks.

Fortunately, Barry hurried around and closed the door. Looking at me kindly he said, 'Come around to the other side, Mam.'

I cleared my throat and, keenly aware of many eyes watching, followed him around the back of the car to the passenger door on the opposite side. Barry opened the door and I murmured my thanks and sat stiffly on the seat, leaving as much space between her and me.

As soon as Barry turned out of the church's driveway and into the main street, Rosalind ordered Barry to put the partition glass up.

I turned to her, my face devoid of expression.

Her face was equally drained of any emotion. 'Can you tell me why we are all being summoned to Barrington for the

reading of the will as if all of this was a particularly bad Hollywood production?'

I frowned at her. 'How else would the solicitor tell us what is in the will?'

She sighed elaborately. 'I realize that you are a bit of a redneck, but it is actually customary for all beneficiaries to simply receive written notification from the solicitor.'

'Right,' I said slowly. She said redneck like it was a bad thing. Still, it was in Hollywood movies that I learned of the custom of reading a will to a gathering of people.

'I'll take it then that you have no idea,' she said coldly.

I put on my sweet face. 'No. Ivan made all the arrangements.'

She narrowed her eyes skeptically and let them slide to my pendant. An ugly look crossed her thin, proud face. 'Do you know the contents of my father's will?'

Suck it up buttercup. He didn't leave it to you. 'Not really. I guess we'll know after the funeral.'

'But most of it's going to you, isn't it?'

I took a deep breath. This needed to be said. 'You want his money, but you never once came to see him in the last six months.'

Her eyes widened with fury. 'How dare you lecture me on my relationship with my father?'

'You hurt him when you never brought your children to see him once in the last two years. He wanted to get to know them.'

'Are you mad? Do you think I would expose my children to that pedophile?'

I gasped in shock. 'How could you say that about your father?'

She looked at my horrified expression with revulsion. 'Why are you pretending to be so shocked? I can say that because it's the truth.'

'It is not,' I said, holding on tightly to my temper.

'How old were you when you came to him?'

'I was seventeen,' I said indignantly. How could she even think that about Robert?

'I rest my case.'

'He ... we ... didn't do anything, then,' I stammered. I wanted to say so much more, but I couldn't. I had to protect my secret. Otherwise it would have been all for nothing.

'God, you disgust me. Both of you.'

She turned away from me and rapped smartly on the glass. When Barry put it down she ordered him to stop the car. As soon as the car came to a halt she got out. Before closing the door, she had one last parting shot for her stepmother.

'Just in case no one told you. It's not the done thing for the grieving widow to deck herself in her best jewelry to attend her husband's funeral.'

Slamming the car door, she walked to the next car in the procession, the car that she should have been in. I turned my head and watched her enter it and shut the door.

 44

I turned back to face the front. 'Carry on, Barry,' I whispered painfully.

My hands were trembling. I touched my pendant and closed my eyes. Oh, Robert. How could she even think that about you? I hoped wherever he was he had not heard our nasty conversation.

Quietly, Barry put on his stereo system and Nick Cave's poignant and heartfelt song *Into My Arms* fills the car. No gesture could have been more appropriate at that moment. The unexpected thoughtfulness of that mostly silent man took me by such surprise that I could not even speak. Our eyes met in the rearview mirror, mine full of silent gratitude, and his kind. I smiled and he nodded.

When we arrived at the cemetery, I got out of the car, and Ivan strode up to me. His face was a like a thundercloud.

'Are you all right?' he asked harshly, his eyes sharp.

His breath smoked. I looked up at him, still dazed. The wintry air invaded my lungs and stung my eyes. Did he also believe that Robert was a pedophile? Was that what everyone was thinking? I nodded.

'Why did she get out of the car?' he demanded.

'It was nothing.' I paused. My mind had gone blank, but he was staring at me with demanding eyes. 'Er ... she ... wanted to know why we are having a reading of the will at the house and not getting written notifications.'

45

'Why on earth did she ask you that? She knows damn well that I'm the executor of the will.'

'Anyway, why are we having it done this way?'

'Because I wanted it this way.'

I looked at him curiously. 'Why?'

'I have my own reason. Now come on,' he urged, and I fell into step with him. We walked briskly, our heads bowed on a path that glistened like white quartz.

It was strange that my hurt and confused heart should find the presence of that cold, hostile man reassuring and a comfort. I stole a glance at him. His face was closed and distant. He gave the impression that he was not even aware of me.

As soon as we reached the freshly dug grave, the woman he had come with caught up with us and linked her arm through his. There was no mound of exposed soil. Everything was white and completely beautiful. A woman handed out pink rose stems. I held it in my gloved hands. I looked around at the assembled. We were the official mourners, come to pay our last respects.

Our breaths rising in little visible puffs.

During the whole simple ceremony, no one spoke. There was just the slight sound of people shuffling. Then the coffin was put on the wooden lattice that had been erected over the hole in the ground.

Someone sang a song. Her voice was beautiful. It rose up in the cold, still air and seemed to hover over us. I put the pink rose I had been given on the casket and kissed the cold smooth wood before I moved on. I didn't stay to watch anybody else. I was freezing cold. I walked quickly to the car and got into it. The interior was blissfully warm. I took my leather gloves off and rubbed my hands together. They were like ice.

That was it. Robert's funeral.

I had survived it.

Now there was the ordeal of the reading of the will to be endured.

CHAPTER 5

Tawny Maxwell

Now I ain't saying she's a gold digger, but old fool that he was, he pulled up in a Benz and no pre-nup.

The reading of the will had been set for 2.00pm in the music room, a bright rectangular space with many tall windows. It had a splendid German grand piano in it that nobody played. Robert told me that it was bought for Rosalind when she was a child, but she had refused to play it after a few lessons.

Chairs had been brought in and arranged in two rows of semi-circles facing the antique writing table. Robert's solicitor, Nathen Jeremly, sat at it. He lifted his head when I walked in and smiled professionally. James, the butler and Mary, the housekeeper were sitting with their spines upright on the last two chairs at the back. I smiled at them and, going to the first row, sat at the end of the semi-circle. Next to arrive were my two stepdaughters. They looked around haughtily before coming to the front row and sitting in the middle seats. Neither spared me a glance.

Dr. Jensen arrived, nodded at me coldly, and took his seat next to Robert's daughters. After him my stepson sauntered in, a glass of red wine in his hand. He caught my eye and smiled lazily at me. He made his way to the chair next to his sisters. They hissed something at him and he laughed.

The chairs were quickly filled by some of Robert's family. Most of whom I had never met. Last to arrive was Ivan. He did not take a chair but closed the doors and stood just inside them. I saw him nod at the solicitor.

Nathen cleared his throat.

'Well, looks like everyone is here,' he began. 'Here is the last will and testament of Robert James Maxwell.'

He picked up the document and began to read it.

'I, Robert James Maxwell, Barrington House, Bedfordshire, England, make oath and say as follows:

For a long time, the words the solicitor was reading seemed like wind in the trees. A rustle. I heard a gasp of surprise and then a grateful sniff from the housekeeper and I vaguely heard the butler's name mentioned. Of course, he made no discernable show of joy.

One by one the drone of the solicitor's voice referred to the relatives I did not even know existed. I only pulled out of my daze when I saw Dr. Jensen jump up from his chair.

'After twenty years. After all I did for him,' he spat. Shaking his head in disgust he stalked out of the room. I was shocked. I couldn't believe that Robert had not rewarded him. He was so loyal to Robert. I frowned wondering why Robert had done that to him. To the best of my knowledge Robert never once mentioned that he did not intend to properly reward him. The door slammed.

I looked at my stepchildren. Their eyebrows were raised and they were exchanging surprised glances with each other.

The solicitor cleared his throat.

I started listening carefully. The next person was Rosalind. The solicitor read out the stipulation that Robert's trust would pay her a lump sum settlement of a quarter of million and twenty thousand pounds monthly for life when she interrupted him furiously.

'Twenty thousand pounds per month? Is this a joke?'

The solicitor looked up, his face impassive. 'Mrs. Montgomery, please be assured that everything you are hearing is the last will and testament of your father. I have arranged for a copy of the will to be couriered to you.'

She jerked her chin towards him. 'I'm not staying for this farce. I'll contest this. It is perfectly obvious that he was not of sound

mind.' She turned towards me, her eyes burning with pure hatred. God! She looked as mad as a mule chewing on bumble bees. She stood and began to walk away, but then changed her mind and headed towards me. She stood over me. 'Well, well, how clever you have been,' she shrieked.

I said nothing. My face was flaming with embarrassment. Everybody was looking at us.

'You think you've won? You think you've got it all?' she spat viciously.

'I haven't got it all,' I said softly.

'He left crumbs for us, his blood children, and the big prize for his trailer park child bride.'

She swung her hand suddenly and it was so quick I did not have time to move my head, but the blow never came. I turned my head and Ivan had her hand in his grip. His face was like stone. She twisted her head and looked at him, her chest heaving with fury. 'Stay out of this. You're not even part of this family.'

'That's my ward,' he bit out. 'I've been entrusted with her well-being.'

'Let go of my arm,' she gritted.

He released her arm. 'Don't force me to take an injunction out on you.'

'She cheated him. He was ill,' she cried.

'He wasn't ill, Rosalind. You may have been able to make that argument if you had not tried to have him declared incompetent six months ago, but he passed the battery of

tests your team of doctors had run with flying colors.'

'He became more ill after that.'

'He wrote his will two years ago.'

She frowned and then gasped. 'As soon as he met her.' She looked down at me and screeched, 'What did you do to him, you little conniving bitch?'

'That's enough, Rosalind. Your husband is waiting outside. You should go home.' Ivan's voice was so cold and hard I jumped.

'This is not the end of it,' she promised before she stalked off. Bianca ran after her, but Dorian remained to hear that he too had been left exactly the same as Rosalind. A lifelong income of twenty thousand pounds and a quarter of a million pounds.

He turned to look at me and sardonically raised his empty glass as if in a toast. I looked away.

Then it was Ivan's turn, and I was utterly surprised to find that there was no money for him at all. Not even a small token sum. All he had been left was a painting that he admired as a child.

After Ivan it was my turn.

The solicitor confirmed what Robert had told me. I had been given everything else. The entire Maxwell fortune.

CHAPTER 6

Tawny Maxwell

The wake was a great success. It was exactly how Robert wanted it, with a sumptuous spread of food, champagne, singers and even fire-eaters performing on the snow covered grounds.

In all the gaiety, music and people, I suddenly realized that I couldn't feel Robert anymore. This was his house and this was a wake for him, but his spirit seemed to be nowhere.

Stifling a desire to tell everyone to go home, I slipped out of the reception rooms filled with people and walked to his library. I paused for a moment before I opened the tall doors and went in. Immediately I was engulfed by the familiar smell of the room. Before he became truly ill this room used to smell of the tobacco from his pipe. Now it just smelt of old leather and that cream he used to use.

Inhaling deeply, I walked into the cold darkness. I felt as if the past lived in that darkness and I could simply walk into it. I journeyed deeper into the room and went up to his desk. I let my fingers trail on the polished wood surface. I switched on the table lamp. It threw a pool of yellow light on the polished wood and I thought of Robert sitting here, his head bowed, reading.

'Oh, Robert,' I breathed.

'Hello, Mother,' a voice drawled from the doorway.

My spine stiffened. I turned around slowly.

Dorian was standing at the doorway holding a glass of red wine. His handsome face was slightly flushed, his lips red, and his hair a little mussed. In the half-light he looked as beautiful as one of those Greek statues, but from the way he held the glass, with it slightly tipped to one side, told me he was more than a little drunk.

'I'm not your mother,' I said coldly.

He took a sip of wine. 'Don't worry. I won't hold that against you,' he said slowly.

I hoped my face did not show the disgust I felt. It never failed to amaze me how little of Robert remained in his children.

'What do you want, Dorian?' My voice sounded harsh in the empty room.

He strolled towards me. Something about his unnaturally casual stance made me shudder. He stopped in front of me and the desire to take a step back was almost overpowering, but I held my ground.

I was in my home. He was the intruder. What could he do to me? One scream and a whole host of people would come running. He was just trying to scare me, but there was

nothing to fear. I was only helpless when my nail polish was wet, and even then I could still pull a trigger if I had to and he was just a spoilt rich kid. I refused to give him the satisfaction of knowing that he had succeeded in rattling me.

'Do you know I've always wanted to fuck you?' he said conversationally.

I stared at him steadily, my face wiped of all expression. Robert always said that the art of war was to never show your hand. Always take your enemy by surprise.

'Well, I've never wanted to fuck you,' I replied with elaborate politeness.

He took a long slow sip of his drink and regarded me quizzically over the rim of his glass. 'Hmmm ... how could he possibly have satisfied you?' he wondered aloud.

I smiled coldly. 'I loved him.'

Amusement flashed in his eyes. 'Come on, the sex was shit though, wasn't it?'

I smiled slowly. 'Not that it's any of your business, but I don't remember ever complaining.'

'If you think that kinky bastard's flaccid dick was good ...'

I laughed throatily. 'Poor, spoilt Dorian. So many women at his command, but all the twisted fucker wants is to do his stepmother.'

His eyes glittered. 'Pull your claws back in, Mother. There's no need for them anymore. You worked hard and fast. One moment you were polishing his nails, the next you were polishing his knob. You've won. Hands

55

fucking down. You've got it all. No one can take it away from you now.' A bitter smile shaped his mouth. He took a step closer. 'You don't even have to pretend anymore. So come on, at least give yourself a little victory fuck. You know you're gasping for it.'

'If you lay one finger on me—'

'So you cheat me out of my inheritance and you won't even put out. Even the lowliest hooker will let you fuck her after she's taken your money.'

'It was not your money,' I said through gritted teeth.

'No?'

'No. It was your father's money and he could have left it to a cat's home if he so desired.'

'But he didn't,' he whispered. 'He left it all to you.'

'Lucky me.'

'So how about the victory fuck then?'

'No, thank you. Now how about you get out of this library and go enjoy the party. Your father would have wanted it.'

His reply was to let his glass drop. It shattered at our feet, the wine splashing up to my calves. He used that moment when I was distracted and surprised to grab me and swoop down on my startled mouth. His lips crushed, his teeth hurt, and the fumes from the red wine choked me. He ground his erect cock into my horrified body. I raised my hands and tried to push him, but he was surprisingly strong.

'What the fuck do you think you're doing?' A voice like whiplash rang around the room.

Dorian released me unhurriedly and turned to look at his stepbrother insolently.

'Do you mind? I'm saying hello to my dear stepmother.'

My shocked gaze flew towards Ivan and found his blazing eyes fixed on me. The gray was like molten silver. Oh my god. What a terrible mess! My hand went up to my throbbing mouth. My knees felt like jelly, but most of all I felt soiled by the accusing look in Ivan's eyes. He thought I was a willing participant.

Feeling sick to my stomach, I stepped away from Dorian, but like a fool I stumbled slightly and from the corner of my eyes I could see Ivan make an involuntary movement as if to help me, but I placed my palms on the desk and stopped myself from falling.

'I should get back to the party,' I said shakily to no one and, without looking directly at either man, I walked past both. When I was outside the room I leaned against the wall and heard Ivan say in a hard voice, 'As a matter of fact I do mind.'

'Oh, don't be greedy, brother. I'm perfectly willing to share. You can have your turn next.'

'You're drunk.' Ivan's voice was hard and cold.

'And you're a hypocrite. Don't tell me you're not lusting after her because I've seen the way you watch her.'

'Go home, Dorian.' Ivan's voice sounded exasperated.

'Always the spoilsport,' Dorian said with a laugh.

CHAPTER 7

Tawny Maxwell

God! How I *wished* I had slapped him hard enough to make his arrogant, drunken head reel. It was a tangled web I was caught in, but I remembered my grandma's words, *In life you have to walk like you're on a runway.*

Dorian's ugly words were still ringing in my ears, but with my head held high, I forced myself to put one foot in front of the other and started walking back towards the sound of laughter and music. Oh, Robert. Why on earth did you think I could do this?

I ordered a glass of brandy from a waiter and drank it really quickly. The fiery liquid spread a warm glow into my numb limbs. I felt myself relaxing. I had not eaten anything for hours and the alcohol was making me feel almost floaty. The tension seeped away. I looked around at the room full of strangers. Soon this would be over. All these people would be gone and I would be alone. I could make my plans then.

At the other end of the room I saw that Ivan had returned to the gathering. He was coming towards me when the woman he had come with waylaid him. Thank god. A waiter approached me with a tray of food and I picked something up and popped it into my mouth. It tasted of nothing. A thin, long-faced woman in a dark gray suit came up to me. Her lips were thin and painted blood-red and her eyes were watery and pale. I had no idea who she was. I smiled.

'I'm so sorry for your loss, my dear,' she said without introducing herself.

'Thank you,' I said, feeling buzzed and hoping it didn't show.

'He was such a good man.'

'Such a good man?' I echoed.

To my horror a mad giggle escaped my lips. I covered my mouth. The woman's eyes grew huge with speculation. There was no way to explain that if she thought that he was such a good man she couldn't possibly have known him. He was a ruthless man. He told me so himself. *A man has to decide whether he wants good friends or he wants to be rich. He cannot have both. I chose to be rich.*

'Can I have a word?' a steely voice on my right asked.

I turned gratefully towards Ivan. His eyes were no longer molten silver but ice cold.

'Of course,' I said coolly.

The nameless woman excused herself and left.

'Don't make my job more difficult than it needs to be,' he grated.

Anger flashed through me. Fuck him. How dare he judge me? Still, I did not let him see

 60

my irritation. I twirled the stem of the crystal flute between my fingers and looked up at him with cold disdain. 'Do you really think I would encourage my stepson to assault me at my dead husband's wake?'

Something shifted in his eyes. He ran his hand through his hair. 'God,' he said. For a moment he looked as if he felt that by taking me on he had bitten off more than he could chew.

'Why did you have the reading of the will in that way? You must have known Rosalind would react badly. Did it please you to see her attack me?'

His jaw tightened. 'Don't be stupid. I needed to see all their reactions.'

'And now that you know, what help is it to you?'

'Time will tell,' he said mysteriously.

'Anyway, thank you for coming to my rescue just now.'

At that moment the woman he had come with slinked over and touched his arm. He stiffened, all expression leaching away from his eyes. Slowly, he moved his eyes away from me and looked down at her.

'Have you met Tawny?' he asked.

She raised one perfectly shaped eyebrow at the mention of my name and deliberately allowed her eyes to fill with condescending amusement. 'Ah, your stepmother? No, I haven't.'

Ivan seemed to wince when she referred to me as his stepmother. 'Tawny, meet Chloe Somerset. Chloe, Tawny.'

'How do you do?' she said in an offhand way.

'Good. Thank you for coming,' I said in an equally careless voice.

'I wouldn't have missed it for the world,' she said throatily and turned towards Ivan, her expression becoming playful. 'Darling, we need to be getting back. I have an early start tomorrow.'

Ivan frowned. 'I can't leave just yet. Why don't you let Paul drive you back?'

Chloe pouted at him. 'How long will you be? You know how ... *restless* I get when I'm in your bed.'

His voice was hard and impatient. 'Then perhaps you should go back to yours?'

I cut in. 'Look, you can go. I'm going upstairs soon, anyway. James will see the party out.'

'We need to talk,' he said sharply.

I nodded. 'Yes, I know.'

'I'm busy all day tomorrow. Are you free for dinner?'

Chloe took a quick intake of breath.

'Yes,' I said.

'Good. I'll pick you up at eight then.'

'It might be better if we just have dinner here,' I said quickly. I could not imagine anything more awkward than going out to dinner with him. Here at least I would be on my own turf.

 62

'See you at eight,' he said and, turning away from me, left the wake. It gave a small jolt of secret pleasure to see Chloe run to keep up with his striding figure.

CHAPTER 8

Tawny Maxwell

I was in the Yellow Room having a dry Martini when James announced Ivan's arrival.

My stomach contracted at the sight of him. He was like a force of nature. Even the air in the room changed. His hands hung languidly at his sides, but his entire body emitted the kind of tension of a prowling animal. From where I was I could make out the contours of his muscles under his shirt. Butterflies started fluttering in my belly. Suddenly the night ahead stretched as an uncomfortable, tense affair.

'Hello, Ivan,' I said nonchalantly from my seat. I had decided that I would be sophisticated and cool.

'Hello, Tawny.'

'Can I get you a drink?' I asked civilly.

He turned towards James. 'I'll join Mrs. Maxwell in whatever she's having.'

'Very good, Sir,' James said, and with a polite bow backed out of the room.

Ivan strolled towards the sofa next to mine, sat down, spread himself with his knees far apart, and fixed his silvery gaze on me.

I took a sip of my drink. 'Good day at the office?' I asked.

His eyebrows arched in surprise. He seemed to hesitate. 'I didn't go in today.'

I suddenly thought of Chloe. About how 'restless' she had been last night. 'Ah, the pleasures of being one's own boss,' I said. It had been my intention to sound light and sophisticated, but it sounded like sarcasm.

The silence stretched and I glanced at my hands. I could feel his gaze on me and, as much as I did not want to admit it, I was starting to get really nervous. I felt as if he was studying me, looking right into me. Interminable seconds passed. Finally, I looked up, my eyes defiant.

'What did you do today?' he asked.

I didn't miss the commanding tone in his voice. This was a man used to giving an order and having it obeyed. I looked into my drink. 'I'm afraid I didn't do much today,' I murmured.

In fact, I had spent my morning in Robert's room. It had brought me to tears because I walked in there expecting it to look like it always did and I found that the housekeeper had ordered the servants to strip the bed and remove the mattress. It had been taken away to be aired, but seeing the bed in that way shocked me and made his death real in a way that seeing him still and wasted inside the coffin had not.

I looked up and found him gazing at me expressionlessly. 'You must get so bored here.'

I met his look levelly. 'No.'

He seemed genuinely surprised and I felt a thrill of joy that I had caught him off guard. 'So you will carry on living here?'

'For the foreseeable future.'

He frowned. 'You don't plan on moving to London?'

'No.'

'Why not? You are a very rich woman now and London is very exciting when you are rich, beautiful and young.'

I felt myself blush. He thought I was beautiful. 'I will go to London when necessary, but I won't be moving there.'

'Do you go up to London often?'

'Well, I haven't used the London flat in nearly six months. I didn't like leaving Robert here on his own so I used to make sure that I finished whatever business I had and returned in time for dinner.'

James came in with a tray. Ivan thanked him and took his drink.

He raised it slightly. 'To you,' he said softly.

I looked at him warily.

'Well, what will you do now that Robert's gone?'

'I'll do what he wanted me to do.'

He stared at me with blankly. 'What was that?'

'For the last three years Robert bought islands with the intention of turning them into turtle sanctuaries.'

Ivan looked at me from narrowed, openly skeptical eyes. 'Robert was setting up turtle sanctuaries?'

I nodded. 'You seem very surprised.'

'I am,' he admitted. He leaned forward and the light from the candles seemed to flicker and shimmer in his extraordinary eyes. His eyes became alive and ... hauntingly beautiful. I blinked at the amazing transformation. With the shadows thrown under his cheeks he was ... suddenly ... wickedly hot! So hot that a strange urge from somewhere unknown dared me to reach forward and lick those curving, sensuous lips. I stared at him, my mind burning with the thought. He leaned back abruptly. 'What?' he asked looking at me suspiciously.

'I shook my head. 'Nothing. Er ... you were saying,' I croaked.

He leaned back in the chair and crossed his arms. 'I was saying Robert was like a father to me for ten years, but in all the time I knew him he never once showed himself to have an altruistic bone in his body.'

'He didn't want anyone to know.'

'Why?'

'I don't know. It was like his redemption or something. If he had told everyone about it, it might have morphed into something else.'

A thought occurred to him. 'Did you ask him to?'

'No, he once went to Asia and someone took him to watch turtles laying eggs. He saw a giant leatherback turtle heave itself up the beach well past the high tide mark, dig an eighteen-inch hole in the sand, lay about a hundred eggs in it and cover it. To his horror, he then saw the locals not only torment the exhausted creature by shining torchlights at it, kicking sand into its face, picking up its flippers and riding it, they also immediately dug up its nest and stole every single egg from it. He said it hurt him to see her cry. At that time, he didn't know then that her tears were actually a jelly-like mucous that she excreted to keep the sand out of her eyes, so he was much moved by her plight.'

He shook his head in wonder. 'Fancy that. The old boy was moved by a big reptile.'

'Leatherbacks are very beautiful,' I said.

'Well, I'm glad for him that he found something to love in his old age.'

I finished my drink. 'He loved you too,' I said softly.

He frowned and looked as if he was about to speak, but James appeared to announce that dinner was served.

I stood and Ivan held out his hand stiffly. I threaded my hand awkwardly into the crook of his, and together we went into the dining room. The long table had been set for two. For a moment I felt a pang of pain. This was our dining room. Robert's and mine. We used to laugh until tears poured down our cheeks.

I sat quietly while the soup was served.

'Bon appétit,' I said, and carefully slipped my spoon into the creamy leek and potato soup.

'Why did you stop visiting Robert?' I asked.

He picked up his glass of Sancerre and took a sip. 'I spoke to him on the phone.'

'I see.' I paused. 'Did he ever mention anything about Dr. Jensen?'

He didn't raise his eyes from his food. 'No,' he said quietly.

'I just can't understand why he was so mean to him in his will. He always spoke so highly of him.'

'The contents of his will were a surprise to me too.'

It was the weirdest thing. Nothing in his expression had changed, but I knew that he was being deliberately evasive. He knew something that he did not want to share with me. I stared at him until he raised his eyes and looked at me. 'He missed you,' I said softly.

His eyes flashed. 'And you? Do you miss him?'

I put my spoon down and looked him in the eye. 'With all my heart.'

He went quiet. Something powerfully intense simmered and rippled underneath the perfectly calm surface. A heavy, sizzling heat hovered in the air between us. We stared

at each other. Then his gaze left my face and swept down to my breasts. My heart jumped in my chest and the tips of my breasts started to tingle and ache.

For his mouth.

Suddenly there were crystal clear images of my mouth on his throat, down that hard chest, and lower still. My tongue trailing, my fingers dragging down a man's tight skin. My lips parted involuntarily and though I did not mean for the small moan of surprise and lust that escaped, it did. I was prepared for everything, but not this. What was this? I didn't go around lusting after men?

Especially not him!

The small sound was as if someone had slapped him, his head jerked upwards, pulling his wandering gaze back up to my face. For a second he continued to look at me as if he wanted to devour me, then he drew a sharp breath, and the sudden crack in his armor was gone. Wiped out. So completely I felt as if I had imagined the entire episode. The classically handsome face tightened once more into a hard mask and his eyes became chips of ice again. Cold. Detached.

'Sorry,' he said not sounding sorry at all, 'but I find this grieving widow act a bit hard to swallow. I don't know what your game is, but quite honestly, I don't give a damn. I'm executor of the trust until you are twenty-one and after that you are on your own, but in the meantime the less contact I have with you the better. Don't call me unless it is absolutely necessary. Please put all your expenses through my office. I'm not Robert. You can't bat your eyelashes and expect me to come running. I don't like chaos. I don't want to be distracted.'

I stared at him open-mouthed with shock. Where on earth did that come from? How could he go from sizzling hot to ice-cold? Then I became furious. How dare he? He was as bad as the other three. I didn't do anything wrong.

'Have I ever asked you to come running? It was you who wanted this meeting today. The arrangement you suggest sounds like a perfect solution to our little problem. I seem to have lost my appetite. Do please excuse me. By all means stay and finish your meal. You are, after all, the executor of my estate.'

I shot up from my seat and would have stalked off in a fit of temper, but his hand shot out and caught my wrist. My anger fled and all that was left was a deep, deep wound. I didn't want to fight with him. I had enough enemies. I didn't need him to be my enemy too. The truth was I was so alone and a little frightened. I stared down at him and tried to control the dam of emotions inside me. As much as I tried I could not stop my eyes from filling with stupid tears. They rolled down my face.

'Oh, for fuck's sake,' he said and, standing up roughly, pulled me against his hard body.

I was so shocked I stopped crying. Inside me strange things started happening. My heart was suddenly beating faster. My fingers curled into the crisp material of his shirt. I looked up at him wide-eyed.

'Oh, shit,' he groaned.

'What is it?' I whispered.

He cleared his throat and, releasing my hand, moved away from me. He ran his fingers through his hair. 'Look, I'm sorry about what I said. I don't know what I was thinking. Of course, you must come to me with all your problems.'

Oh my God. I wanted him to kiss me. I looked at him stunned. I felt confused. At the place we found ourselves.

He pushed his hand through his hair again. 'I really should go. Thanks for the meal and I'm sorry it turned out this way.' Without looking at me he turned and started to stride out of the dining room.

'Ivan,' I called.

His head swiveled back, his face only half-lit.

'About Rosalind and ...'

'Legally they don't have a leg to stand on, but stay well away from them. They're poison,' he said harshly.

Suddenly it seemed very important that he left on good terms. 'I plan to. They give me a serious case of the creeps,' I said, and pretended to shudder so exaggeratedly it must have made me look a downright fool.

An involuntary smile slipped onto his lips. 'Right. Call me if you need me,' he said.

'You are my friend, aren't you, Ivan?' I asked. I don't know why I asked. Maybe I just couldn't bear him to leave yet.

'Friend?' He laughed, a hollow sound. 'Yeah, sure I'm your friend. The best fucking friend you have. Goodnight, Tawny.'

CHAPTER 9

Tawny Maxwell

I slept badly and woke up feeling restless and dissatisfied. After a big breakfast of toast, ham, eggs, pancakes smothered in butter and jelly and coffee, I dressed in my riding gear and went outside. There had been more snow during the night, and the top layer was perfect powder. There was a freezing chill in the air, and above me the sky was an uninterrupted clear blue.

Thin frozen puddles by the entrance of the stables crackled under my winter boots. Jack, the groom, had already saddled up my horse, Dutch. Jack's ears were reddened with the cold.

'Thanks, Jack,' I said, looking at Dutch with real pleasure. He was such a beauty, slender limbed and glossy as silk. I could see his breath come up in great puffs in the freezing chill of the air. I took a sugar cube out of my pocket and held it in the palm of my hand. His breath felt lovely and warm and his lips scraped my skin.

'It's cold so don't work him too hard now,' Jack cautioned.

'I won't,' I said, nuzzling my face into Dutch's cold fur and listening to the sugar crunch between his teeth.

'Great. Give us a shout when you get back,' he said.

I climbed onto Dutch, gave him a pat on the neck, and picked up his reins. I shifted my weight and dug my heels into his sides and he took my lead perfectly, and began to trot, his mane bouncing with each stride. In perfect rhythm we went out into the frigid, ice-kissed world.

The leaves and berries in the bushes were bejeweled with frost. No one had disturbed the snow and except for a few fox marks it lay in a pristine layer on the ground. I looked at the beauty around me, breathed in the still silence, and felt pure joy. Dutch too seemed pleased to be out.

We had travelled peacefully for about fifteen minutes when my skin began to tingle. Not from cold. It was an unfamiliar sensation. My hands felt as if they were numb and yet so sensitive I could feel the blood throbbing inside the vessels. I squeezed my hands into fists.

However, the odd feeling persisted.

Then my head started to feel light and strange. Concerned, I slid off Dutch and my boots sunk into the snow. I held on to Dutch and tried to understand what was happening to me. The tingling in my hands spread to my arms and culminated in a delicious warm glow all through my body and brain.

I should have been frightened, but I wasn't. How could I? It felt incredible. I felt as if I could taste the air. It tasted clean and I could actually feel the oxygen in the air I was breathing. Every little movement and thought made me extremely happy. Everything felt good to touch. Even my clothes against my skin was pleasurable. I rubbed my face against the fur lining on my collar and it felt as if I was not rubbing a strip of dead fur, but the indescribably soft warm fur of a baby chincilla that was alive and curled around my neck.

I experienced the beauty around me the way I had never done before. I started to feel as if I was one with the landscape, as if I knew how the trees and animals felt. We were all one organism. It was, you know, peace and love. At that moment I loved every single person on earth. I guess I was being in the moment. There was no yesterday and no tomorrow. There was only now, where everything was perfect.

I saw the most *gorgeous* squirrel run down a tree and come towards me. He stopped about ten feet away. The little creature's eyes were so bright and alive I felt as if he was my special mate.

I dug around in my jacket and tried to share my cookie with him. I was disappointed to the point of tears when his beautiful bright eyes stared greedily at the cookie in my hand, but he refused to come closer.

I became sure that the reason he was refusing to come to me was because I had once eaten squirrel meat.

'Look, I'm really sorry,' I told him. To my ears my voice sounded high and cartoon like. I paused, giggled, and continued. 'Now that I know you I'll never do such a thing again.'

I threw the cookie towards him. He scampered away at first and then came back to snatch the cookie and rush away back up a tree. Sitting on a branch, he began to nibble at the cookie. I laughed so hard I had to hold my belly. His antics seemed to me the funniest thing in the world. To my delight it started to snow again. Big, fat flakes. What grace. What elegance. I opened my mouth and they melted on my tongue. Delicious. Absolutely delicious. I lifted my face to the heavens, and with my hands outstretched, I twirled around just savoring the marvelous sensation. It made me dizzy and I fell to the ground. Feeling deliriously happy, I stared up at the white sky.

One moment I was eating snow and laughing, and the next I was a snow-covered lump in the bleak landscape. I don't know how long had passed. I was conscious I was becoming cold, but my legs felt funny and I didn't trust myself to ride home. Anyway, the horse was nowhere to be seen.

I should call someone, but the only person my buzzing brain wanted to call was Ivan. He had such a sexy mouth. I remembered again the way he had looked at me for that one second during dinner last night, and I was determined that I really, really, really should kiss those lips. At least once.

I fumbled around in my coat pocket, found my phone, and peered at the screen. The colors on my screen seemed so bright. Strange but I couldn't remember his number. Finally, I managed to locate it in my phone. I hit the call button and missed. That seemed funny and I giggled and tried again.

Yes. Result.

But it rang out.

I put my phone back into my pocket and looked up at the sky. Wow! Psychedelic man! I lay back on the soft snow and smiled.

'You missed out, Ivan,' I said into the silent air, and nearly jumped out of my skin when my phone suddenly rang.

'Shit,' I exclaimed, sitting up and grabbing my phone.

'Hello,' I said.

'You called,' Ivan said. His voice made me feel really happy.

'I think you have a really, really, really sexy mouth,' I told him.

For a few seconds there was pure silence and a quick intake of breath. Then his voice came down the line, as mad as a wet hen. 'You dragged me out of a meeting to tell me that?'

'I just wanted you to know. Just in case you didn't,' I sang, oblivious to his irritation.

'Tawny?' he said quietly.

'Yes?'

'Where are you?' His voice was cautious.

'I think I might be about five minutes away from Jupiter house.'

This time the silence stretched even longer.

'Robert told me all about your tree house,' I explained.

'Are you all right?'

'Well, I think someone at the house spiked my drink with ecstasy, and I'm totally off my cake, but otherwise I am just fantastic.'

'What?' he barked suddenly in the receiver.

I jerked the phone away. Whoa, his voice had been like a mini explosion just outside my ear. 'It's all right,' I said with a laugh. 'I have popped a pill once before so I'm not frightened or anything.'

'Tawny, are you dressed warmly?' he asked urgently.

'Oh yes,' I said confidently.

'Good. Do you think you could last out there for another hour?'

'Sure. I was thinking of walking back to the house.'

'No,' he said urgently. 'Listen to me. Don't go back to the house. Can you see the tree house from where you are?'

'Yup.'

'Can you make it there?'

'Why wouldn't I be able to?'

'Good. Can you go there, close the little trapdoor and wait for me?'

'Yeah, I can do that.'

'Great. You will be out of the elements. Call me when you reach it, OK?'

'OK,' I said breezily.

'Be careful,' he said.

'I will.'

'Go on. Get moving.'

I stood up unsteadily. 'Whoa.'

'What?' he growled.

'Nothing. Just gravity problems.' And that seemed funny to me and I began to laugh uproariously.

'Fucking hell, Tawny. Get a hold of yourself.'

'OK, OK. No need to shout. I'm on my way,' I said, wanting to feel grumpy, but totally unable to. He was sweet that Ivan. Real sweet. I could eat him. I smiled to myself. He didn't know that I had a thing for him. I stopped short. Did I? Nah. He was not for me. He should be with a woman, what was her name again. Oh yeah, Chloe. I bet she read Robbs Report every month. I know Rosalind reads it. Robert said he never wanted me to read such a magazine.

'It's for snobs who want to find out the most snobbish way of spending their money,' he used to say.

I trudged through the snow, falling a few times, until I reached the tree house. My ears were numb and the bitter cold had seeped into my gloves, numbing my fingers until they were so thick and stiff I could not bend them properly.

How I climbed the tree was a miracle in itself. But somehow, despite my shaky legs, I managed to get to it. Using my already frigid hands, I scooped the snow drift away from the rough wooden door and used my body to wedge it open. I crawled in and closed the door. I curled up in the opposite corner and, although there was a draft that oozed in from under the door, it was much warmer inside Jupiter. I must have dozed off again because the next thing I knew someone was calling my name.

'Here,' I called. 'I'm here.'

And then Ivan was there. He was scowling, but I looked at his lips and I wanted to kiss him. I reached out and, hooking my hand around his neck, pulled him down until his mouth was inches from mine.

'My, my, what a lovely boy you are, but one kiss, and I could turn you into a man,' I whispered.

I saw his eyes darken.

'One kiss ... and oh, oh, you'll never want to leave.'

Then I kissed him. His lips were full of magic, a warm curse, that is until he grabbed my forearms and pushed me away, but oh, boy, oh boy, that was the best and most incredible kiss of my entire life.

I stared up at him in wonder. 'You're such a great kisser. Are you from New Orleans?' I asked in a hushed awed voice, as if I was imparting some great cosmic secret to him.

'God, you're fucked,' he said.

'Profoundly fucked,' I corrected him, my voice slurring.

Then I passed out.

Lord Greystoke

I looked down at her blue-tinged lips on the dusty, rough wood floor of my old tree-house and felt like upper-cut punching the coward who had done that to her. I took it personally. As if every inch of her body belonged to me and some god-dammed bastard had harmed what was mine.

I felt such fury that it drove me to tears. It actually filled my eyes and leaked down my face. I swiped them away with my palms. Fucking hell! Where did that come from? Never thought I had it in me to care that much for a woman. Let alone the gold digger!

Easy, Ivan. You've never met anybody like her.

I knew I needed to get her somewhere warm fast so I concentrated on that. But I swore that if it was the last fucking thing I did, I would find the worthless piece of shit/shits who did that to her and get even.

Fuck it to hell. Robert gave her to *me*.

CHAPTER 10

Tawny Maxwell

When I came to I was alone in a huge bed, in a room I had never seen before. The heavy curtains had been pulled shut and it was very dim, but I could make out that it was large with high ceilings and sparsely furnished. I sat up and listened intently. Nothing. It was dead quiet. No music. No sound of human activity.

I shouldn't really have been frightened, but because I had no idea where I was and I felt so disorientated, I became suddenly petrified. How did I get here? Who brought me here? What was their intention? Was I someone's prisoner? The fear totally changed the trip of the drug I had been given. It was like going from thirty miles an hour to one hundred and fifty. The wonderful high from when I was outdoors in the snow felt like a dream.

I felt my heart start beating so hard and fast that I could hear it. My breath came out in short sharp gasps. Then my hands began to tremble uncontrollably. I looked at them in horror. Indescribably frightened and horrified at what was happening to my body,

I curled up into a tight, shivering ball, and peered out into the gloom. I was absolutely and inexplicably convinced that monsters were going to come out of the darkness.

Suddenly my petrified gaze was pulled to one corner of the room. I thought I had seen movement. With my heart racing like a mad thing, I fixed my eyes in that bit of gloom, and to my horror I found that there was a crack in the wall ... and oh God! The crack was growing, becoming bigger and bigger. Inside the crack were moving shadows. A cold wind blew through it.

I suddenly understood its significance.

The crack was a door to another dimension and something was trying to come through, but I knew without any doubt whatever it was, it was not a good thing.

I wanted to stand up and run out of the room, but I had no control over my body. It was locked solid in its fetal position. Frozen with unnameable terror and dread I stared at the widening gap. Suddenly I heard a scuttling noise, an eerie scratching.

Oh sweet Jesus! It was coming!

I wanted to scream for help, but my mouth was numb and useless. All I could do was stare helplessly at the gap in the wall.

Something was coming.

Another scratching sound. This time closer. Louder. It sounded like nails or claws.

I began to pray fervently. I had never been so afraid.

Then it popped out.

 84

The squirrel.

My eyes bulged with surprise. The squirrel I had given the cookie to? No, this one was different. This one had fierce eyes. I knew instantly without being told that it was related to the squirrel I had eaten all those years ago. It was hopping mad at me. It began to grow. Until it morphed into Rosalind!

She advanced into the room and looked around with crazy, bulging eyes. Spotting me cowering in the bed, she gave a murderous howl of rage and began swaying like some kind of demon from a horror movie towards me. My teeth chattered and my whole body was shaking with abject fear.

I wanted to beg her not to hurt me, but I could not. My heart was pounding so hard I thought it would burst. I had never felt such fear. She was coming closer and closer. Silent tears started to pour down my face. This was it. I was going to die. Killed by my stepdaughter. Somehow I managed to force open my mouth and let out a scream.

The door to the room flew open and a man came in. Instantly the squirrel disappeared into the crack and the crack began to close. I turned gratefully towards the man who had come in, but he had a mean face and he was nearly as tall as the ceiling. He was saying something, but his voice was so distorted it sounded like a demonic wail.

I was very frightened of him, because there was no doubt in my mind his plan was to hurt me. It was clear that he had brought me here to hurt me.

I opened my mouth and screamed for Ivan.

He suddenly strode towards me and cradled me in his arms. The gesture surprised me. He was the bad guy. What was he doing? I felt cold. So cold that my teeth were chattering. His body was warm and though he was the enemy I snuggled up to his splendid warmth.

He said something and I knew it was urgent, but I could not make the words out. The edges of his face were blurred. I tried to form words, but even to my ears they sounded like the sound of wind wailing in the distance.

'Mommy,' I yelled.

He said something else, but I still I couldn't understand him.

'I want my Mommy,' I begged.

The stranger rocked me in his arms and crooned something, but the words ran into each other so I couldn't understand a word he said.

'Where is Ivan?' I cried, clutching his shirt. 'I'm not allowed to trust anyone else. You must find him for me.'

The man stilled as if I had said something shocking.

He pulled me even closer and continued rocking me while he stroked my hair as if I was a sick child. I let him. I knew that if I let him stay and rock me Rosalind could not get to me.

I don't know how long he rocked me, that big, boulder-like stranger. Then another man came into the room and he was holding a black bag. I was certain he was the serial killer from the movie Child 44, and I cringed away from him and clung desperately to the stranger.

'Don't let go of me,' I sobbed. 'Please. He wants to kill me.'

The gentle giant's voice echoed in my head. I couldn't understand him, but it was OK because he did not let go of me. The other man tried to touch me but, like a madwoman, I went into spasms of fear and eventually he said something to the stranger and left. When I was alone with the stranger I began to sob loudly. I don't know why I felt such grief that I wanted to end my life. If he had given me a knife I would have stabbed myself.

'Who are you?' I asked him.

He told me but I could not understand him. His voice was faint like how fading flowers must sound if they could talk.

Every time he tried to extricate himself, I clung harder to him until eventually darkness came to take me.

'I don't know who you are, but please, please, I beg of you, don't let go of me,' I whispered as the darkness was taking me away.

Lord Greystoke

When she passed out from sheer exhaustion I put her to bed, and as the doctor had ordered I sat next to her all night. I never closed my eyes once. She was not walking out of any of my windows. I stared at her the way a man stares at a thing that he craves even though it frightens the shit out of him.

Once she moaned in her sleep and thrashed her arms about, but I held her close, kissed her cheek and whispered, 'Shhhh,' until she became quiet and still.

Then I sat and planned how I would keep my distance from her, because the truth was she was not mine. And never would be. She belonged to no one. All this unfortunate incident had proved was that I was fucking putty in her hands, and if she even suspected it she'd milk it for all it was worth.

I promised Robert I'd help her, but once she was firmly on her own two feet, I would have to let go pretty quick. She was dangerous the way heroin was dangerous to the ordinary human. I knew a man who stepped over his dying girlfriend to get his fix.

It was not too late: she was not already in my blood calling to me. A cunning gold digger entwining herself into my soul.

CHAPTER 11

Tawny Maxwell

When I opened my eyes again, I seemed to be gazing at a different ceiling. This one was recessed with cream moldings and was much bigger. My head was fuzzy, my mouth tasted dry and bitter, and I felt as weak as a kitten. I swiveled my eyes slowly around the room. It was large and masculine with glossy blue walls, gleaming walnut furniture, a large surreal oil painting of a white castle floating in a blue sky, red suede bedside tables, and a large, dove-grey armchair by the bed in which was slumped ... a sleeping Ivan!

I had to blink a few times to make sure he was real and not another hallucination like the squirrel. When did he get here and how long had he been sitting there?

Bemused, I turned my head and watched him curiously. Actually, I drank in the sight of him. He did not look so dark and dangerous in sleep. His head was tilted slightly to the left, his hair had fallen over his forehead, his unfairly thick lashes were resting on his gorgeous cheeks, and there was a dark shadow on his hard jaw which, strangely, made him look vulnerable and wickedly sexy at the same time.

The other man, the giant, probably called him, and he must have come. Where was I? Was I in his home? I suddenly realized that under the duvet, I was totally naked under a huge T-shirt. What the devil?

'Oh,' I exclaimed with surprise as his eyes snapped open, the grey finding me instantly.

I froze at the suddenness with which they focused on me, laser-like and disconcertingly sharp. We stared at each other. The air between us crackled as if there was a big storm coming. The sensual lips thinned into a straight stern line. He broke eye contact, sat forward, then glanced at his watch.

'How're you feeling?' he asked.

'You undressed me,' I accused.

His eyes flickered, but his face was shuttered. 'Yeah, but don't worry I've kind of seen it all before.'

''You didn't have to. I could have slept in my clothes,' I said resentfully.

His lips twisted wryly. 'You pissed yourself.'

My eyes popped open and my entire body flushed with crushing embarrassment. 'Oh God,' I gasped. I wished the ground would open up and swallow me. I couldn't be more completely mortified.

'I had to move you from the spare bedroom into my bed. A new mattress will be delivered later today and you can move back in there for tonight,' he explained.

I drew a shaky breath. 'I'm so sorry,' I whispered.

'Don't be,' he said carelessly and stood up. His clothes were crumpled as if he had spent all night in the chair.

'I'll pay for the new mattress, of course,' I added quickly, exhaling in a rush.

'That won't be necessary.' His voice was cold as if I had offended him.

'Please. It would make me feel better,' I insisted, too humiliated to look him in the eye.

'Do as you wish,' he said, as if he was already bored with the conversation and would prefer to be somewhere else.

'Thank you.' I bit my bottom lip. 'Ah ... where is the other man?'

He narrowed his eyes. 'What other man?'

'From last night. The big guy.'

'There was only me and the doctor last night.'

'Oh,' I said in a small voice.

The night before seemed blurred and fuzzy in my mind. I was sure there had been another man. A kind man who held me close to his heart and rocked me for hours. Was he another hallucination? But he had felt so real. Could Ivan be that man? I looked up at him. He looked back distant and cold. No way. It must have been another hallucination.

'Do you feel like some food? Soup? Toast?' he asked.

Even the thought of food made me feel horribly queasy, and I shook my head. 'Thank you, but no. I'd like to have a shower though, before I go home.'

He looked down at me expressionlessly. 'I'm afraid you won't be able to go home for a while.'

'Why not?'

'Because whoever drugged you yesterday wanted to frighten you. Wanted you to know that you are not safe, and whoever it was, is either living in the house with you, or more probably has one of your staff working for them.'

I closed my eyes for a second and tried to think. In my weakened state the problem seemed insurmountable. I opened my eyes. 'Never mind. I'll sort it out. Tomorrow. When I feel better.'

'I've already warned James that you will not be back for a bit.'

'Thank you. Yes, I think it would be a good idea for me to stay in London for a few days. After I have had my shower I'll get a taxi to Robert's.' I paused. Of course it was all mine now. 'I meant, to my apartment in South Kensington.'

'No, I don't think that's a good idea.' His voice was flat and unyielding. 'You would be vulnerable on your own there. Besides, the doctor said you could have flashbacks for the next forty-eight hours and you shouldn't be out on your own. The most practical solution

is for you to stay here for a few days until we come up with a workable plan for you.'

'Wouldn't I be in your way?' I asked cautiously.

'I wouldn't have thought so. I'm hardly ever here anyway.'

'Well, I'll go as soon as I can.'

'Yeah, whatever.'

'I feel grimy and my head feels like it's full of cottage cheese. I should have a shower first,' I said, and sitting up pushed the bedcover away from my body.

His eyes strayed to my breasts and then moved away quickly. 'You'll find the bathroom through that door. I'll get you some towels.

'Er ... have I got anything to wear?'

'Your clothes must be dry by now. I'll go get them.'

'Thank you, Ivan,' I said, a small smile curving my lips.

'Think nothing of it,' he said and left.

I slipped out of bed. My legs felt weak and the ground was like a waterbed as I slowly dragged my feet to the bathroom. In the mirror I looked like something out of a horror movie. My plait had come undone and my hair was all over the place. My eyes were bloodshot and my pupils were popping. There were dark circles under my eyes and my skin looked unnaturally white and sickly.

Ugh. I shivered and turned away, but too fast. It made me feel dizzy. I gripped the sink and waited until my head felt normal again.

94

Then I ran the shower and stood under it; the water felt like heaven. I stood in the hot stream and tried to think straight.

But all I could think of was: Oh, damn! I pissed myself in his bed. The shame of it. Of all the people I wouldn't have wanted to see me in such a humiliating situation, he was at the top of the list.

Still, the hot shower made me feel more human and I consoled myself that I was drugged and not of sound mind. I came out of the shower, wrapped myself in a large towel, and went back into the bedroom. I'll just have to take it in my stride. I found my clothes on the bed and, once dressed, ventured outside into the corridor.

CHAPTER 12

Tawny Maxwell

I padded down a corridor with oversized modern art on the walls, not sure where I was going, but utterly unafraid of what I would find. I knew where I was and whom I was with.

The corridor opened out to a large living room with a high ceiling and light pouring in from tall windows. The décor was minimalistic with a spare color palette of white stone with black accents, and a mixture of modern and mid-century pieces. It was a perfect man cave. It even had the black bear rug.

How strange though? I did not have even the faintest memory of any of this. Whatever drug they had administered to me, it was certainly powerful. I should ask Ivan what the doctor said, if there would be any long-lasting side effects.

I walked through that space and found Ivan in a large, spotless, black and white kitchen, beating eggs. The radio was playing *How Long Will I Love You* and the air was scented with the aroma of the brewing coffee.

He turned to look at me with a puckered brow. 'Could you not find your shoes?'

'I know where they are, but I'm a Southern girl. We like being barefoot. I used to walk to the store in my bare feet all summer long.'

He looked at me as if he didn't quite know how to respond to that bit of unsolicited information. 'Right.' He paused and scratched his chin. 'Well, there's a hairdryer in the second drawer to the left of the door in the bathroom.'

'Thanks, but I usually just let my hair dry naturally.'

'Fine.' Again he seemed at a loss. He looked down at the bowl of eggs he had been beating when I came in. 'I'm having eggs. You should have some too. You haven't eaten anything since breakfast yesterday, have you?'

I ran my tongue along the inside of my right cheek and winced. 'I don't think I'll eat anything. I have sores on the inside of my mouth and my jaw hurts.'

He frowned. 'Yes, you were grinding your teeth in your sleep. Want me to heat up some soup instead? I think there might be some cans somewhere around.'

'No, I'll just have coffee first and see how I feel after.'

He walked to the coffee machine and facing me asked, 'Cappuccino, espresso, filter, latte?'

'Filter, please.'

He put a mug into the slot and hit a button. Coffee splashed into the mug. 'Milk, sugar?'

'Milk and two sugars, please.'

I lifted myself onto one of the tall stools around the island and he placed a steaming mug in front of me. I smiled my thanks and, grasping the mug with both my hands, brought it to my lips. I blew at the surface before taking a small sip. The fragrant heat travelled down my gullet, warming me.

'Mmmm,' I said.

He glanced at me, but did not say anything.

Quietly, I watched his strong, sure hands pour the beaten eggs into a pan greased with butter and scramble them slightly before scraping them onto two plates. He then buttered four slices of toast, placed them on the sides of the plates and put one plate in front of me and one at the opposite side of the island.

'Bon appétit,' he said.

'Same to you.'

Sitting down he began to dig into his food.

I picked up the fork and put a small piece of egg in my mouth. I didn't think I could eat, but the coffee had stirred my appetite and the eggs were surprisingly tasty. The sores only hurt if I let food scrape against them. I took a bite of toast. Our eyes met. His were level.

I carefully chewed on my good side, swallowed, and said, 'Thank you for my breakfast.'

 98

'I would have done the same for anyone,' he said expressionlessly.

This was exactly why I hated this man. He could drive a preacher to drink. I put the fork down. 'Why did you do that?'

'Do what?' he asked forking more egg into his mouth and chewing unconcernedly.

'Throw my gratitude back in my face and try and turn every encounter into an argument,' I said fiercely.

'I don't want you to be grateful to me and neither am I picking an argument with you. We argue because you insist on having a conversation when none is necessary.'

'Wow! You sure know how to deflate a girl.'

He stopped chewing. 'I'm not trying to deflate you. We are two people who have nothing in common. However, we seem to have been thrown into each other's company for the time being. Until I find a workable scenario, I guess we'll just have to tolerate each other, but I'm not going to pretend to be excited about the prospect, and I don't expect you to be either.'

I jumped out of my seat. 'Well don't bother. I can take care of myself,' I said furiously.

'I made a promise to Robert and I'm keeping it,' he said quietly.

That stopped me in my tracks. 'You made a promise to Robert?'

He nodded.

I climbed back into the seat that I had vacated in a daze. 'When?'

'I used to go and visit him when you were in London.'

'What?'

'Yeah. He knew how I felt about you so he used to invite me around when you were gone.'

I shook my head in disbelief. 'Oh my God. He never breathed a word about it. Not once.'

He shrugged and bit into his toast.

God, he had really good teeth. I mean like really white and really straight. I shook my head to get my thoughts back on track. 'What did he make you promise?'

He sighed. 'I suppose it's not a secret. He made me promise that I would make sure his children did not hurt you. He wanted me to watch over you until you reach twenty-one. After that he said you would be able to take care of yourself.'

'That's crazy ... he wanted you to watch over me until I am twenty-one!'

'It may be crazy to you, but it was very important to him. He had never asked me for anything before that.'

'Twenty-one. That's more than a year away.'

'I know,' he said gloomily.

'How long do you think it will be before you find a,' I lifted my hands up to face level and made air quotes, 'workable scenario'?'

He sighed. 'Just give me a few days to think about it and come up with something

workable. We don't want a repeat of yesterday.'

My shoulders slumped. He was right. I shouldn't be sitting here hollering at him. I should be trying to figure out how yesterday happened.

'What exactly did you tell James?'

He picked up his mug and took a sip. 'As a matter of fact, James is no longer working at Barrington Manor.'

'What?' I cried in shock.

'I gave all your staff their walking orders.'

I stared at him in amazement and mounting fury. 'You did what?'

'I gave them all six month severance pay in lieu of notice. Theresa will hire a few people to close down the house and hire a caretaking couple. The gardening and stable staff will continue to maintain the gardens and grounds,' he explained arrogantly.

'Why?' I spluttered in disbelief.

'Because I don't know who to trust and I don't have the time to find out right now.'

I stared at him in horror. 'So you fired them all!'

'Yup.'

I shook my head. 'That is unbelievably high handed, and anyway you can't do that. You can't make decisions like that without consulting me. You're the executor of the estate so I need to come to you if I need to make a large purchase, but you can't fire my staff or stop me living in that house. It's mine.'

He shrugged casually. 'You're welcome to speak with a solicitor. You will find that I am able to take any decision that I think is in your interest. The house and its management also come under my jurisdiction.'

'How is it in my interest to close down the house and fire all *my* staff?' I demanded angrily.

He looked at me as if I was stupid. 'Tawny. Have you fucking forgotten what happened yesterday? Someone you know and trust at the house drugged you. Effortlessly, I might add. Just think what would have happened if I had been overseas, or if I had not seen your call when I did. You would have spent the night outdoors, terrified out of your mind. You might even have frozen to death. You were blue by the time I found you.'

I subsided and covered my face with my hands. This couldn't be happening. I needed time to think.

'I need my wardrobe,' I whispered almost to myself. I was thinking of that wonderful space that I used to steal into when I needed to be alone, but Ivan's lip curled with distaste.

'You're rich enough to buy yourself a whole new wardrobe.'

'I didn't mean the contents. I meant ... never mind,' I said wearily.

'Look, I've got to go out. Please don't leave the apartment. The doctor said you could get flashbacks. I'll get Theresa to call you and you can ask her to bring what you want.

Food, clothes, toiletries, magazines.' He spread his fingers out. 'Whatever you need.'

He pointed towards a closed door to the left of the kitchen. 'That's the spare room. A new mattress will be delivered later this afternoon. You can set up in there until I figure out the next course of action.'

I glanced in the direction he had pointed. 'Um ... I know I don't seem like it, but I am very grateful for what you did yesterday.'

'No problem. I'll be back for lunch. We can go out if you want.'

'You don't have to take me out. I'll be OK.'

'As you wish,' he said indifferently, and walked away from me. I heard him go into his room and shut the door.

The eggs were cold so was the coffee. I sat on the stool and sighed deeply. What an ugly, ugly mess. Robert had been right to be worried. His children were far, by far, more venomous than I had given them credit for.

I fell asleep on the sofa an hour after Ivan left for work. I guess I must have been more devastated than I thought. When I woke up I felt horrible, depressed and kind of numb. Dead inside. And so lonely. Horribly lonely. I knew some of it would be the comedown effect of the drugs, but another part was the

way life was turning out. The truth of my situation hit me. Without Robert I had no one.

No family. No friends. Not a single person in the world actually cared for me. Even Ivan made it blatantly clear that I was a nuisance to him and that he couldn't wait to be rid of me. I was all alone in this world and now I didn't even have a home I could go to.

Oh yeah. I seemed to have acquired a bunch of enemies too.

My head hurt.

I walked around Ivan's beautiful apartment listlessly. Then at 2.00 p.m. Mrs. MacDonald came around.

'Please, call me Theresa,' she invited.

'Then you must call me Tawny.'

'Come and have a look at what I've got for you,'

She had brought some groceries, toiletries, and some clothes. A pair of jeans, a couple of T-shirts, a pair of sweats, and a shimmering cocktail dress. They were all in super bright colors that I would never have chosen for myself. It was as if she thought I was still a teenager.

'Look, I even brought you some make up,' she said cheerfully.

'Thank you,' I said politely. 'But I definitely won't be needing that.' I held up the cocktail dress.

'Oh, I believe you will need that. His Lordship is taking you to dinner tonight,' she informed me with an approving smile.

Well, that was a strange way to find out someone was taking you to dinner. 'No, I don't feel up to it yet. Would you be kind enough to convey my apologies to him.'

'Should I call a doctor?' she asked, a frown creasing her forehead.

I shook my head firmly. 'No. I just feel a bit down. I'd be terrible company.'

'If you're sure. Do you want me to get you anything else?'

'Thank you, but no, I'm fine.'

'All right. I have to be somewhere else, but your new mattress will be coming in the next hour.'

Once the mattress had been set up, I found sheets in one of the cupboards and made up the bed. Then I flopped into it and fell into a deep, black sleep.

I never even heard Ivan come in.

Lord Greystoke

I stood outside her door, one hand on the knob. I wanted to go in. I really did. No one would ever know if I did. I'd simply look at her and then I'd walk out. No one would be harmed. Nothing would change. I felt a twinge in my body. Fuck the twinge. What about the upheaval and the loss of control

and power going on inside me? The urge was so strong my hand gripped the knob until it felt as if it would break.

I snatched my hand away.

I took a step away from the door.

Jesus, this was so screwed up. What the fuck was I doing? There was a world of possibilities and choices out there. Beautiful, willing, anonymous women who didn't make me feel as if I was worthless without them. Women who didn't gnaw in my blood like fucking viruses when I stayed away from them. Women who did what I wanted.

I needed those women.

Not this sick addiction for her body, her skin, her smell, her smile, her fucking lying lips.

She never wore shoes in summer. Yeah right. She always let her hair dry naturally. A little harmless Southern girl. She doesn't fool me. Not for one cotton pickin' second. I'm not Robert. She's no good.

And yet I want her. So bad.

Fuck!

I should stop thinking about her. I should stay away from her. I should go out and bury my cock in other bodies. Eventually one of them will immunize me against her. Surely that cannot be too difficult to do.

Not for the man who won the title of Ivan the Terrible.

CHAPTER 13

Tawny Maxwell

By the time I woke up it was nearly six o'clock in the morning, but the long sleep had cured me somewhat, and I felt much stronger both mentally and physically.

I washed and dressed quickly in the sweats that Theresa had brought. They were a little big, but they would have to do for the meantime. I put my hair in a plait, and opened my bedroom door.

The apartment was dark and still. Ivan's door was firmly shut and there was no noise from within. Quietly, I passed his door and, picking up the set of keys that were in a silver bowl by the front door, let myself out into a corridor.

I stood for a moment taking in my surroundings. It was quite spooky that I totally could not remember passing through any of it. There were only two doors with numbers on them on that floor, Ivan's and another on the opposite end of the corridor. I passed a lift and made for another door that looked like a fire escape.

I opened it and ran down two flights of steps to the ground floor. I exited out into a classy lobby with a highly polished floor and granite walls. There was a large vase of fresh flowers at the reception desk. A man in a cheap grey suit was standing at the glass front looking out. He turned around when he heard the door open.

'Hello,' he greeted, his tone polite, but his stare was full of suspicion.

'I'm staying temporarily at Apartment 5. Just going for a jog,' I felt compelled to explain.

'Have a good run,' he said formally, as he moved to hold the door open for me.

I thanked him and ventured out into a dark and mostly deserted London. Unlike Bedfordshire, there was no snow at all in London. It was just cold. I turned left and began to jog down the empty street. The cold wind whistled around my ears. I made a few turns, all the while carefully memorizing road names and landmarks, and eventually ended up in Brook Street. I ran down it until I came to Grosvenor Park.

There were other joggers and people with their dogs. They smiled at me or called out greetings. I passed the familiar American Embassy building and ran further up the road until I got to Hyde Park where a group of people were practicing Tai Chi, their movements slow and graceful. I kept going until I reached the Serpentine Lake before my lungs felt as if they were on fire, and I turned around and started to retrace my steps.

The morning sun was beginning to filter through the buildings and London was coming alive with pedestrians and morning traffic. Almost everybody was dressed for a day in the office and not as friendly as the dog walkers and joggers I had passed on my way out. By the time I got back I was drenched with sweat, but feeling absolutely exhilarated.

I let myself into the apartment and I could tell immediately that Ivan was up and about. His bedroom door was yanked open suddenly and he stood at the doorway in his pajama bottoms, shirtless and frowning. My eyeballs nearly exploded. Whoa! I'll be dog-gone! Who knew that underneath all those perfectly tailored suits the icy English Lord had a chest full of tats?

Designs like you would see in Chinese landscape paintings decorated his pecs. Like dragons or flying beasts, the inked creatures flew down the powerfully developed muscles of his upper arms.

It was shocking to think that half-asleep and grumpy as a grizzly, a man could *ooze* raw sex appeal like that, but before he could think I was a special kind of stupid I dragged my eyes back up to his brooding face.

'Good morning,' I said cheerfully.

His eyes moved arrogantly over my hot, sweaty face. 'What's good about it?' he asked moodily.

'I don't know. The sun is shining? We're alive?'

'Of course you'd have to be a morning person,' he groaned disgustedly.

I smothered a laugh. 'And of course, you'd have to be a mean sow in the morning.'

He threw me a filthy look, and was about to turn around and disappear into his room again when I spoke up.

'I could make us breakfast?' I suggested brightly.

'No. I have a breakfast meeting.' He paused. 'Maybe coffee?'

'Aye, aye, sir,' I said with a mocking salute.

He nodded and went back into his bedroom.

After he shut his door I went into the kitchen and switched on the machine. While it was heating up I hit the shower. I hurried through my toilette, but by the time I came out of my room he was gone. There was an empty coffee cup in the sink.

The sight deflated me further.

Oh, well. I had the whole day to myself, maybe I should do some shopping. All the stuff Theresa got for me was too big and clumsy. Yes, I should go out and get a few things that I needed. With some amusement I realized that I, the dreaded gold digger, didn't have any money.

I called up the bank and asked them to courier a replacement debit card to Ivan's address. They were extremely accommodating even when I told them that I had no ID on me. They said they would send a teller who could recognize me with my new card. I would have it in less than two hours. I put the phone down and reflected that the world really did bend over backwards to accommodate people with money. I remembered when I had none at all, how the bank manager looked at me as if I was a bit of shit at the end of his shoe.

Well, no more of that. Robert had seen to it that I would never again have to endure such a situation. I put the phone down with a feeling of accomplishment.

Right, breakfast. I went back into the kitchen and looked around.

I was actually ravenous and ended up eating a bowl of cornflakes, two fried eggs, bacon, and two slices of toast. I washed it all down with two glasses of pomegranate juice. Afterwards, I placed all the dishes in the dishwasher and cleaned up after myself, then got ready to go out.

I was pulling on my shoes when the phone by the front door rang. The concierge was ringing from downstairs to say that there was a flower delivery.

'Shall I send her up?'

'OK,' I said.

I opened the door and a woman wearing a smart uniform said brightly, 'Hello. Where do you want these?'

'Wow!' I said, looking at the riot of colors. It was a really big and gorgeous bunch of flowers. So beautiful it was more like a work of art. I opened the door wider and bade her to put them on the dining table.

'Thanks,' she said after I signed her little pad and gave it back to her.

After she left I went to look at the flowers in surprise. Whoever they were from they must really be crazy for Ivan. I went closer to the arrangement and to my surprise I saw that the card was actually addressed to me.

Bemused, I tugged it out and opened the envelope.

Happy Valentine's Day

Underneath was a large scrawling signature that clearly read Ivan. With everything that had happened, I had even forgotten it was Valentine's day.

Obviously, it did not mean anything.

I was staying at his flat and he must have felt sorry for me. I walked around the bunch admiringly. Gosh, it must have been really expensive. Hmm ... I wondered why he had decided to spend so much money on me. Did he expect something back in return?

The phone went again. It was the bank employee with my replacement card.

'I'll come down and get it,' I said.

She was very pleasant. 'Anytime you need our help, please don't hesitate to call,' she said.

I got the card from her, then took a taxi to Fenwicks of Bond Street where I picked up a whole bunch of lovely lingerie, matching bras and panties, garter belts, camisoles, slips, a totally sexy and unspeakably naughty blue brocade corset, and a peek-a-boo black baby doll. I knew I would probably have no use for them for the foreseeable future, but purchasing them was therapeutic. Buying gorgeous underwear always made me feel better, and already I felt a whole lot perkier.

Carrying my bags quite jauntily, I stopped for lunch at a pretty little crepe café. As I was enjoying my goat's cheese, scrambled eggs and herb crepe, I overheard a snatch of conversation between two women who were passing by my table.

One was telling the other, 'I've booked a cab, but I might stay on at the party. It all depends what everyone else wants to do after that, I guess.'

Both women moved out of earshot and I did not hear more, but that little snippet of their conversation made me feel unaccountably sad. That was exactly the kind of life I had always wanted for myself. Having workmates and good friends and going to parties that I have to book cabs home for.

Slightly depressed, I paid for my food and walked up the road to Liberty's. It was a grand, two hundred year-old nineteenth century Tudor revival department store that was an Aladdin's cave of fabulous things. I spent the afternoon acquiring two pairs of skinny jeans, a few tops, a couple of tracksuits for running, a pair of cowboy boots, a cream cashmere coat, a soft woolen scarf and leather gloves.

I was already weighed down with packages and bags and thought I was done, but as I was leaving the store I noticed a mannequin wearing a black silk, sleeveless, wraparound evening dress. It had a wide, deep V-neck and a bowknot sash at the waist. It had been accessorized with an intricate necklace made of red stones. I bought both without trying them on. On another floor in the shoe department I found a pair of red high heels to match.

It was nearly six o'clock when the taxi dropped me at the entrance of my temporary home. When I got into the apartment I realized that Ivan was already in. I always knew when he was around. The atmosphere became electric. I went into the kitchen and, firing up the kettle, switched it on. I was sitting at the island with my sweet tea when he walked in wearing a dinner jacket and pale yellow shirt.

I did not dare stare but, my, my, what a very attractive specimen he was. Speaking totally neutrally of course. I'm not interested in him like that.

'Thank you for the flowers,' I said. 'They're very beautiful.'

'Yes, I guessed you'd need a bit more time before you snared your next conquest.'

My shoulders slumped. For a second I looked at my bare feet. Wow, that hurt. I felt wounded, actually. Maybe because I had not been expecting it. I looked up at him. 'Did you send me flowers so you'd have another excuse to insult me?'

He stared at me and I could tell that he regretted what he had said. 'That was uncalled for. I'm sorry,' he muttered finally.

'It's OK,' I said softly.

'You're going to be OK on your own?'

I smiled. 'Yeah. I like my own company anyway.'

'Good night, then,' he called moving away.

'Ivan,' I called.

He turned back around, one eyebrow raised.

'Have a nice night.'

'Thanks,' he murmured, and hesitated as if he wanted to say something else. He must have thought better of it because he shook his head, smiled at me, and walked away.

CHAPTER 14

Tawny Maxwell

I sat staring at my cold tea. Without him the apartment felt so empty. I stood up and paced the kitchen restlessly. I couldn't get the image of him as he hesitated, out of mind. The moment was like a splinter in my flesh. He was out having a good time. Everybody was out.

I felt lost and lonely.

Maybe I should go out for a walk, but it was probably a bad idea to be wandering about aimlessly on my own on Valentine's night. What I needed was something to do. I should watch a movie. Or read a book. My eyes fell on the lemons in the stainless steel lemons basket. I knew what I wanted to do.

Bake a cake. A lemon cake like the ones that my grandma pulled out of her oven. Lemon cakes were simple things to do and all the ingredients were sure to be in the house. Besides, baking always calmed me. I'd probably have to beat the cake by hand, but that might be a good thing considering the state I was in. Burn off some of that excess energy bubbling inside.

I looked in the fridge and the cupboards, and the only things I was missing were a pound of unsalted butter and kitchen scales, but I had made this sort of cake often enough that I could probably guess at the measurements and get it right. As for the butter, I could pop down to the Newsagent that was less than a ten-minute walk away for it.

I put on my coat, picked up the extra key that Ivan had left out for me and went out of the door. As I pulled it shut behind me I saw a gentleman put his key into the apartment door at the opposite end of the corridor. I only hesitated for one second.

'Excuse me,' I called out.

He turned around slowly. He was good looking in a very English sort of way, dark brown hair, pale skin, nice, boyish eyes and proper. Very proper.

'Yes, can I help you?'

I walked up to him and smiled. 'I'm temporarily living at the end of the corridor and I was wondering if you have a kitchen scales that I could borrow?'

His eyes filled with amusement. 'I thought neighbors usually wanted to borrow a cup of sugar?'

I grinned. 'I've got that. I'm trying to bake a cake.'

He put his hand out. 'Ralph Drummond-Willoughby.'

I placed my hand into his. 'Tawny Maxwell.'

His eyebrows rose. 'Ah, the American heiress everyone is talking about is hiding out in my block.'

I grinned. 'You won't tell anyone will you?'

He smiled rakishly. 'Not if you promise to share a slice of your cake.'

'Deal.'

He pushed open his door. 'Come in. There should be a kitchen scales around somewhere.'

I followed him into his apartment. To my surprise it was decorated in a very similar manner to Ivan's apartment. 'Who decorated your apartment?'

'My mother. Why do you ask?'

'She wouldn't have decorated Ivan's apartment too, would she?'

'I doubt it,' he said dryly. 'Why do you ask?'

'They are both startlingly similar in style and taste.'

He turned around and looked at me as if did not believe me.

'I promise you they are. You must come and see it,' I insisted

He nodded and, going into the kitchen, came out with the scales. 'So you are baking on Valentine's Day.'

I nodded. 'And why are you not out on a date? You seem ... most eligible.'

He grinned. 'I like eating cake on Valentine's with astonishing blondes.'

I took the scales off him and smiled. I liked him. He was good in the most unthreatening way possible for my battered ego. 'I'll bring you some later.'

'Well then, I suppose I'd better help you carry this into your kitchen.'

'Are you sure?'

'Positive. This weighs an absolute ton.'

I looked at the little plastic thing cradled in his hands. 'Listen,' I said, and smiled to take the sting out of my words. 'I'm still in mourning for my husband so I hope I'm not giving you the idea that I'm available or anything like that.'

'Perish the thought. You're absolutely ravishing. Of course, you're not available.'

I laughed and he followed behind. I opened the door to Ivan's apartment and he carried the scales in and set them down on the island. He looked around him.

'You're right. The color scheme is remarkably similar.'

'Thank you for the scales.'

'Right. I guess I'd better be off. Bring the cake around anytime it is ready. I'll open a bottle of champagne and we'll have cake and bubbly to celebrate our ... um ... friendship.'

'All right, see you about ten o'clock,' I said happily.

This day was turning out way better than I had thought it would. After he left I popped around to the corner shop for the butter. Then I set about baking my cake. It was nearly ready when I heard the key in the door. I felt my body tense up. I was not expecting Ivan to come back for ages and he

had not warned me that anyone else had the key.

'Who is it?' I called out.

Ivan appeared at the door. 'Me,' he said.

I breathed a sigh of relief.

He sniffed the air. 'What's that smell?' he asked.

'I'm baking a cake.'

He seemed surprised. 'You bake?'

I smiled. 'Yup. I love baking. I usually bake in the middle of the night when there is no one around. It calms and relaxes me.'

'Really?'

'What are you doing home so early?'

He walked over to the fridge and pulled out a bottle of champagne. 'If I tell you, you'll never believe me.'

I leaned a hip at the counter top. 'Try me.'

He plucked two tall flutes from one of the top shelves and placed them on the island top. Deftly he untwisted the metal from around the top of the champagne bottle and removed it together with the foil. The cork came out with a quiet hiss and he filled the two glasses. Picking them up he came towards me. He handed me a glass and I took it.

His gaze met mine. 'I thought you shouldn't spend Valentine's night on your own.'

My eyes widened with surprise.

'Happy Valentine's Day, Tawny.' His voice was strange, thick.

We clinked glasses. 'Happy Valentine's Day, Ivan,' I echoed.

I watched him over the rim of my glass.

'Does it taste like the greatest champagne ever made?' he asked.

'Why? Who says it is?'

'The head of Sotheby's Wine Department.' I let my gaze float down to the faded label on the bottle. Krug Collection 1928. 'Wow!' I exclaimed. 'It's older than both of us put together.'

'It was served for King George VI and his guests at the first royal banquet in Buckingham Palace.'

'Hmm ... I'd have saved it for a more special occasion,' I murmured.

'It is a special occasion.'

'It is?'

His fingers flexed restlessly. 'It is.'

I cocked an eyebrow. 'So what's the occasion?'

He shrugged. 'Something at work.'

'Oh. Great.'

His eyes were hooded and watchful. He raised his glass as if in a toast. 'Do you like it?'

I took a sip and considered the taste. 'It's ... racy?'

He nodded and drained his glass. Then he began walking away from me and poured himself another glass. There was something different about him. A coiled tension. If I didn't know better, I would have said it was sexual in nature.

'What happened to your date?' I asked as he turned to face me again.

He looked at me expressionlessly. 'What do you think happened to her?'

I shook my head.

'God, I really hate Valentine's Day. First you have to send out for overpriced flowers, and then you have to take them out to restaurants where you are cajoled into the set menu that you would never choose ordinarily, and then the couple sitting at the table next to you starts arguing.'

'Ah,' I said, trying not to smile.

'And this year I was one half of that arguing couple.'

'Oh dear! I'm sorry to hear that.'

A ping went off and I walked over to the oven and looked in through the glass doors. The cake looked fabulous. I switched off the oven and, donning thick mitts, opened the door and brought my cake out. Ivan came over and stood beside me looking at it. I heard his breathing deep and quick and felt his powerful body almost vibrating with tension. My pulse started leaping.

'Impressive,' he said. 'I'm surprised you managed to find all the ingredients in my kitchen.'

I moved slightly away and forced myself to smile. 'Almost. I went down to the corner shop for the butter, and Ralph lent me the weighing scales.'

His body became peculiarly still. 'Ralph?' he queried softly. There was menace in his voice.

'Yeah. He had a real posh, double-barrel last name, but he lives at the end of the corridor.'

He frowned. 'I've been living here for years and I've never seen my neighbor.'

'You should meet him. He's really nice.'

He lifted his glass and took a sip, but there was a new tension about him.

'In exchange I promised him some cake.'

'How civil,' he said, his voice dripping with sarcasm.

'What's the matter with you?'

'And when did you plan to take the cake over?'

I flushed bright red. I couldn't explain. No matter what I said, champagne and cake would look bad.

'Oh my. Have I interrupted a late night cake eating date?'

'It was not like that. I was just being friendly.'

'Friendly?' he snapped.

'I was being neighborly. He was good enough to bring the scales over,' I explained.

'He came here,' he growled, suddenly aggressive.

'Well, yes. He helped me to carry it over.'

His eyes moved to the scales. 'What? That heavy thing there?'

I felt my face grow hot again. 'Don't you judge everybody by your standards, Mister,' I hit back angrily.

'What's wrong with this story, Tawny?'

'All right,' I conceded. 'He did try to hit on me, but I set him straight. I told him I was still mourning Robert, but we could be friends and he was totally fine with it.'

He laughed, a brutal, cutting sound. 'I can't decide if you're dangerously naïve or a total idiot.'

'Just because I'm a country girl, doesn't mean I'm illiterate or stupid,' I said with as much dignity as I could muster. I felt crushed by his assumption that I was stupid and naïve, and disappointed that again we were at loggerheads over something totally innocent. I would have turned away and stalked out of the room if he had not caught my arm and spun me around. My heart jumped.

He pulled me towards him. 'Let me tell you something about men, country Princess. We *don't* befriend attractive women. *Never.*'

'Just let go of my arm, please. I want to go to bed,' I said through gritted teeth. I had been looking forward to having champagne and cake with Ralph. He was the first man who offered me the hand of friendship ever since I came to England, and now Ivan had completely spoilt it.

'I'll be damned if I left my date because I didn't want you to spend Valentine's night on your own, and you go off to bed in a huff because you don't like the sound of the truth.'

I looked up at him, the warmth from his hand seeping into mine, and something in my stomach suddenly fluttered. Jesus, his eyes really were insanely beautiful. Like liquid silver. They poured over my face hungrily. Something dangerous whispered in my blood.

He's your stepson, Tawny.

The air was suddenly deadly silent. I could hear myself think.

Hell to the no. He's your freaking stepson.

I blinked. 'Do you want to have some cake?' I asked jerkily.

'Cake? Yeah, I want cake,' he whispered hoarsely.

I stared up at his lips as they moved in their sensuous dance of making words. Something bloomed between us. I wanted more. Much more. Unconsciously, I licked my lips and, from the way his eyes flared, it was clear that it was actually an invitation, pure and basic. A female calling to her male.

He brought a hand to my hair and fisted it. Pulling me back, he covered my neck with his hand. His skin practically burned me. There was something dark and desperate about the gesture. My pulse raced wildly under his fingertips.

'Oh, fuck it,' he swore suddenly and before I knew it, his muscles flexed, my body slammed into his, and his mouth crashed onto mine.

Oh, badass!

His tongue pushed into my mouth and the sudden explosion of lust between us was unbelievable. Never in my wildest dreams. Fireworks went off in my core. The passion was like wildfire that threatened to consume me.

'I'm sorry I questioned your intelligence, but you're fucking driving me crazy here,' he growled, and swept his mouth along my jaw while his hand trailed down my neck and captured my breast. He rubbed his palm over the sensitized tips. Heaven.

'Don't you want this, Tawny?' His voice rang too raw, too hungry. This couldn't be the same man I knew. His eyes burned into me. No sarcasm or distaste there at all.

God help me. 'Yes,' I gasped. My entire body felt like a twisting, wanting mess.

He pulled back and looked into my face. His eyes were heavy lidded, the pupils dilated to huge black pools.

He was unbuttoning my top when the doorbell rang. Both of us froze. For a moment he looked down at me, and there was an expression of disbelief in his face. Then he left me and strode to the door and yanked it open.

From where I stood I could see Ralph standing with a bottle of champagne in an ice bucket, and two flute glasses. My stomach churned.

'Sorry, have I come at a bad time?' Ralph said.

'Get lost,' Ivan replied, his voice remote and cold.

I shivered.

'Right. Got it,' Ralph said.

I pinched my eyes shut. Oh damn.

Ivan closed the door and came within a few feet of me. A furious stranger with desolate eyes glared at me. His lips curled in a sneer. 'Any dick would do. Huh?'

'It wasn't like that,' I whispered, cringing at the horrible bitterness in his tone.

'Go to bed, Tawny.'

'Wait,' I called, but he was already across the dining room and in the corridor. I heard his bedroom close with a slam that made me jump. If he had slapped me I could not have felt worse. He had treated me like a whore.

I swallowed the stone in my throat. The tears that welled into my eyes were hot and bitter, like poison.

'Oh dear God.' *What have I gotten myself into?*

Lord Greystoke

Fuck her.

Fuck this bullshit.

What a horny fucking slut!

I was so furious I wanted to punch a hole in the wall. *Damn her to hell.* I couldn't

believe that I fell for her shit. My hands clenched into tight fists. I could feel my fury burning like molten lava in my guts, but my cock was so hard it was like a piece of fucking wood stuffed into my trousers.

I strode over to the bed and sat down. I undid the button on my trousers and ripped the zip down. *Little cheating bitch.* I slid my trousers down to my knees and my cock was thrusting out of my underpants. Grabbing the material, I yanked them down roughly, closed my eyes and, loosely fisting the base of my shaft, started moving the throbbing mass of muscles in slow, pleasurable strokes.

The door suddenly opens and she is standing there, her hair flowing down her shoulders and back like a golden river, and her eyes huge and unfuckingbelievably gorgeous. She looks like a goddess.

'What the fuck do you want?' I snarl.

She smiles sulkily, pulls her skirt up to her waist and shows me her naked pussy. 'Look at what you have done to me,' she complains in a wheedling voice. 'I am dripping. Dripping all over the floor. I want you to put your cock in it.'

'Come here now and let me see,' I say sternly.

She comes forward, her skirt hitched up to expose her pussy, and stands right in front of my face.

'Look at how ready I am,' she mewls.

I see that she is absolutely right. I don't think I have ever seen a woman so fucking wet. It is dripping down her thighs.

'Don't you want to put your dick into my hot, tight pussy?' she asks eagerly.

'Talk dirty to me first,' I say.

'Oh, Daddy, pound your little slut pussy. Make your whore cum,' she says rubbing her slippery clit.

'What a nasty girl you are.'

'I'm not a girl. I'm your stepmother. Fucking me is forbidden.' She licks her lips lasciviously. 'It's taboo.' She shakes her head from side to side. 'Not allowed. Bad. Filthy.'

'You need to have your mouth washed out with my cum.'

'Yes, yes, I want to feel your cock in my mouth right now,' she gasps desperately and gets immediately to her knees. My entire cock disappears into her mouth before I know it. Her cheeks suck inwards. What a fucking whore. Her mouth is warm and wet, but it is not enough. I need something better. I need to punish her.

'Actually, I think I'll fuck you in the ass,' I say, and pull out from the depths of her throat.

She looks at my dick, glistening with her saliva and her eyes become enormous.

'Oh, you're so big. It'll hurt me so much, but I still want it,' she says and gets on her hands and knees. She twists her neck to look at me.

'Fuck my ass. Stretch it good,' she begs.

I don't use any lubricant. I just plunge straight into the lying, two-timing bitch's ass. She screams ...

... and I shot my load. It jetted out of me in streams of white like I hadn't come for ages. I fell back on the bed, alone, my right hand still curled around my dick. Fuck. I needed a whole new strategy to deal with her.

A completely different strategy.

CHAPTER 15

Tawny Maxwell

I slept badly, my night filled with weird dreams. In one, I had sex with Ivan and when I woke up my whole body was tingling. In another, I was in Barrington Manor with Robert. Not only was he still alive, he looked as he had before he became really ill. We were sitting in the rose arbor at the edge of the vegetable garden and I was trying to tell him something, but he said, 'I can't hear you, my darling. You'll have to stop that dog from barking first.'

I looked in the direction he was looking and there was Chloe on all fours. She was naked but for a dog collar, and barking her head off. She had a long pink tail, which stood up and away from her body, and she was waving it really hard. Weird.

Consequently, I could not wake up in time to go for my run, and I was in the kitchen cutting a slice of cake while waiting for the coffee machine to heat up when Ivan walked in.

Last night was etched in my mind, but it was almost as if what happened between us, the hunger, the crazy kiss, was just one of my weird dreams. The passionate man from last night was firmly locked away in a deep dungeon. There was only the suave businessman Robert introduced me to that very first night. Cold-eyed and totally unreachable, he stood in the middle of the kitchen and addressed me.

'Good morning.'

'Morning,' I said, and lifted my hand in an awkward wave.

'Do please sit down,' he said, waving his hand towards the island stools.

'Formal,' I commented, and popped myself on the stool furthest from him.

'Well, yes. I've decided what I want to do with you.'

'Very dramatic,' I said lightly, but already I didn't like the sound of his voice.

He cleared his throat. 'The simple fact is; the terms of Robert's will mean should your stepchildren manage to arrange for your demise, or your incapacitation, his fortune is basically up for grabs. However, if you are married, your husband will inherit everything, and if you have children of your own that puts even more layers between them and your inheritance. At that point it would be pointless to eliminate you.'

He looked at me with raised eyebrows.

'The marriage would only be a temporary arrangement. At twenty-one you will be able to set up trusts of your own and put in stipulations so your stepchildren are completely eliminated from being in positions of rightful heirs.'

I tilted my head to one side and considered him with narrowed eyes. What he just said sounded like three gallons of crazy in a two-gallon bucket.

'Let me get this right. Are you actually suggesting I get into a sham marriage to keep my stepchildren away from my fortune?'

'Yes. That is exactly what I am suggesting,' he said blandly.

I laughed, humorless and short. 'And you have a man ready to marry me as well, I suppose?'

'Yes,' he agreed quietly.

I moved back, stunned. Good gracious me, it never crossed my mind that he already had a candidate lined up and waiting for the job as well. No doubt he expected me to marry some employee of his or servant who would be compensated with *my* money for this ridiculous charade.

'And do I know this accommodating man?' My voice was low even though I was furious.

'You're looking at him.'

Well, butter my butt and call me a biscuit. 'You?' I uttered incredulously. 'You hate my guts.'

He shifted slightly. 'Hate is a bit intense.'

'Well,' I breathed. 'We certainly don't love each other.'

He looked at me as if I didn't have the sense that God gave a goose. 'What's love got to do with it?'

'Do go on,' I said dryly, still unable to quite believe he was being serious.

'Quite frankly, I don't see why not. You seemed to manage very well once before without love.'

The cocky bastard. I shot venom from my eyes. 'This is exactly why we should *never* get married. I'd end up poisoning you and going to prison.'

'The truth does tend to hurt,' he observed.

'The truth? You wouldn't know the truth if it hit you where the good Lord split you.'

He grinned suddenly, which just made me even madder.

'And while we're at it,' I cried hotly. 'You don't know the first thing about my marriage to Robert. You might need to take a seat for that. Actually, you might need to take a whole bench to yourself to sit and listen without judging,'

He raised both his hands, palms facing me. 'Fair enough. I take that remark back, but if you keep the high emotions out of this scenario you'll quickly appreciate the fact that I'm the best option and this is the best solution to your troubles.'

I opened my mouth to let off another tirade, but he raised his hands again.

'Hear me out. The marriage ceremony itself will be quick and less painful than a trip to the dentist, and in about two years' time we'll get divorced. You'll get your inheritance back under your control, I'll sail off into the sunset, and we never need meet again.'

I looked at him suspiciously. 'What do you get out of it?'

'Just the sex really.'

'What?' I exploded.

'Where's that famous sense of Southern humor gone?'

'It got chewed to bits when you unveiled your grand plan.'

'It's a good plan, Tawny. Strictly speaking we don't even have to live together after a reasonable amount of time.'

I scowled. Why would he want to put himself out to the extent of marrying me, when it was perfectly obvious that he didn't even like me? In his eyes I was a gold digger. Aha! Correction: I used to be a gold digger. I wasn't anymore. As a matter of fact, I was now the rich American widow. Easy prey for all kinds of avaricious men. Perhaps even men with titles and no fortune.

I leaned forward. 'And how much of my inheritance do you get to keep when we divorce?'

His eyes were suddenly freezing chips of ice, and I realized that I probably shouldn't have put it quite so crudely. There was still a small, unlikely chance he was doing all this to help me. To be fair I should have given him the benefit of the doubt.

'I'll get my lawyer to draw up a pre-nup where neither party benefits from the other, and have a draft sent to your lawyers. Any other objections?'

Another very obvious objection occurred to me, but I didn't voice it. I didn't even look at him suspiciously. What if he was in cahoots with my step-children? They kill me, he inherits the whole thing, and they split it among the four of them. Nice plan.

'I'd like a bit of time to think over this new scheme of yours.'

'Be my guest. Believe me I'll be more than glad if you could come up with a strategy that is less involving.'

After Ivan left the apartment, I cut a large slice of cake and sat down to eat it while I thought about Ivan's surreal and totally unexpected proposal. No matter which way I looked at it, it simply didn't feel right even to pretend to marry Ivan. Not when I had only just buried Robert.

Poor Robert would have been horrified to see the situation I was in. He wanted me to be independent. Yet here I was, Barrington closed up, all the staff laid off, and me stuck in Ivan's apartment and at his mercy while his stepchildren plotted God knows what to get their hands on my money.

I thought again about Robert saying to me, 'Trust me, my darling Tawny. I have thought long and hard about this. I promise you my plan is a sound one.' His illness must have ravaged him more than I thought. As far as I could see there was no plan to speak of, and he left such a large loophole for them to exploit.

I tried to imagine his reaction to me marrying Ivan. The thought made me sigh. Yet what choices did I have right now? I had no access to the money. If I tried to go it alone I would just make it even easier for them to knock me off. Perhaps they had even meant for me to perish that day. Like Ivan, I was a hundred percent certain that they would try it again. One look into Rosalind's mean, dead eyes told me that she was a total psychopath. One hundred and ten million was a lot of money.

I put away the breakfast dishes and called Angela, who worked at the One Turtle Foundation.

'Oh, Mrs. Maxwell. I'm so sorry for your loss. I was at the church service, but I did not come forward because I didn't want to intrude.'

'Thank you, Angela. That was very kind of you.'

'Mr. Maxwell was very generous to Steve and me in the will. I did not expect it. He was such a kind man. I miss him.'

'Yes, he was,' I said, a lump forming in my throat. For the first time, I was speaking to someone who loved Robert in the same uncomplicated way I did.

'Are you coming in to see us? Please say that you are.'

'Yes, I was thinking of dropping in this morning. Maybe we can do lunch?'

'That will be fantastic. It's been so long since we talked,' she said happily.

I met Angela for lunch at a small Chinese restaurant on Baker Street. We talked about Robert, her new baby, and the charity. Then she came up with a very good suggestion.

'Why don't you take a trip to one of the islands? It will do you good to get away. Recharge yourself and then you can throw yourself back into work.'

I smiled at her. 'Yes, I am missing my bikini a little bit.'

She grinned. 'Go on. I love you with a tan.'

'You know what, Angela? That's actually a brilliant idea. I will go to one of the islands. I think it will make me feel closer to Robert.'

'There you go,' she said expertly picking up a piece of lobster between her chopsticks.

Filled with excitement about the prospect of leaving all my troubles behind and going away, I went shopping for a bikini and some light clothes. I also bought a suitcase. By the time I got back it was nearly six in the evening. A mousy woman with dark eyes

came out of the kitchen. She was wearing overalls and holding a feather duster in her hand.

'Good afternoon, Mrs. Maxwell. The master told me you stay here with him. My name is Helena. I am cleaning flat for him.'

I smiled at her. 'Hello, Helena.' I looked around the super-clean place. 'I see you have been busy. The place smells wonderful.'

She held up three knobby fingers. 'Three times a week. Monday, Wednesday and Friday I come here. I am finished now, but if you have any clothes you want me to wash with hand, no problem. I take home. Just tell me what you want. Anything is no problem for me.'

'No, I have nothing for you to do, but thank you for offering. It is very kind of you.'

'You give me clothes next time, OK?'

'OK,' I agreed.

She smiled sweetly. 'You want I make tea or coffee for you?'

'No, it's OK. Don't worry. You go ahead and get home. It's getting late. We'll have a coffee together next time.'

She smiled broadly. 'I come again on Friday.'

'Great. I'll see you then.'

After she left I realized I was very tired. That drug episode must have drained me far more than I had imagined. I ordered myself a pepperoni pizza delivery and ate it in front of the TV. Weird thing was, I kept listening for

Ivan's key in the door, but there was no sign of him even when I went to bed about eleven.

My last thought was: He's probably with that snooty Chloe, and the thought didn't sit well at all.

CHAPTER 16

Tawny Maxwell

I woke up with the chickens and went out for a run in the dark. It was a good decision. Finally, I felt as if my body had completely recovered from being laid up. I felt strong again, and it smelt like it was going to be a sweet day. In my experience those mornings always turned out best.

As I was coming into the foyer of the building, I bumped into Ralph. His boyishly handsome face creased into a genuine smile.

'Hey stranger,' he said.

'Hey yourself,' I panted and, putting my hands on my knees, caught my breath before I straightened again and tried to talk. 'Listen, Ralph. I'm really sorry about the last time. It was my fault. I should have checked with Ivan first before I invited anyone around into his place.'

He grinned. 'Make up for it by having breakfast with me.'

I jerked my head back. 'What, now?'

'Sure.'

'I'm all sweaty and smelly.'

'Don't you know? Guys love sweaty smelly girls,' he teased.

I laughed.

'How about I meet you back here in twenty minutes?' he suggested.

I hesitated and thought of Ivan's reaction.

'It's just to that little café across the road. They do the most amazing blueberry muffins I've ever eaten.'

I turned and looked to where he was pointing. It was practically across the road, and it looked warm and cheerful inside with yellow lights, wooden tables and chairs, a long counter full of all kinds of baked goods, and waitresses in white shirts and short black skirts.

I bit my lip considering his offer. Well, I had nothing better to do. Why shouldn't I go? After all, Ivan spent his night with Chloe.

I smiled. 'OK, see you here in twenty.'

'I'll be waiting right here.' He grinned broadly, so obviously and sincerely pleased that I instinctively warmed towards him.

I waved and jogged up the two flights of stairs. I let myself into the apartment as quietly as possible, almost tip-toeing into my room. I showered, moisturized my face, dried my hair, and got into my new purchases; jeans, blue and white sweater, and cowboy boots. Then I slicked on some lipstick and opened my door.

All was silent and there was no movement at all inside the dragon's den. It did feel as if I was sneaking around, but honestly, Ivan was like a bear with a sore head first thing in the morning, and I didn't relish telling him I was having breakfast with Ralph. I scribbled a note and left it propped up on the kitchen island.

Ralph was seated on the long cream sofa in the lobby. He looked like he was playing a game on his phone. When he saw me coming, he stood up with a smile.

'How do you manage to look so good so early in the morning?' he asked.

I smiled at him. 'Tell me your secret and I'll tell you mine.'

He laughed. 'Keep that up and lunch and dinner are on me.'

'So what's the story with the frosty bugger?' he asked with a sideways glance.

'Every dog should have a few fleas,' I said firmly.

He looked at me quizzically. 'What does that mean?'

'Nobody's perfect. He's frosty and cocky, but his heart's in the right place.' I smiled. 'He rescued me.'

'Right,' he said, and held the door open for me.

As we walked across the road towards the café, he had his hand solicitously and lightly placed on the small of my back, but as soon as we were on the other side he dropped his arm. I was impressed. It was exactly the kind of Southern courtesy my mother had taught me to expect from a man.

He moved ahead of me, opened the door, and held it open for me. Hmmm ... more brownie points. We sat at a table by the window and ordered blueberry muffins and coffee. I had a cappuccino and he had a tall latte.

The muffins arrived and they were a hair's breath away from being as good as my grandma made them, he was easy to talk to, and he kept the topics light. I was feeling totally relaxed and happy when Ivan suddenly loomed next to us.

He didn't look at me. He put his hands on the table and stared aggressively into Ralph's face. 'You're obviously a thick bastard. Here, let me make it clearer for you. She's out of bounds. Now fuck off.'

Ralph was cool in that stiff British way. He leaned back and said, 'You don't own her, Greystoke. And last time I looked you're not my father, or my boss, so you don't get to tell me what to do.'

'Well, I've got news for you, shithead. She's my ward. So you don't get to date her unless I fucking say so.'

At that point I shot up. I was furious. 'No, Ivan. You don't get to say who I date. I'm only your ward as far as managing my inheritance. Nothing more.'

He turned to me, his eyes glittering savagely. 'If you just hang on for one minute I'll deal with you.' Then he turned his attention back to Ralph. 'If I see you with her again, I'll punch your lights out. You've been warned.'

To my utter humiliation, Ivan then grabbed my wrist and pulled me out of the restaurant with him. Everybody was looking at us in amazement. I was so embarrassed my face was flaming. Never in my wildest nightmare had I dreamed I'd be in a situation where two men were squaring up over me in a café full of ogling customers. Once outside, I let him pull me along until we were past the glass fronted shop window before I jerked hard at his hand.

'Let go of me, you brute,' I yelled. I was desperate to kick his stupid, sexy legs.

He stopped and turned towards me, his jaw tight.

'How dare you embarrass me like that?' I demanded furiously.

'Awww ... my heart is bleeding.'

'What is the matter with you?' I exploded.

'What is the matter with *you*?' he countered.

'I was having breakfast with Ralph. He's a friend. It was an innocent thing until you came barging into that café to harass us. I am so humiliated I will never be able to go back there again. For your information Ralph is a perfect gentleman. Unlike you. He never tried it on once with me. And here's something else for you to think about, you big tree. I really don't appreciate you thinking that you can run my life or pick my boyfriends for me. I'm old enough to pick my own, thank you very much. Now, let go of my hand before I cream your corn,' I roared.

'I'll let go when you stop behaving like you've been given cornbread for brains.'

My jaw hung loose. People were passing us on the pavement and giving us a wide berth. 'If you must know I happen to *love* cornbread, so when you get a chance to get off Twitter, you ... you troll you, you might want to come up with a more inventive insult,' I yelled in frustration.

He let go of my arm.

I rubbed it. 'What have I done that is so bad, anyway? I had breakfast with a neighbor,' I demanded.

'I think it's a phenomenon called karma. You know, what goes around comes around. Since you're now worth over a hundred million, *you*'ve become the target for every fortune hunter in the country.'

I shook my head in disbelief. 'Wow! I can't believe I'm hearing this. So you assumed that Ralph is a fortune hunter? Just like that. No evidence?'

'No,' he stated clearly. 'I didn't just assume. I *know* he is. He's a city boy who hasn't made any money for more than a year. He's had to take a third mortgage out on his flat, and his credit cards are all maxed out. He hasn't a bean to his name.'

The first sensation was one of hurt. The knowledge that the lovely, ordinary life I had dreamed about was never going to be mine. From now on I was always going to have to examine the motives of everyone who came into contact with me. *You can either have good friends or you can have money.* I covered the wound with indignant anger.

'You had him investigated? How dare you poke your nose into other people's business like that? So what if he's poor. It doesn't make him a bad person.'

'I didn't have him investigated. Just ran a credit check. Anyway, I don't know what you're so mad about. It's what you should have done before you agreed to go for a cozy muffin breakfast with him.'

The suspicion that I had been bottling up bubbled over. 'Maybe I should have you investigated.'

His eyes narrowed. 'What's that supposed to mean?'

His voice was suddenly deadly quiet, but I had got this far and I wasn't backing down. 'Maybe I should have you investigated. Find out why you're going to all this trouble for me when you don't even like me.'

He crossed his arms. 'I told you why I'm doing it.'

'The deathbed promise to Robert to take care of me? Or maybe ... you're so eager to marry me for my money. It is a lot, isn't it?'

His eyes widened comically. Then he laughed, a sarcastic, arrogant laugh. 'That's rich. Really rich. *You* are accusing *me* of being a gold digger?'

I shrugged. 'Why not? You're making love to Chloe while asking me to marry you.'

He looked at me strangely. 'I don't make *love* to Chloe. We have sex. I fill up all her orifices and ejaculate in them. Her pussy, her mouth, her ass.'

My mouth dropped open at the last orifice he mentioned.

He smiled wickedly. 'Why, Tawny honey,' he said in an irritating parody of a Southern accent. 'I didn't know you were into ass play. All you had to do was ask.'

'I am not, and if I was you'd be the last man I'd ask,' I gritted furiously.

He threw a fake grin. 'Shame. It might have been real fun filling up your cornbread eating ass.'

'Trust you to be as disgusting as possible. However, I noticed you didn't deny wanting to marry me for my money.'

'That's what our pre-nup is for, darlin'. I don't take yours and you don't take mine.'

'Yes, but I bet being married to me would mean you could live better and bigger, wouldn't it?'

His expression changed. He paused as if debating whether to tell me something. It was hard for me to know what was going through his head. Finally, he said, 'Come on. I want to show you something.'

'Forget it. I'm not going anywhere with you,' I said stubbornly.

'It might clear up the misunderstanding you have about me and my ... er ... intentions towards you.'

I hesitated.

He turned and began to walk away. For a few seconds I hesitated, then he turned around and cocked an eyebrow, and I knew I was going to follow him. How could I pass up such an intriguing offer to know my husband to be?

'This better be good,' I mumbled, taking a step towards him.

'It is,' he said, and smiled as I drew up alongside him.

He took me around the block to where his car was parked. Oh. My. God. Of course, he would have to be one of those guys who spent all their money on a car. It was a mean looking black Lamborghini with red leather seats. The car doors lifted up.

'They say men who buy these kinds of cars are compensating for a lack of size or performance elsewhere,' I said airily.

'Have you ever noticed how haters are never as successful, as clever, or as good looking as the people they're hating?' he asked, and slipped into the car.

I got in, the wings came down, and he turned the ignition on.

'Where're we going?' I shouted over the fantastic roar.

'Buckinghamshire,' he said shortly.

For crying out loud! '*Why* are we going there?'

'Let's just call it a surprise,' he said casually and switched on the stereo. He pressed a few buttons and Johnny Cash's *Ring of Fire* came on. 'It's a long ride. Lie back and enjoy the music.'

I crossed my arms huffily. Fine by me. If he imagined he was insulting me by playing country music, he could think again. I *loved* country music and I was proud of where I came from. Besides it would mean he would quit his belly achin'.

We drove without exchanging a single word for almost an hour. Eventually he turned off the motorway and drove down a dual carriageway for another ten minutes before we got on to quieter country lanes.

A brown road sign indicated that Foxgrove Hall was nearby. I had heard of it. It was meant to be very beautiful. I saw a picture of it in a magazine once at the dentist's office.

To my surprise he turned into the road that lead to Foxgrove Hall.

'Are we going to Chiltern House?'

'Yup.'

I turned in my seat to face him curiously. 'Why are we going there?'

He glanced at me briefly before turning his eyes back to the road because we had reached a gated entry manned by a man in a uniform.

The man smiled and respectfully called, 'Morning m'Lord.'

Then the gates swung open.

CHAPTER 17

Tawny Maxwell

He nodded and we drove through with my brain racing in overdrive. The road climbed a hill. On either side was beautiful rolling countryside. My gaze was drawn to a herd of deer resting under a massive, old oak tree. The car came to a halt at the crest of the hill and from our vantage point, Foxgrove Hall sprawled out in the stately grandeur of a time past. I took a deep breath. Well, knock me down and steal my teeth!

'All this belongs to you, doesn't it?' I breathed.

His response was a shrug.

Well, shut my mouth. There I was thinking he wanted me for my money and the man had enough to burn a wet mule. No wonder he was drinking a bottle of champagne worth thousands of pounds for no good reason. Now I understood why Robert had entrusted my entire inheritance to him.

I felt a great sense of relief: he didn't want to marry me for my money. He genuinely wanted to help me. I gazed in wonder at the splendid building. I had never seen anything so grand in my life. It was at least five times larger than Barrington Manor.

'How big is this place?'

'It's set on seven hundred and fifty acres.'

I whistled.

'You're wishing you hadn't insisted on that pre-nup now, aren't you?' he teased with an irrepressible grin.

'No,' I said slowly, 'but I am *very* embarrassed. Turns out you're waaaaay richer than me. Why didn't you correct me?'

'I'm correcting you now,' he murmured.

'You live in London. So who lives here?'

He started the car. 'Me sometimes.'

'Jeez! What a waste!'

'I guess I'll use it more when I have a wife and kids.'

I felt a strange hollow feeling in my stomach. I knew he was not referring to our pretend marriage. One day, after he divorced me, he would fall in love and marry someone for real.

'My mother lives here for certain parts of the year,' he said.

I filled my lungs with air. 'Is she here now?'

'No, you'll never catch her in England in the winter.'

As we drove closer to the house I saw just how tall and imposing the thick front columns were.

'So you inherited all this, huh?'

'The house has been in the family since the eighteenth century, but almost the entire

west wing and its contents were destroyed in a fire in 1995. There was no money to rebuild it so it remained that way until I inherited it. I was seventeen when it became mine and I remember coming here that first time and not only the west wing was a burnt shell, but the whole place was in a terrible state of disrepair.'

He shook his head with the memory.

'I was advised to turn it into a trust building, but I refused. It took me ten years to return it to its former glory. You are looking at the only classical Greek revival stately home in all of Buckinghamshire,' he said with quiet pride.

'If your father couldn't afford to rebuild it, where did you get the money from?' I asked curiously.

'Well, I took a big risk. I knew there were billions to be made in the emerging property market in China, so I mortgaged everything I had and invested every penny I had. I could have lost everything.'

'But you didn't.'

'No, I didn't. You know all those images of ghost cities that are on the net?'

'Yeah?'

'I helped build some of them.'

I frowned. 'How did you make money building those? Aren't they supposed to be failures? Years later and nobody is living in them.'

He smiled and shook his head slowly. 'No. They are the opposite of ghost cities. A ghost

153

town is one that is abandoned when the town's fortunes decline and the people move away. These are the opposite. The people have not come in to occupy them yet. The Chinese are long-term planners. They can defer pleasure for years in the pursuit of a cherished goal.'

'So you must be a real catch. What are you, like Britain's most eligible millionaire or something?' I clapped my hands over my mouth.

'Billionaire,' he corrected.

'Sometimes you need a billion dollars,' I quipped.

'That's truer than you realize,' he said. 'There's almost nothing to beat the feeling of being so completely and utterly financially solvent.'

I looked at him and for the first time I felt as if I was seeing the real him. I felt a sense of peace spring up between us and I felt connected to him. We didn't have much in common but we had this. We didn't try to pretend that money was not important. We both knew it was. Without it this world was a cruel place indeed.

I knew what it was to have nothing, not even a roof over my head, and it was the scariest, most horrible feeling in the world. I will never be able to scratch from my mind the sensation that felt as if my stomach was slowly digesting itself, and how that hunger robbed my spirit. I don't care what anybody says: hunger butchers love.

When Robert took me under his wing and said, 'From now on until the day you die you'll be able to afford anything you want,' I cried with relief.

I looked into Ivan's crazy-assed, silver eyes and that nameless thing between us started crackling again. If I had carried on looking at him the atmosphere in the car would have changed. The peace would have dissipated. Electricity and an aching longing would have taken over and I would be under his spell again, boneless, unable to do anything but what his body demanded of mine. I didn't want that. Not now when I just found a real connection to him.

'Oh my God!' I cried in a mock-horrified voice. 'The tabloids will have a field day. I can just see the headlines now.' I zipped my hand in the air to punctuate every word that followed. 'Greedy American Widow Steals Britain's Most Eligible Billionaire.'

'No, they'll say, "Lucky bastard marries breathlessly beautiful, leggy blonde."'

I swallowed. If only it could always be like this between us. 'No they won't,' I croaked. 'They'll hate me. I don't have the right accent.'

He opened his mouth to speak but I interrupted him.

'But don't you worry about nothin'. I'll be a darling at being a billionaire's bride.'

He threw his head back and laughed, the first real laugh since I knew him, and that made me smile. Sometimes, I decided, I really liked Ivan de Greystoke.

Ivan parked the car on the vast gravel car park and we got out. A white delivery van drove in after us and drove around the back. We were walking towards the imposing frontage when a man in a cream sweater and white slacks ran out, his face wreathed in a large smile. He might have been gay. He flapped his hands expressively.

'Good morning, my Lord. How wonderful to see you again. Will your Lordship be staying? Should I get your room ready?'

'No, I'm not staying, Lee. Just wanted to give my fiancée a tour.'

Lee's eyebrows shot into his hairline.

'Why, my Lord, I had no idea. Congratulations are in order.' He turned his face towards me, his expressive brown eyes zig-zagging down my body and lingering one second longer on my cowboy boots. Yes, definitely gay. 'Welcome to Foxgrove Hall, Mrs. Maxwell.'

I raised my eyebrows, surprised that he knew who I was, but I guess I was talk of the town.

'Thank you, Lee,' I said politely.

He smiled and turned towards Ivan. 'Well, I can serve brunch or lunch if you prefer anytime you feel like it.'

'Does Mrs. Kennedy know how to make muffins?' Ivan asked.

'I only have to inform her.'

Ivan looked at me. 'What flavor?'

'Blueberries,' I said.

'Done,' said Lee with a smirk.

Then Ivan put a possessive hand on the small of my back and led me up the grey stone stairs, and it was nothing like the polite one that Ralph had used to guide me across the road. This one said, this woman is *fucking* mine.

This was turning out to be a sweet day, but a surreal one.

In the tall stone hallway where the house branched into three parts, Ivan stopped. He said he had a few phone calls to make and asked if I wouldn't mind doing a bit of exploring on my own for a bit.

'Yeah, I can do that,' I agreed.

He suggested we meet back in the breakfast room in an hour. He waved his hand down the corridor on the left. 'It's the last room at the end of that corridor.'

'OK,' I said casually and wandered towards the main part of the house. But as I wandered wide-eyed around that sumptuous, awe-inspiring edifice, I realized that Foxgrove should not be confused with being merely a house.

It was a blatant status symbol built to show the rest of the world in no uncertain terms that its occupants were superior, untouchable beings. It took me almost an hour to see just one room filled with sculptures and artifacts from around the world. The sensation I had was similar to walking into one of the rooms in the British Museum. All these amazing sculptures, no doubt some illegally brought back from their countries of origin to England.

I turned around and went back to the breakfast room. Foxgrove's idea of a breakfast room was my idea of a palace. There were gilt moldings, ceilings painted with angels and people in robes. There was velvet and brocade and different types of marble on the walls and floors.

'Hey,' Ivan said from behind.

I turned around. 'Nice home you have,' I said politely.

'Yes, it is nice. I sometimes forget.'

Lee came into the room, walked to the long table, and pulled out a chair for me on the nearest corner.

I took it and Ivan sat next to me so we had the table corner between us. The muffins were brought in. They were still warm and delicious. Lee disappeared and we started to talk. Cautiously. A bit about me, but I kept the conversation flowing mostly about him.

I learned that he had spent a few years in America. Mostly in New York, a place that he loved and still went to a lot as he had a lot of business dealings there. He loved the fact that you could travel for hundreds of miles in America and still be in the same state. He thought America was one of the most beautiful countries in the world, but he hated the American prison for profit system.

Just as I was getting to know him, he got another phone call and we had to return to London. At my request he dropped me off outside One Turtle, and I didn't see him again for the rest of the day.

CHAPTER 18

Tawny Maxwell

I opened my eyes the next morning and knew without a doubt that the wisest thing I could do was to go out and get myself a lick of space. Taking off to the island alone was the best option for me. Right after our wedding I should take off and get some perspective, figure my shit out. Because only a fool couldn't see that I was blindly waltzing in the wrong direction.

Yesterday, I allowed myself to get too close to Ivan.

Yesterday, I started to think foolish nonsense about Ivan. Things I had absolutely no business thinkin' about since it was obvious as hell that any feelings I developed for him would be doomed from the start.

Sure, the sexual thing was there in spades, but there was something else too. Something not right. A thing I couldn't put my finger on. He was hiding a secret from me as sure as I was hiding a secret from him.

Even though I was dying for my morning coffee, I waited in my room until I heard him leave the apartment before I opened my door. After a strong coffee and a quick breakfast, I took a cab to the One Turtle Foundation's office. I had only managed to clear a tiny amount of work yesterday, and there was actually quite a lot of stuff that needed my attention. I threw myself into it gratefully. For a while I even forgot to think of Ivan.

The proper return back to work was also nice because one of the first islands that Robert had turned into a sanctuary had just been gifted to the locals to manage on their own, and they had sent lovely thank you cards with pictures of baby turtles enclosed. There were also many unopened condolence messages waiting for me. I replied to all of them.

By the time I looked up from my desk it was already lunchtime.

After a hearty meal at a Moroccan deli with Angela and two other girls from the office, I went out to the shops to buy a few more bits and pieces that I would need for my holiday. Mosquito repellent and all the other stuff that was essential on an island.

Although I planned to go barefoot most of the time, I bought two pairs of flip-flops because the monkeys are always stealing them. I also bought lots of boxes of chocolates and biscuits for the volunteers who crave chocolates made in the West. Local chocolates simply didn't taste as good as they had to be made with palm oil to stop them from melting in the heat.

It was nearly four by the time I let myself into the apartment, and I was dropping my shopping bags on my bed when the doorbell rang.

Curiously I went to answer it. It was Chloe.

'Hello,' she said, miraculously managing to make a harmless word sound like an insult.

'Ivan's not in,' I said.

'I know. I'm not actually here to see him. I left something in his bedroom and I've come to collect it.'

'Oh, OK.'

I opened the door wider and she sailed in. She was wearing a beautifully cut navy blue coat. She undid the buttons. Under it she was wearing a blue dress. Someone should have told her that just because it zips up doesn't mean it fits.

I moved back. 'Well, you know where everything is,' I said noncommittally, and began to walk towards the kitchen. I stood in the middle of the kitchen and heard her enter Ivan's bedroom and close the door.

I looked around the spotless space. My stomach felt funny and there was a vicious taste in my mouth. I didn't know why I had gone in there. I was not hungry and I was not thirsty. I went to the cupboard and opened it. My fingers were gripping the knob of the cupboard so hard my knuckles were bone white.

I really did need that holiday.

I stood staring at the contents in the cupboard. I swallowed hard. I should bake something. *Good idea, Tawny. Bake something.* I blinked blankly at the canned food and condiments on the shelves.

Cornbread.

That's what I should do. Make a show stealing, rich, tender, moist, flavorful, crunchy-edged, buttery tin of cornbread.

Bitch.

I turned away from the cupboard and went to the fridge. The first and most important ingredient: unsalted butter. I placed it on the counter. *Deep breath. Nothing to do with you. Don't you be minding other people's business, young lady.* Right. OK. Fine.

I closed the fridge and opened the cupboard where all the dry ingredients were kept. Brown sugar, corn flour, all-purpose flour, baking powder. I started pulling the ingredients I needed out, unconsciously slamming each one on the counter.

The last one penetrated my fog of fury.

I stopped and took a hold of myself. I had no right to be angry. Ivan and I were getting married, but it was a fake marriage. He didn't belong to me. Besides, it was my idea to not drag sex into the equation. So really he could sleep with as many slutty Chloe clones as he wanted. I heard a noise behind me and whirled around.

Chloe was standing at the door, well posing, actually.

'Found it,' she announced with a smile and waved something in the air. 'My butt plug.'

My expression must have betrayed my thoughts because she frowned and came towards me.

'I know you. Don't get ideas about Ivan. He's no Robert Maxwell. He's a man who needs things you know nothing about. You haven't got the slightest clue how to keep him satisfied. Do you know how I met him? I met him in a club called The Dirty Aristocrat. Do you know what he was doing? He was finger-fucking a random woman on the dance floor.'

My mouth dropped open.

'Yeah, I thought so. He's wild. Like me.'

I snapped my mouth shut.

'So here's some good advice. Stay away from him. He's mine.'

My skin bristled and the hairs on my body stood on end. I felt like one of those cats you see with their backs arched, their fur ruffled, their heads thrust forward, and their mouths opened in a threatening hiss. Then she made her first big mistake. She reached out and poked me in the chest with her forefinger. I forgot to say, I'm a bit fussy about who touches me.

I grabbed her finger so suddenly her head snapped back. I turned it upwards while I watched her eyes widen with shock and her mouth open in an inelegant (but extremely satisfying for me) grimace of pain. She tried to pull her finger out of my grasp, but I was the stronger of the two of us and I had no problem holding on.

'Listen, honey,' I said quietly. 'I didn't go to finishing school to learn how to eat a fourteen course meal in the proper way, but where I come from girls like me eat bitches like you for breakfast. Let this be your first and last warning. If you touch me again, it won't be a butt plug being stuffed up your skinny ass, but my rolling pin.'

Her eyes bulged with fear. Her mama had obviously not told her to never corner someone meaner than herself.

I let go of her finger. 'Now get out of my sight.'

She clasped both her hands together and took an unsteady step back from me.

'What are you doing here, Chloe?' Ivan asked from the doorway of the kitchen.

We were so engrossed in our little spat we had not heard Ivan come in the door. He had addressed her but he was looking at me with an odd expression on his face.

'Chloe came for her butt plug,' I said sweetly.

Ivan's eyebrows flew upwards, and I swear, the beginning of an irritating smirk was starting to curve his mouth as he turned his eyes on her.

'Oh good, you're here. I was actually hoping to catch you,' Chloe said, her voice quivering with relief.

'Well, come into the living room then,' he said, and turned his body sideways to make space for her. She practically ran out of the kitchen.

He looked at me. 'I won't be too long,' he said, and followed her wriggling plug-hungry butt.

I curled my fists into balls of frustration. Ugh! What the hell was I doing living in his house and being forced to endure such humiliating scenes? It was intolerable. I was so glad I was going off to the sun in a couple of days.

I switched on the oven and dialed it to 400 degrees. *Next:* melt the butter. I dumped the butter into a bowl and stuck it into the microwave. I found my fingers tapping the countertop as I waited. I forced my fingers to stop. I looked at my watch. Three minutes had passed since they went into the living room and closed the door.

Is that not enough time to fit a plug into an itchy bitch?

Obviously not.

I took the bowl of melted butter out and thumped it on the island surface to cool. A little bit slopped out of the sides and puddled on the granite.

Next: DIY Buttermilk. I put three teaspoons of white vinegar into a cup and added whole milk into it. Unlike me, that was going to need five minutes to sour. I greased a round pan, then stopped, and listened. There were no sounds at all coming from the living room. I glanced at my watch. Honestly.

I began measuring the dry ingredients. Indian head stone ground yellow cornmeal, flour, baking powder, salt. Next job: whisking the cooled butter, brown sugar and honey. I whisked the mixture so hard it began to froth. I poured in the buttermilk.

The bastard.

I whisked again. The door to the living room opened.

'Bye, Tawny,' the shameless slut called out in a fake-happy voice.

I didn't answer.

Calm down, Tawny, I told myself as I mixed the dry and wet ingredients with a lot more violence than necessary.

Ivan arrived at the door. I glanced up indifferently. He seemed very indifferent too. I didn't comment on the lipstick staining his cheek and squashed the urge to straighten his skewed tie. I even managed to ignore the smell of her perfume.

He walked to the fridge and took out a beer.

'What are you making?'

Oh! the cheek of the man. 'Cornbread.' My voice sounded vinegary.

I threw a sideways glance at him and the sorry ass actually looked amused. I felt like smacking his head against the fridge.

He sat on one of the stools on the other side of the island. 'I've never tried cornbread,' he said conversationally.

'No, I wouldn't have expected you to.'

'Are you mad about something?' he asked innocently, and I swear he was trying not to laugh.

'No, whatever makes you think that?'

'I don't know. It could be the dark cloud over your head.'

I walked past him, picked up the greased pan, and on my way back to the bowl managed to accidentally purposely whack the side of his head with it. Hard. There was a satisfyingly hollow metal-meeting-skull thud.

'Ow,' he exclaimed.

There! That sure wiped the smug look off his face. 'Oh, sorry. Did I hurt you?' I purred.

He rubbed the side of his head and looked at me sheepishly. 'What are you so furious about?'

'Nothing.' I flashed him my fakest smile.

'Look,' he said. 'Chloe is not my girlfriend, OK? I don't do girlfriends. I've had longer relationships with the cartons of milk in my refrigerator.'

'Oh, is that why she smelt so off,' I fumed.

'You don't believe me?' He seemed shocked.

'Do you want your answer in one word or two?'

'Go ahead be a devil. Use two,' he taunted.

'FUCK NO,' I yelled.

Those incredible silver eyes fixed me in a deadly stare. 'You go ahead and believe what you want. I didn't mislead her and that's the fucking truth. She knew exactly what she was getting with me. She just came by to piss you off. For your information she won't be coming around again, and if she does, please don't let her in.'

I poured the batter into the tin and clunked it on the table surface to even it off, before I looked up at him. 'Piss me off? I thought she came for her butt plug.'

'Tawny,' he sighed, his voice exasperated. 'I don't have to explain myself to you, but I'll do it this time and only this time. I'm a man and I have needs. Since you're not planning to take care of them there *are* going to be other women, probably lots, in my life. However, none of them will come around to wherever we are staying.'

I put the tin in the oven and banged the door shut. I crossed my arms over my chest. 'You're absolutely right. I agree with you. I won't bring my sexual partners around to wherever we're living either.'

He jumped out of his chair and crossed the room so freaking fast I gasped with astonishment when he grabbed my upper arms. His face was tight with barely leashed fury and his eyes were glowing. Oh my god! He could pierce someone's soul with those wolf eyes. My mouth dropped open and I stared at him, shocked.

The air between us crackled with tension. He opened his mouth to say something, then he appeared to remember himself. His breath came out in a rush. He let go of my arms and stepped back. His hands hung by the sides of his body, but they were hard fists.

I stood rooted to the spot staring at him. It was amazing how suddenly and violently his mood had changed. One moment he was relaxed and placatory, even amused, and the next he was charging at me like some thunder god.

I was startled by the lightning change in him, but even more shocking and confusing was the way my traitorous body was *still* reacting to him. My eyes couldn't help staring at his broad chest, the way it rose and fell with every breath he took, the snug fit of his trousers over his lean hips.

What was wrong with me?

How could I be aware of his innate sexiness and his primal virility when we were slap bang in the middle of a slanging match?

He took another step away as if I was something that was dangerous to him, his eyes were hooded and guarded.

'I came home early because my ever resourceful secretary managed to reduce the twenty-eight days of notice necessary at the Registry Office to six days. She made us an appointment for three days' time. We're getting married at 2.00 p.m. this coming Monday, and I was going to take you to dinner tonight to celebrate,' he said softly.

A strange silence crept in between us.

He just stood there, his eyes steady on me. It was like we were at two ends of a bridge. We could see each other but we could not touch. Two much bad stuff lay between us. I felt the pressure to say something. Anything. I had to make it right. I had been a bitch. The rusty wheels in my brain turned round and round. *Anything at all would be good, Tawny.*

'So take me out then,' I said, my voice barely a whisper.

'Do you like Japanese food?' He said the words slowly.

'Not to celebrate our wedding,' I said.

He smiled crookedly. 'French?'

'Nearly there.'

He smiled. 'Italian?'

'You have one last try.'

He cocked an eyebrow. 'English?'

I smiled. 'I can live with that.'

'Pick you up at your door at half-eight?'

'Sounds like a fine plan to me.'

He broke eye contact, nodded, and turning away disappeared into his study.

I stood there looking at the empty doorway. What the hell just happened between us?

It looked very much as if I was throwing away my best laid plans and going out on a date with Lord Ivan de Greystoke.

CHAPTER 19

Tawny Maxwell

I washed my hair, dried it, and painstakingly put corkscrew curls in it. Then I painted my nails ice cream yellow, colored my eyes smoky and moody, glossed my lips, and got into the new black dress I bought at Liberty.

Mama always said, it is better to be late than arrive ugly, but I was standing in front of my mirror by eight-thirty sharp, and nobody could have guessed I once ran barefoot and tangle-haired to the creek to swim naked.

Ivan knocked on my door and I saw my eyes light up like a Christmas tree in the mirror. Girl, that's a bad sign right there. Taking a deep breath, I walked over to the door and opened it.

Oh my!

Darkly urbane, radiating a wild, feverish excitement, he stood, dressed all in black except for a fabulously cut cream jacket. His blazing eyes lusted for me. It made my knees go weak but I smiled all sultry and sexy-like, and didn't let on that I thought he was prettier than a glob of butter melting on a stack of pancakes.

'Can I keep you?' he teased.

'Only if you keep me in a jar and give me lots of treats!' I replied.

He laughed. 'Don't worry there'll be all kinds of lovely things in there for a good little girl like you to suck and swallow.'

"You'd charm the dew right off the honeysuckle,' I said sarcastically.

'I settle for charming the dew right off you,' he leered.

'I'll be darned. You managed to turn that old saying into something dirty.'

'It's a talent,' he said with a filthy snigger.

I batted my eyelashes the way that was more parody than sexy. 'Do you think they'll let me into The Dirty Aristocrat like this?'

'The Dirty Aristocrat is a sex club,' he said, his lips twisting upwards so sexily, and darn it to hell, but I wanted to lick that dirty smile right off his face. Men like him should be kept locked up in special places to be used purely for copulation purposes.

'I know what it is,' I said coolly. 'I asked if they will let me in dressed like this.'

His jaw twitched. 'Baby, there isn't a bouncer born who's going to turn you away from anywhere.'

'Good,' I said calmly and walking to my bed, collected my coat from it. 'Because we're going there later.'

His eyes glittered. 'We are?'

'Aren't we?' I asked innocently.

'They don't play country music there,' he said, helping me into my coat.

I tilted my head to one side as if I was processing the information. 'They don't?'

I turned around and he shook his head gravely.

I put on my best I'm-so-country-sticks-fall-out-every-time-I-open–my-mouth' expression. 'You mean to say nobody in England ever thought to have sex to Dolly Parton's songs?'

He kept his face straight. 'Afraid not.'

'It seems to me the English are missing out.'

'It would seem so,' said the slick weasel, hiding a smile. 'Nevermind, you wouldn't have liked it, anyway.'

I looked up at him through my eyelashes. 'Why honey, you're so full of shit it's surprising your eyes ain't brown.'

He grinned. 'You'll get on well with my mother.'

'Good, it's all settled then. The Dirty Aristocrat it is,' I said.

'This should be an interesting night,' he said, a twinkle in his eye.

I buttoned up my coat.

'Shall we?' he murmured.

We went out into the street. It was only a little cold. I lifted my collar against the wind and snuggled down into the warmth of my coat. His car was parked down the road and we strolled down to it. He walked close enough for people to realize that we were together, and I immediately appreciated the fact that I loved being with Ivan. Every woman we passed looked at him with hungry eyes first, then at me with wishful envy.

He drove us to a very exclusive restaurant. Stopping the car at the entrance he turned to me. 'Here we are?'

'Very fancy,' I commented.

'Like you wouldn't believe,' he replied and hit the button that worked the car's wing doors.

I swung my legs out and put them on the pavement, then someone held a gloved hand, palm up, so I could put my hand into it. As soon as I did, he gently and expertly tugged me so I floated upwards as if we were part of an immaculately choreographed dance.

I thanked his impassively polite face and saw that Ivan was already waiting for me. I linked arms with him and we went up the stairs into a grand, green, marble foyer. Staff came to help us with our coats, and show us into a high ceilinged room. It was all white with recessed mirrors on the ceiling and eggplant leather seats. It was all very civilized. People in fine clothes and that deliberately languid air of very fat cats were seated at the white tables sipping at their drinks. It seemed as if some of them knew Ivan. There were waves and nods in our direction. The women reminded me of different versions of Chloe. Ugh.

'Would you like a drink at the bar?' Ivan asked me.

'No, I'd like to go straight to the table, please,' I said.

'Of course, Madam,' the courteous man hovering at our elbows said.

He took us through a vibrantly emerald corridor hung with extraordinarily complicated and clever light-staircase chandeliers made out of bronze plumbing pipes.

The corridor opened out to a truly unique and marvelous dining area. A rectangular room sculptured out of a variety of materials to give you the impression that you had entered a glass box. It was decked out with hoop-shaped lights suspended from the ceiling, pink leather banquettes, and futuristic looking diagonal brushed steel panels with lighted butterflies on them.

The waiter showed us to our table. I remembered reading that every restaurant had golden tables, ones that were kept for their best customers, their most famous, or their best-looking. Well, we were being seated at their golden table. It was actually elevated as if we were on a stage holding court.

I looked at Ivan.

'Is this table OK with you?' he asked.

'Sure,' I said, and let the waiter pull a chair out and carefully push it back as I bent my knees so I was perfectly seated without having to pull my chair towards the table.

They brought us menus, we made our selections, and they bowed, smiled, approved

of our choices, and respectfully withdrew. There was no music in the place, only the subtle murmur of polite conversation. I looked up at Ivan and he was watching intently.

'Do you come here often?' I asked.

He leaned back and put his wonderfully shaped hands on the table. 'Sometimes. The food is generally superb.'

A sommelier appeared with a bottle of wine. After the usual fluffing around that they inevitably do in fancy restaurants, he poured it out into our glasses.

'To our wedding,' Ivan said, holding his glass aloft.

'To our wedding,' I echoed and took a sip. It was dry with subtle tones that I was too nervous to note.

Another waiter came to the table. He placed a plate with a selection of canapés in the middle of the table and started to explain what they were, but his accent was so thick I only picked up random words, tomato, snow crab puree, caramelized onion ...'

Satisfied that he had done his job, he bowed from the neck and made himself scarce.

I leaned forward, my hand accidentally pushed one of the knives: it clattered onto the glass-like floor. Without music the noise of its landing was exaggerated and heads turned in our direction. I felt myself flush.

'Sorry,' I apologized awkwardly, and I was about to bend and pick up the knife when he leaned forward and caught my hand.

'For what?' he asked, a frown making his eyebrows come together in a straight line. A waiter was already picking the knife up.

'For being so clumsy,' I said, winching inwardly.

'Social etiquette is how the moronic silence the intelligent. What does it matter if you drop your knife, or eat with the wrong fork? Don't ever apologize for such things again.'

I stared at him. How wonderful to be born in a class where you don't have to emulate anyone. Anything you do is seen as wonderful simply because of your bloodline.

As if he had read my mind he said, 'I was very rebellious when I was growing up and I hated being a Lord. My heroes were all anti-establishment figures. To my mother's horror I put up a massive poster of Gandhi in my room. She thought he was a ridiculous, half-naked fakir, but I admired him because he refused to allow anyone to make him feel he was less because of his color, descent, or traditions. I loved that he came to England to meet his colonial masters dressed in rags.'

He flashed a cheeky smile. 'I can imagine how infuriating it must have been for them.'

'You said you hated it when you were young. So you don't hate it anymore.'

'Well, I acted up a lot when I was a kid. I did the most outrageous things, but no matter what I did, I was always forgiven because of who I was. And in the end I thought if people were going to be stupid enough to put me on a pedestal simply because of an unearned title, who was I to pull myself off it? I milked it for all it was worth.'

I laughed.

'What's funny?' he asked.

'It's funny how you and I are from the exact opposite ends of the spectrum. When I first came to this country I tried, without much success, to fit into the very society that you tried without much success to escape from.'

He looked at me. 'Don't let anyone change you, Tawny. You were always beautiful. There was not one thing about you that needed to be changed.'

I looked carefully at him to see if he was taking the piss out of me, but he was sincere.

'I thought you didn't like country bumpkins,' I said lightly.

He grinned. 'What are you talking about? I adore country bumpkins. I secretly even like that twangy American accent that you arrived with.'

'I can still talk like that,' I said, returning to my old way of talking and letting go of everything Robert had taught me. It felt good to talk like that again. When I first came I didn't want to be the one with the funny accent. I wanted to belong so I tried to change to suit my environment, but maybe I didn't need anybody's approval anymore.

I could talk like them, I just didn't want to anymore.

'That's more like the glorious Tawny I first met,' he said and grinned at me. An open boyish grin that took my breath away. Wow! It hit me then, that despite all my efforts to keep him at arms length, I was crazy about this guy. I always had been. From the first moment I laid eyes on him I wanted him, but he had always looked at me with such cold, disapproving eyes. I was forced to hide my feelings even from myself. I did not hate him. Far from it.

His eyes narrowed. 'What?'

I shook my head and reached for my wine glass. 'Nothing.'

'Sure?'

'Yes,' I said. No way was I telling him that he was my man crush. I leaned forward. 'What would happen if we left now?'

'We'd be still hungry?' he said, one eyebrow raised.

'No, I mean if we left this place and went and got a juicy cheeseburger instead.'

He leaned back in his chair. 'You want a cheeseburger?'

'With fries.'

He clasped his hands and stared at me. 'With fries,' he echoed.

'And two strips of bacon.'

He shook his head. 'Right now?'

'Yeah. I haven't had one in ages. Robert could never eat burgers, what with his diet being so restricted, so I never did either.'

He lifted his hand. A waiter came. 'Bill please,' he said, not taking his eyes off me.

'Is something wrong, Sir?' the waiter asked worriedly.

'Nothing's wrong. We have to be somewhere else.'

He hurried away. The manager came. His brow was creased and he seemed extremely concerned. 'Is something amiss, Lord Greystoke?'

Ivan did not even spare him a glance. 'Not at all. We just remembered that we have to be elsewhere. If you would be kind enough to bring the bill.'

'No, no, Lord Greystoke! We couldn't possibly charge you. You haven't had a bite to eat. The wine will be compliments of the house.'

God! Rich people sure got away with murder.

Ivan dropped a wad of fifty-pound notes on the pristine tablecloth and escorted me out of that august establishment.

CHAPTER 20

Tawny Maxwell

We stopped in front of the cutest little white American restaurant in Mayfair. Chuck's Diner had a white and red sign that read, Bringing New York to London. Decorated like a steakhouse it had dark-wood paneling, inviting red booths, a bar counter running the length of the restaurant, and chatty staff that practically sat down to eat with us.

Ivan ordered the two hundred and fifty gram fillet and I very nearly had the four hundred gram rib-eye, but in the end I had the Chuck's Hefty Hamburger with an extra side of fries.

The salad arrived and while Ivan drizzled dressing onto it, I observed his movements with fascination. The more time I spent with him, the more interested in him I became. I liked watching him perform even the most mundane action and I wanted to do more than just watch him.

I wanted to touch.

As Chloe had pointed out, he was someone so out of my league that even contemplating such an idea was playing with fire. I was bound to get hurt.

Fortunately, before I could become too morose, my burger arrived and it was something else. Nearly as big as the dinner plate and dripping with melted cheese, bacon grease, and beef juice, it looked and smelt like the food from my childhood.

I grinned at Ivan. 'Now that's what I call a burger.'

'Bon appétit,' he said mildly, picking up his steak knife and fork.

I picked up my burger in my hands and took a really big bite. 'Mmmm,' I said, and rolled my eyes like I was eating ambrosia.

Ivan stared at me. 'That good?'

I nodded enthusiastically since my cheeks were so stuffed talking was not possible.

'Good. I'm glad you're enjoying it,' he said and cut and speared with his fork what my granddaddy used to call a civilized bite.

I swallowed my food. 'You don't know what you're missing. This is so good it practically dissolves on your tongue.'

'I don't think I've quite seen a woman enjoy her food this much,' he said with a chuckle.

'Where I come from they say, fries before guys,' I said, as I used two thick, golden, salty fries to soak up the excess juices from the meat on the plate and put them into my mouth. I half-closed my eyes and fluttered them as fast as I could, as if I was in the throes of ecstasy.

'Give me one of those damn fries,' Ivan said and, reaching over, grabbed one.

I watched him put it into his mouth and chew thoughtfully.

'Isn't it brilliant?' I asked, picking the dripping burger up in my hands.

'Yeah, it is good,' he conceded.

I widened my eyes. 'Good? It's freaking wicked.'

I took another hefty bite. Ketchup ran down my finger and I licked it.

He stared at me.

'Sorry,' I said with a grin.

He shook his head. 'Don't be sorry. You look cute when you're stuffing your face, besides, it's a pleasure to see you truly enjoying something. You're normally so ready to fly into a rage anybody would think you've a fucking cactus up your ass.'

'Why, Lord Greystoke, I could have said exactly the same thing about you,' I said.

'So you're a Southern girl. I don't have much to do with the South. Where exactly are you from?' he asked flashing one of those smiles that made my stomach go funny and made me glad I was sitting down.

'Tennessee. I'm from a little town close to the border of Virginia.'

'What was it like?'

'Oh, parochial. Our nightclub only opened on the weekends.' I wiped my lips.

'Keep me away from there,' he said, with mock horror in is voice.

'No, you'd hate it,' I agreed.

'So tell me something about you?' he invited, slipping a piece of potato into his mouth.

'Like what?'

He pretended to consider. 'Hmm ... start with your weaknesses.'

I grinned. 'The only real weakness I have is cowboys.'

'Get me a hat and I can ride longer and harder than any cowboy.'

I laughed. A funny little flutter in my stomach.

He took a gulp of beer straight from his beer bottle and eyed me seriously. 'What do you love, Tawny?'

I said the first thing that came into my head. 'Horses, turtles, my shoes, oh, oh and I really love Christmas. Well, I suppose everybody does.' I poured ketchup on the side of my plate.

He smiled. 'Not me.'

My mouth dropped open. I had never met anyone who did not like Christmas. 'Why? What's not to like?'

He made a face. 'The presents, the stupid decorations, the Christmas jingles, the dry turkey. Ugh. Everything. What do you like about it?'

'The presents, the stupid decorations, the Christmas jingles, the dry turkey. Everything.'

'Every Christmas I'd disappear off to Barbados or somewhere they don't make such a fuss.'

'Didn't you even enjoy it as a child?' I asked curiously.

'No.'

'Unbelievable. Christmas was such a special time when I was a child. My mama and I used to drive down to my grandma and granddaddy's. It was so wonderful. We used to eat until we couldn't move. Then we'd sit in front of the TV and slowly my granddaddy would start farting. I can still remember the horrible smell of his sprout farts mixing with the Christmas candles. Then mama and I would giggle when my grandma brought out the air freshener can and started blasting the room.'

He chuckled. 'Well, if you want to celebrate Christmas when we are married, you can.'

I dipped a chip into the pool of ketchup at the side of my plate. 'I was going to ask you, where will we live after we're married?'

'Well, for the first few months we'll keep the present arrangement going, and then if you prefer living in the country you can move to Foxgrove Hall.'

'What about Barrington House? Will I ever go back there again?'

His face hardened. 'I'm afraid you won't be able to live there for some time. I wouldn't feel safe with you being so far away.'

We had apple pie and ice cream for dessert. The crust was golden and crunched satisfyingly when my spoon sliced through it. I put it into my mouth and Ivan was sitting back looking at me.

'Good?' he asked.

'Almost as good as my grandma's,' I said.

He looked at me curiously. 'Robert told me you have no one.'

I put my spoon down, suddenly wary. 'Yeah. That's me. Little orphan Tawny.'

'What happened to your parents?'

I took a deep breath. I was getting into dangerous territory here. *No, lies, Tawny. You don't have to reveal the truth but no lies.* 'My father left before I was born and my mother died when I was seventeen.'

'Robert also said that your mother passed away before you came to England.'

I sobered up. 'Yeah, my mother died.'

'You miss her very much, don't you?'

I looked up at him and took a deep breath. A lump was forming in my throat. 'Every day.'

His expression was serious. 'I'm sorry, Tawny.'

'Yeah, me too.'

'What was she like?' he asked softly.

'When I was growing up my mama was amazing. She had read Paper Moon when she was a young girl and the main character's mother used to paint her nails, and while they were drying she spread her fingers out and waltzed around the room. My mama was so impressed by that, that she used to copy the action. If I close my eyes now I can see her floating about our trailer to Celine Dion's *It's All Coming Back To Me Now.*'

I smiled with the memory.

'She sounds sweet,' he said.

'She was. Every Saturday evening she used to lay me on the kitchen counter and wash my hair in the sink. Then she'd put rollers in at night, and then next morning just before we left the house she'd blow a whole can of hair spray on it so I could go to Sunday church looking like a poodle.'

He laughed softly.

'But she became sick and then it was horrible. I couldn't bear to see her suffering. We didn't have insurance and there was nothing I could do for her. After she died I lived in her car for a few weeks.'

He looked at me horrified. 'What did you after that?'

I looked down at my pie. I couldn't remember the last time I opened up to someone like that. I couldn't even blame the alcohol. I only had a few sips of my beer.

'I came to England. I met Robert and the rest is history.'

He looked at me curiously. 'So how on earth did you meet Robert?'

I shook my head. 'I'd rather not talk about it.

For a second his eyes narrowed suspiciously. I stared at him steadily.

He looked at his watch. 'You still up for The Dirty Aristocrat?'

I nodded. 'Yeah. What actually goes on in there?'

'It's an anything goes kind of place.'

I leaned forward. 'Why do you go there?'

He looks at me expressionlessly. 'Usually for an anonymous fuck.'

I looked at him long and hard. 'Why?'

'Because I like it.' A smile spread across his face. 'Because I get bored easily.'

'Don't you ever want to be in a relationship with someone?'

'I don't know. I've never met a woman yet who has stopped me from wanting other women, so what's the point of pretending to her or me that we're in a relationship when I'm not truly committed?'

'Fair enough.' I said, fixing my eyes on him, not liking what I was hearing. Chloe was right. He was a womanizer. An unapologetic, unabashed, unrepentant manwhore. Yet I could not stop wanting him.

He raised his eyebrow at a passing waiter and signaled for the bill.

CHAPTER 21

Tawny Maxwell

The foyer of The Dirty Aristocrat was claustrophobic, small and dark and hot. We went down some red steps and into a place with red lights and purple velvet curtains everywhere. A queen size bed with purple sheets and red cushions had been roped off. Presumably it was meant to evoke the sensation of entering a brothel, or a courtesan's boudoir.

I could feel the heat from Ivan's hand around my waist as we moved deeper into the club. It was heaving and the music was very commercial. They were playing *Gangnam Style* as we made for the bar. Somehow it seemed perfect in such sleazy surroundings. A gay couple sat on top of a massive speaker kissing passionately, and the dance floor was jam-packed with writhing, half-naked bodies.

Ivan led me to the bar. There was one empty stool. He curled his hands around my waist and, picking me up, popped me on the seat. I squealed with surprise.

'Why did you do that?' I asked, a little bit embarrassed and a little impressed with the show of brute strength.

'You wanted to be here. Remember? Anything goes,' he replied with a glint in his eye.

'Oh yeah?' I challenged daringly.

He gave me a look that made *something* happen between my legs. Jesus! Such a thing had never happened to me before.

'What're you drinking sexy lady?' he asked staring into my eyes.

For a moment my mind was a complete blank. Then I said the first thing that came into my head. 'Tequila with salt and lemon.'

He smiled. 'A fire drink. Excellent choice.'

He didn't even have to order the drinks. A switched on barman had not only heard the order, but had already fulfilled it. Two glasses came sliding across the bar towards us and stopped dead in front of us.

'Impressive,' I said.

The barman smiled, put down a saucer with lemon wedges and a salt shaker, and went on to another customer.

I looked at Ivan. 'Don't you have to pay for this?'

'I have a bar tab running. The bill is settled monthly.'

Wow! A regular haunt then. We did the salt, alcohol and lemon thing.

'Whoa,' I said, my face scrunched up with the sour taste of the lemon. I had never had tequila before.

'Another?' he asked.

'OK,' I agreed immediately.

We did it all again.

'Whoa,' I said, trying not to cough.

'Another?' he asked with a devilish grin.

'OK, but this is the last one,' I said firmly. 'I already feel ten times merrier for no good reason.'

'This time let's do it the Mexican way.'

'What's that?'

'Warm without the salt and lemon.'

I raised my eyebrow. 'Surely that would take all the fun out of it.'

The corners of his eyes crinkled. 'On the contrary.'

He spoke to the barman and two shots came sliding towards us.

He clinked his glass to mine, his eyes telling their own story. 'Anything goes.'

'Anything goes,' I agreed, and let the drink slip down my throat. Without the salt I could actually taste the peppery taste of the drink.

'Like it?' he asked.

I nodded. 'I do actually.'

PSY's *Daddy* came on and it could have been the Tequila or the feeling of being so damn close to him, but my foot started tapping.

'Wanna dance?' he asked.

'Thought you'd never ask.'

He laughed and pulled me off the stool. The palm of my free hand somehow ended up on the wall of his chest. Heat radiated out of him into my skin.

'Damn, you're solid,' I whispered, my knees all of a sudden quite wobbly.

His hand tensed around me. He was just keeping me upright, I guess.

We got to the floor and suddenly all those people trying to be so sexy seemed funny so I started clowning around doing all the totally unsexy moves from PSY's video. I flicked my hair back from my face and, pointing my forefinger at him, screamed the words, 'Hey, where'd you get that body from?'

He was good for it. He copied my earlier goofy dance moves and shouted back, 'I got it from my Daddy.'

I laughed.

He fell to his knees and to my surprise executed some unexpectedly cool moves while on them. The tequila started buzzing in my head and we carried on like two fools until the song ended and I smiled sunnily up at him.

The next track was Galantis's *Peanut Butter Jelly*.

'Spread it like,' he prompted, miming the action of combing his hair.

'Peanut butter jelly,' I bellowed, and turning wriggled my butt provocatively at him. He slapped it and I whirled around with exaggerated surprise and showed him my middle finger. Laughing he spread the fingers of both his hands and made circles with them.

He looked so ridiculous I had to laugh.

It was the most fun I'd had since the hogs ate grandma and I was giving it all I got, widening my eyes, and making silly faces, when he suddenly grabbed me, pulled me towards him, and kissed me. The laughter died in my throat. His cologne flooded my senses. Delicious. Everything around us melted away.

Oh my God! It was like our mouths were made of chocolate. They melded into each other. We were just a hot mess of lips, tongues, saliva and desire. I became lost in him.

Spread it like. Spread it like. Spread it like.

I felt the effects of his kiss down to the tips of my toes. When he raised his head I could only stare at him dumbfounded.

'Oh wow!' I said, my lips tingling.

Reaching my hands around his neck, I pulled his head back down and carried on kissing him. I was like a hungry animal that had been kept in a cage and not fed for days, while it could see the food just outside its reach. I could have stayed like that forever, just drowning in the sensation of that mind-blowing kiss if he had not pulled me off him.

'Hey,' I protested, frowning up at him.

'This club is not wild enough for what I want to do to you,' he muttered thickly and dragged me off the dance floor.

We were standing facing each other at the coat counter, waiting for my coat, when I saw a woman behind Ivan approaching us. She was slim with shiny, dark-chocolate hair and her skin was smooth and olive toned. She was staring at me intently. Not taking her eyes off me she tapped Ivan on the back. I watched him turn and look down at her.

'Isla is having a party,' she told him. 'You can come. There will be girls there for you.' She let her eyes slide toward me. 'I can take care of her while you are busy.'

Hot bling was blasting in the background. The expression on Ivan's face did not change in the slightest, except for the sudden tightening of his fingers on my hand.

'Maybe next time,' he told her flatly.

'Shame,' she said looking at me. 'I really like your little friend.'

'Have a great time at your party,' Ivan said and turned his back on her. I looked up at Ivan. His face was a frozen mask.

The girl who had taken our ticket emerged from the back room with my coat. She put it on the counter and he took it and helped me into it.

We walked out into the cold air and Ivan took hold of my elbow. I looked into his eyes.

'Did you want to go to that party?' I asked.

He shook his head. 'No, I can go to parties like that any day of the week.'

'Good,' I said.

He hardly spoke in the car. I stole a few glances at him, but he seemed to be in his own thoughts. He parked in the underground car park. I turned to look at him.

'Thank you for a lovely evening.'

He smiled. Slow and sexy. Oh! I'm so screwed.

'It's not over yet,' he said softly.

'No?' There were butterflies in my tummy.

'Come on, I'll walk you to your door.'

'Makes sense,' I joked, but my voice sounded nervous.

He came around and helped me out. We walked without touching, but the air between us was throbbing. I did not look at him in the lift. When we got inside the apartment he closed the door behind him and I turned to look at him. His eyes were veiled. I stared at him nervously. It had been fun in the nightclub, but now that we were at the point where it all got serious, I felt incredibly nervous. Whatever buzz from the alcohol seemed to have completely exited my system.

'Should we have a drink first?' I asked.

He shook his head slowly and began to advance. Sensuality dripped from him. 'Shit, Tawny. I'm going to make you scream so hard tonight,' he promised.

I opened my mouth. There must be something clever to say to that. My mind was a blank. Oh sweet Jesus. Then my legs began to move. Backwards. I was retreating. Damn. Who'd have ever thought I was such a coward? My mouth started making words.

'Hang on a minute. Can you just give me one minute to ... ah ... get into something more comfortable? Erm ... something easier for you ... to ... um ... take off,' I babbled nervously.

He stopped advancing. 'You have exactly one minute,' he said silkily.

'Perfect,' I said, and almost ran to my room.

I closed the door, leaned against it and took a deep breath. My heart was racing like a mad thing. *Take stock, Tawny. You definitely do want to sleep with him, right?* Oh boy, did I want a lick of Ivan. OK, just nerves then. Perfectly normal. I can do nerves.

I rushed to my lingerie drawer and pulled out my new baby doll. I hurried out of my dress and into the lacy bit of material. I dashed into the bathroom and stood in front of the mirror.

Wow! I sure looked different. My cheeks were flushed and my eyes were glittering with excitement. In my haste I had snapped one of the delicate white ribbons on my baby doll. If I switched off the main light he would never notice. I fluffed my hair frantically and gargled with mouthwash. I walked into my bedroom and froze.

Ivan was standing at the door. He had taken off his jacket and three of his buttons were already undone. Smooth tanned skin gleamed through the V.

'Is it already one minute?' I heard myself asking.

'Sorry,' he said not sounding sorry at all. 'Couldn't wait another second.'

'Oh.'

'My barefoot beauty,' he said staring at me. No one had ever looked at me like that. With such naked hunger.

'Bare feet go with every outfit,' I babbled.

Reaching out a hand I quickly snapped off the switch for the main light. Illuminated only by the bedside lamps, the room was a little less intimidating.

He smiled slowly, confidently. There was something almost devilish about that smile. I was so anxious my heart was fluttering like a trapped bird, but I wouldn't be outdone for bravado.

'I bit my lower lip and said in the sexiest voice I could muster, 'What're you waiting for? Come and get it, babe.'

It was like a red flag to a bull. What happened next was a total shock to me.

In the blink of an eye, I found myself pinned face down on the mattress. A large, powerful hand landed between my shoulder blades to hold me in place while his other hand unclasped my bra.

I was too shocked to even think. Adrenalin surged through my blood and my body felt as if it was about to ignite. I could no longer keep my breathing calm. He twisted his fingers into my hair and jerked my head back until my ear was next to his mouth. I was so hyped up I felt no pain.

'Is this what you want?' he growled softly, his voice grating with lust. 'You want me to take you? To fuck you? To make you scream?'

The blood roared in my ears. I was shaking with a strange excitement.

'Everyone thinks you're such a nice, sweet girl, but I know the truth. I know how bad and naughty you truly want to be ...'

'Yes,' I whispered.

'I didn't hear you,' he said arrogantly, his breath hot on my neck.

'Yes,' I said, my voice louder.

'Yes what?'

For God's sake. 'Yes, I want you to take me?' I admitted through gritted teeth.

'The word I was actually looking for was, Sir.'

'Yes, Sir,' I squeaked.

'Good,' he said with satisfaction.

He released my hair and my head flopped forward. He flipped the hem of my baby doll upwards. I felt the soft material land on my head. I knew my entire back and panties were completely exposed.

For a while he did nothing. I just heard him breathing hard. Then he roughly seized the silky material of my panties in an iron fist and yanked it up hard and forward, forcing me onto my knees, my ass high up in the air. The crotch of my panties was pulled so tight against my pounding clit that I lost even the ability to think rationally. Scrap that. I couldn't think at all.

I wanted to scream at him to ease up, but when I opened my mouth only a raw groan escaped. I knew at that moment that I was in over my head, but I was already in the position he wanted me to be in and his fingers released the material suddenly. I took a shaky breath as blood started flowing to my clit again.

His fingers brushed against the wet material of my crotch. I shivered uncontrollably and started panting like a dog on a hot summer day. I could think of nothing except what was happening between my legs. Oh God, I had been reduced to the insistent pulsating between my legs. Nothing else mattered, but for the man who stood behind me to satisfy the gnawing ache inside me.

I felt his hand, rough and impatient, push aside the soaking material, and his long fingers plunge into me with a squelching sound. The foreign sensation, the wet sound, and the bestial nature of his action, shocked me and made me freeze.

His fingers stilled without warning inside me.

It was as if we were both suspended in time. Neither moved. The atmosphere changed, chilled, congealed. Slowly, I turned my head and looked up at him. He was staring at me in disbelief. He shook his head as if in denial. My mind was blank. There was not one thing I could think of to say that would make the situation better, less embarrassing for me.

He retracted his fingers hastily, as if he just realized that he had in fact, thrust his hand into a viper's nest.

With his hands at his side he continued staring at me, his face shocked.

'What?' I asked, my voice horribly squeaky.

'You've never been with a man, have you?' he accused.

CHAPTER 22

Tawny Maxwell

I swallowed. I really thought I could wing it and he wouldn't know, but it was not to be.

'No,' I whispered.

'What?' he bit out incredulously.

'It's true. I never have,' I admitted.

'How can that be?'

'That's how it is,' I said in frustration.

He continued to stare at me. Neither of us moved, then he took a long step back.

'Right,' he said, and for the first time since I knew him he sounded like the upper-crust Englishman that he was. 'I have to go somewhere for a bit. Can you give me a few minutes? I need to do something. It's … rather important.'

I stared at him wordlessly. It was the weirdest thing ever. There I was with my ass swinging in the air and he needed a few minutes to do *something*.

'OK,' I said. What else was I going to say?

'Good.' He nodded and, as if talking more to himself than me, said, 'Good. Don't move. I'll be back. Wait for me.'

I nodded, wondering if I was trapped inside a really bad slapstick comedy.

He strode out of the room and I heard him cross the living room and go into his bedroom. I stayed where I was for a few more seconds because I was in such a state of shock, then I vaulted off the bed. For a while I stood in the middle of the room not sure what I should do. What a disaster. Still, he did say he was coming back. Maybe he had to consult a How to Have Sex With A Virgin manual or something.

I went back to the bed and sat on it. I shouldn't wait indefinitely. That would be weak and spineless. I should give him a time limit. Five minutes. If he did not make it back in five minutes the deal was off. I sat staring at the bedside alarm clock.

Four minutes left, buster.

Then I heard his bedroom door fling open and his footsteps quickly cross the living room.

I jumped and immediately turned to face the doorway.

He stood framed in it. With the light behind him he was large and forbidding. An overlord come to claim his prize.

Lord Greystoke

The light shone on her beautiful golden hair making her glow softly like an angel from a Rembrandt painting. The whole night stretched out before me and there were so many things I wanted to do to her, but all I wanted to do at that moment was simply look at her a little bit longer, so I'd capture her in my mind, so I'd never forget how faultless a moment can be.

I watched her hug herself nervously, open that plump mouth that I had jerked off to for two fucking years, and let stumble out nonsensical, meaningless, trite words into my perfect moment.

'Let me explain. Robert and I—,' she began.

Instantly, I crossed the space between us and placed my fingers across those crazy-sexy lips of hers. They felt soft and full.

'I don't want to know. At least not right now,' I said.

You see, my obscenely sexy little angel, you just gave me the piece of the puzzle that was missing. The thing I could never figure out. The big secret. BTW the plot twist was brilliant. I never would have guessed.

She stared mutely up at me, her eyes shining like blue stars, and the heat of a blush burning her cheeks. God, she was so fucking beautiful. My cock hardened and strained.

'OK?' I asked.

She nodded slowly.

I removed my hand and smiled.

The answering smile that trembled on her lips was so decadent and so utterly delicious that I wanted to fucking cage her. I could feel the muscle ticking furiously in my jaw.

'Now where was I?' I said.

She looked down at the floor, looked up again, tucked a stray lock of hair behind her ear and said, 'You were about to spread it like peanut butter jelly.'

I smiled. That was the thing about her. She was supposed to be trailer trash, but she had more class in her little finger than some of the so-called royals I've met. I felt something inside me swell and grow. Our eyes locked.

'Yes, well, I might have been in a bit of a hurry before. This time I'm going to take my time and savor you. Then I'm going to spend the whole night doing things to your body that you never even thought were possible.'

She licked her lips nervously, her breath washing over my cheek, warm and soft. Thoughts flitted across her face like clouds. She inched towards me and I touched her waist.

'So you ... uh ... don't mind popping my cherry?'

'Tawny honey, it'll be a fucking honor to pop your cherry.'

Tawny Maxwell

His eyes held mine almost ... lovingly. They were so different from the wild man who had pinned me down on the bed and roughly shoved his fingers into me that I could only stare back, bemused.

He laid a hand gently on my cheek and tenderly brushed his fingers down my neck. It made my stomach clench. As if he knew the effect he had on me, he smiled, brushed my hair back from my forehead, and kissed the hollow of my throat.

'Oh,' I breathed, my throat suddenly dry.

God, I wanted so much to please him. I wanted to be wanton and passionate. The possibility that I might disappoint such a sexual connoisseur as him clung to me like bad debt. I wanted to be like the women who frequented The Dirty Aristocrat. Utterly unashamed of my sexuality. His hands moved down and massaged the sides of my breasts while his teeth gently nibbled on my lower lip.

Without warning his tongue thrust into my mouth and withdrew again. Then back in again. My toes curled. Lord have mercy, the man was fucking my mouth with his tongue! It was dirty and it was wonderful. Like a little rehearsal. I knew that he knew that, that was what I was craving for between my legs. The harder and faster his tongue thrust in and out of my mouth the more my sex clenched, as if he was already inside me. He was so masterful at tantalizing my body, my bones were starting to feel like wax in the midday sun.

He knelt before me and let his hand slip up my thighs.

I bit my lip and tried not to tremble. He lifted the baby doll and looked at the way the wet silk clung to my shape highlighting every curve and groove. I felt myself blush. He hooked his fingers into the waistband of my panties and, with aching slowness, pulled them down my skin while he stared unblinking at my exposed sex.

'Do you know that your clit is *so* swollen it is poking outside your pussy lips?' he asked softly.

I licked my lips and shook my head.

'Step out of your panties,' he ordered.

I rushed to obey and he picked them up. Fixing his amazing silvery eyes on me, he dragged his tongue across the crotch panel and licked the sticky fluid there.

'Oh,' I whispered, my head swooning.

Lord Greystoke

I licked the wetness along the virgin's inner thighs and instinctively her legs moved apart in invitation. I separated her swollen lips and brought my nose close to it, inhaling her state of arousal. Why, she smelt exactly as I always knew she would. Ripe. Juicy. Ready to be consumed.

I nuzzled the soft golden curls of her adorable pussy. The sweet sensation blew my mind after years of fantasizing. I kissed her on her steaming core and, while she watched with dazed eyes, I let my tongue make contact with the cream of her desire. Fucking heaven. I drank her in. She moaned helplessly. It occurred to me on some vague level that I was never going to get enough of this woman.

I looked up at her. 'I like the taste of your wet cunt,' I whispered.

She gasped with a mixture of shock and excitement.

I wrapped my fingers around my lover's left leg and draped it over my shoulder. Her pussy opened up like a pink fruit. I kissed her again, my tongue moving slowly between her glistening lips.

Her breath came in short and quick gasps. Her hips pressed against my face and her hands curled around my head and pulled me in. She wanted more.

I swooped on her clit and feasted on it while she moaned, whimpered and groaned until her leg began to tremble and she was swaying unsteadily. Immediately I planted my hands firmly on her pert rear and, taking the hood of her clit between my teeth, I bit down. She threw her head back and swore at me.

Very unladylike, soon to be Lady Greystoke.

I smiled against her pink flesh as I felt the shudders that coursed through her. At this rate she wasn't going to last very long.

Tawny Maxwell

My head was buzzing as intense pleasure radiated from my core and rolled into every part of my body. A massive climax like I had never experienced was ripping right through me. I had to grasp Ivan's shoulder to prevent myself from falling over. I screamed incoherently and exploded while he carried on slobbering all over my sex as if it was chocolate or ice cream.

His greed was obscene and filthy and wonderful.

My muscles were still convulsing and throbbing when he stood up. Hauling me into

his arms he carried me to the bed and threw me on it. Bending over me he opened my legs wide and pushed a long, thick finger inside my swollen, pulsating sex.

My body arched. 'Oh God,' I gasped, clenching his finger.

'That's right. Call to your maker. You're going to fucking need him tonight,' he growled.

He pulled his finger out and with a slow smile brought it up to my face. He stroked my lips until I opened my mouth a little. Immediately his finger slid inside and I tasted myself.

'Suck it,' he ordered, and pushed his finger deeper into my mouth. As soon as I obeyed he smiled again, removed his finger, and plunged it back into my sex.

'Ahhhh,' I cried out.

Watching me intently he began to thrust that finger. In. Out. In. Out. All the while watching me moan.

'I know,' he said soothingly, 'but I need you to be very, very wet tonight so you can take all of me.'

Then he took the finger out and once more brought it close to my lips. I opened my mouth to take it in, but he put that finger into his mouth instead and sucked it hard.

Wow! That was so hot.

His mouth fused with mine and I kissed him back greedily. Kissing him was like being in the eye of a tornado. Time stills. You lose a part of your soul. By the time he removed his mouth I was a boneless mess. He licked, nibbled and sucked my jaw, my throat, my shoulder. He used his teeth to snap the little white spaghetti strap. He pushed the silk down and exposed one breast.

'Look at that. Full, round and just begging to be sucked,' he whispered and drew my sensitive, aching nipple into his mouth.

I grabbed his head in my hands and, arching my back, tried to push more of my breast into the warm wet cave. He responded by sucking harder. I welcomed the painful pleasure of his lips. Jolts of electric sensations went from his mouth to my groin. I felt my nipple swell and become a hard little stone in his mouth. His tongue swirled around the hard nub.

He lifted his head. 'You're so beautiful,' he breathed, looking down at me.

I was suddenly aware of my disheveled state. One breast exposed, the baby doll torn and crumpled around my waist, my legs askew, my sex swollen and dribbling.

'The other nipple,' I urged, my voice urgent and shameless.

His eyes glittered triumphantly at my brazen need. With a dark laugh he grasped the neckline of my baby doll and viciously ripped it down the middle. I lay before him, on display, every inch of me offered up to his eyes and his touch. He swooped down, engulfed the other nipple, and sucked it until I was writhing with pleasure.

He stood up and, feasting his eyes on me, began to undress. I watched wide-eyed as he flung his shirt and roughly yanked down his trousers. Hot damn! The man was right beautiful. My eyes flew to his cock, jutting aggressively out through the waistband of his white underpants.

I watched him yank the thin material down his muscular legs, and for the first time in my life I saw a real life erect cock at such a close distance. It was enormous and beautiful with thick veins twisting up it like dancing snakes. Amazing how it bounced back like an angry rubber thing. It had. Taking my hands, he guided them to his throbbing, jerking flesh.

His big, beautiful cock was lightly clasped between my palms. My heart was beating hard and I could hear the blood rushing in my ears. I touched the tip with its bead of liquid pearl, and looked up at him in wonder. He seemed unrecognizable, his face tense and foreign.

'I wanted to see my cock inside your mouth from the first moment I saw you.'

I lifted my head off the bed and, rising to my elbows, set my mouth on the short journey to the head of his cock. On the way there I breathed in the smell of him and it made me almost dizzy. Musk. Faint. Then I was there, and his hot, satiny-soft skin brushed my lips. Looking up at him, I took him between my lips, my mouth stretching to accommodate his girth.

I tasted him then. He had a taste! He was resting on my tongue, heavy and hard when I withdrew and licked him experimentally. Slightly salty and something else. Something that I really liked. Like the water from the creek after it had rained. I licked him again. Gently and with total dedication. Like a dog.

'Oh fuck. That's it. That's good,' he groaned.

That encouraged and emboldened me. I could do this. My lips closed on the shaft and my tongue slid around and explored the shape of the swollen head. His hand curved around the back of my head. Clawing into my hair, he guided my face forward and forced my mouth to take more of him.

'Fuck, Tawny,' he groaned. 'I always knew you'd feel amazing.'

His hips moved forwards and back as his cock slid gently in and out of my mouth and I sucked him with deep, drawing pulls. Then he pulled out of my mouth with a wet slapping sound.

'What's the matter?' I whispered, surprised. I wanted to satisfy him, to feel him climax, to return the pleasure he had given me.

'Absolutely nothing,' he said softly and, bending down to the floor, picked up a foil packet.

'Oh,' I said. It was strange, exciting and a little frightening. I shivered at the thought of something that long and thick and solid was going to go into my body.

He fitted the rubber on himself, pushed me back down on the bed, and opened my legs wide.

'Keep your knees up,' he instructed, and positioned himself between my legs. I loved our bodies being entwined and joined, his chest crushing down on my breasts, his hard naked body pressing down on mine, and those strong powerful thighs spreading me wide open. Even more, I think, I loved the anticipation.

My fingers gripped his gorgeous arm muscles. I could feel them flex when he raised himself slightly and, pointing the enormous head of his cock over the entrance into my body, pushed in.

I inhaled sharply, my eyes widening with surprise.

Good God. He was only partially inside me, but it felt like a thick, deep intrusion. Painful and not pleasurable at all. My thighs were spread wide, but my body was distressed. How would all of him fit? Suddenly, I felt tiny and helpless under his big powerful body.

I must have whimpered because he paused.

Dipping his head down, he murmured, 'It's OK, Tawny. Just relax. It won't hurt in a while.'

He looked down at me almost hypnotically, while his hands stroked my body, soothing and calming me. Then his tongue entered my mouth and my fear faded almost instantly. The kiss was hard, demanding and fiery and I became lost in it. I sensed my body supplicating to his, my legs spreading even further apart. His mouth was locked to mine, his tongue deep inside my mouth, I was vaguely aware of the turgid shaft slowly working deeper and deeper into me with each gentle thrust. Slowly but surely, he was travelling into the depths of my body.

I sucked his tongue blindly. Nothing else existed but us and what he was doing to my body. When he tried to pull away I moaned into his dominating mouth.

Lord Greystoke

Tawny's body was like heaven. Wet, warm, tight, and so fucking responsive. I luxuriated in the way her slender thighs cradled me and I enjoyed her little groans and whimpers, the plaintiveness of them, the excitement on her face, the strained look of surprise and pain in her glazed eyes, and the way her hands grabbed handfuls of the bed sheets as I forced my cock into her.

It had taken every ounce of my willpower not to fuck her hard. Hell, I wanted nothing more, but I didn't. Not this time. There would be other times for that. Many other times.

Stilled inside her tight, hot, slippery channel, I could feel the heat of her sex and the soft downy feel of her pubic hair against my shaft. My cock was pulsating and my balls were so heavy and full they were like ripe fruit ready to burst.

Hell, I couldn't wait anymore, but the icing on the cake is when you can get her to come at the same time as you. I hadn't gone all the way to the hilt, so I reached my hand between us and began to circle her slick clit with my finger.

Her eyes widened in surprise.

I felt her clench my shaft tightly as she arched herself beneath me, her feet kicking high towards the ceiling, her hands clutching my biceps as she climaxed at the same time I did.

CHAPTER 23

Tawny Maxwell

'**T**hat's going to be a very hard act to top,' I breathed into his ear, as he lay on top of me, his cock still buried inside me.

He chuckled.

'What?' I asked.

'Nothing.'

'No, really, what's so funny?' I insisted.

'That's not an act. That's the twenty-minute induction class,' he said.

I giggled. 'Really?'

'Yes, really. Don't forget you still have sex to Dolly Parton's dulcet tones to look forward to.' His voice was dry. Obviously he didn't think sex to Dolly was going to be anything special.

I grinned. 'That's true. Shall I go put her on?'

He didn't seem too impressed with my idea. 'Ah, give me a few minutes. Aren't you sore, anyway?'

'Noooo, I *love* having you inside me,' I said enthusiastically.

'Good, because you are going to be having me inside you a lot, Missy,' he promised.

I squeezed him experimentally. 'If we're going to have a break can we eat something? I'm hungry.'

He lifted his head and looked into my eyes. 'Tawny. You're a girl after my own heart.'

'What do you want?'

'Surprise me.'

'OK. Get off me then,' I said and deliberately clenched his shaft as tightly as I could.

He looked at me warningly. 'Do you know what happens to little girls who go and pull the tails of tigers?'

'What?'

'They get fucked in the ass.'

'Oh shit.'

'Exactly,' he said and, pulling out of me, rolled to his side.

I missed him inside me immediately. I realized that I loved the feeling of being so stretched and filled. I sat up and he stayed on his elbow watching me.

'Don't look at me,' I said.

'Why not?'

'Because I'm not used to having anybody look at me naked.'

'Get used to it, because I love seeing you naked.'

I jumped from the bed and ran out of the room to the sound of his laughter. Once out of his view I stopped and grinned to myself. Wow! Who'd have thought sex could be that great?

I never dreamed having a man inside me could feel *that* good.

I walked into the kitchen and gingerly touched myself. My sex was so hyper-sensitive it felt as if it was swollen to at least two times its normal size. The folds felt as if they were hanging between my legs. I bent down to look and they were actually hanging. I hadn't bled, but that was probably because of all the horse riding and rough sports I'd done during my lifetime.

I quickly cut and put a few slices of cornbread on a plate and loaded that onto a tray with a jar of honey, a spoon, some savory cheese balls and a jar of pickled Okra that I'd ordered from a Southern food specialty website, and carried the tray to the bedroom.

My breath caught. Buck naked and totally unashamed of the fact, Ivan was lying propped up on some pillows. I almost couldn't believe how beautiful he was. It was actually very distracting to be with such a hot man. His dusky-gold skin was gleaming in the dull yellow light.

'That was quick,' he said.

'Err .. Greystoke, what's with the giant erection?' I asked softly.

'Come over here and I'll tell you all about it,' he invited, patting the space on the mattress by his side.

I went to the bed, put the tray down on it, climbed up, and sat with my legs folded under me, and my knees together.

'We're about to eat. Why do you have a hard-on?' I asked in a cheeky voice. The truth was I was trying to cover my embarrassment about being naked on a bed with a naked, fully erect man.

'Why do you think?' he mocked.

'It's not some kind of medical condition, is it?' I ventured solemnly.

'I'm afraid so,' he said gravely.

I put on my I'm-so-sorry-your-lottery-ticket-didn't-win face. 'Does the disease have a name?'

'Hotfortawnyitis,' he said, his eyes beginning to twinkle.

I hid a smile. 'Oh,' I said very slowly. 'How awful. Is there any cure?'

He nodded. 'Friction. Lots of skin on skin friction.'

I suppressed my laughter and played along. 'Should we do something about it?'

He pretended to look pained. 'The sooner the better.'

I glanced at the plate. 'Don't you want to eat?'

'I do,' he said softly, his splendid eyes gleaming like jewels in the shadows.

I wrinkled my nose. 'If that's a joke I don't get it.'

'I love to eat and fuck at the same time.'

'What?' I shook my head. 'How?'

'Sit on my poor sick dick and I'll show you.'

'No way. I won't to be able to eat while you're inside me.'

'Of course you will,' he said and, reaching for a condom, sheathed himself.

'No, I won't,'

'Yes, you will.'

'No.'

'Yes. Now come and sit on my fucking dick,' he ordered.

'Well, if it's really going to help,' I murmured and started to crawl towards him. Strange fact: I was actually wet and wanting to impale myself on that glistening pillar of hard meat too. I straddled him, my knees on either side of his body.

'Is your sweet pussy wet?'

I felt my vagina pulse with excitement. 'You bet.'

He smiled. 'This time you get to decide how far into you I go. Think you can take me to the hilt?'

'Either that or I'll die trying,' I said with a grin.

I gripped the thick shaft in my fist and, positioning it under me, slowly lowered myself onto the blunt head.

He grabbed my hips and pushed me a few inches down his shaft. My mouth opened in a silent gasp of surprise.

'The rest is up to you,' he said quietly.

I exhaled the air slowly from my lungs and savored the sensation of his thick heat stretching me. A man inside a woman must be remembered in the DNA because it felt familiar, as if I'd had him inside me a thousand times before. I realized being stuffed full must be a primal pleasure.

'Your pussy is so tight it feels like it's sucking my cock in.'

Holding his eyes, I pushed myself down on him. A slow burning heat flowered at my core and rippled through my entire body as I went on that long, slow slide down that thick pillar of meat.

I imagined him as a beautiful stallion, big and powerful, sculptured with muscles, taking my weight and movement in his stride whilst I rode us both to the ultimate pleasure. My nerves felt raw and my skin tingled with his every touch.

Not taking his eyes off me, he reached for the tray and slid it along towards him.

'What's this?' he asked, holding up the cornbread.

I stopped my downward movement. 'Um ... corn ... bread.'

He took a bite and chewed. 'It's like a hug from God,' he said appreciatively. He held the cornbread six inches away from his mouth. 'Go on take a bite,' he urged.

I leaned forward.

'Mind my fingers,' he cautioned.

I bit into it.

'Bounce on my dick,' he said.

Still chewing, I slid up and down his shaft. It was the strangest sensation. I swallowed it as quickly as I could.

He thrust upwards while I was on my way down. 'What are the balls?' he asked.

I was almost incoherent with the jolt of electric pleasure that went through my body. 'Ahhh ... what?' I asked blankly.

He played with my clit. 'The balls on the tray. What are they?'

'Uh ... cheese. Ohhhh ... Ahhh ... Cheese balls,' I gasped.

Using his left hand, he popped a cheese ball into my mouth and watched me as I writhed under the ministrations of his right hand.

'Very tasty. Did you make them?'

'Yessssss,' I hissed.

'Here,' he said and pushed another cheese ball between my parted lips. I rolled it in my mouth and tried to chew it while his hands circled my clit and manipulated it until I thought I was going to climax and choke to death or spew the food all over him. But he took his hand away and I quickly swallowed the food in my mouth. He needed both hands to unscrew the jar of pickled okra.

'What on earth is this?'

'Pickled okra,' I said pausing in the act of jumping up and down on his shaft.

'Don't stop. Continue bouncing,' he instructed.

He extracted a vegetable in his hand. 'Are they supposed to go with the cheese balls?'

I nodded.

He smelt it, made a face, and brought it to my mouth instead. I quickly took a bite and, tasting nothing, swallowed it. He popped another cheese ball into his mouth. I stared at how unaffected he seemed to be when I could barely think with his hard cock so deep inside me.

'Fuck my dick harder, Tawny,' he said, casually dusting the crumbs off his hands.

I rode him faster until finally I could see that he was no longer in control. His eyes were becoming darker, his jaw was tight and his mouth was starting to become a snarl. He was very close to climax.

'Lean forward and grind your clit on my groin,' he commanded.

As soon as I leaned forward and tried to obey his order, his cock was suddenly too deep. 'Oh, sweet Jesus,' I panted.

'An inch too far?' he growled.

'Make me,' I cried. 'Make me take all of you ... every last inch. Push me down on you. All the way.'

He frowned. 'That would hurt you.'

'I want it,' I whispered fiercely. 'I want to take all of you. I want you to cram it all in. Every last inch.'

'No.'

'Other women have taken it all in.'

'They didn't have the tight cunt you have.'

I let him slip out of me and rubbed my wet cleft shamelessly along the length of his cock. 'Please. Just this once. So I know what it feels like. If it gets too much I'll scream and you can stop.'

He hesitated.

'Just this once.'

In a flash he grabbed my hips, penetrated me, and pushed my body down until my sex was flush with his skin. My mouth was open in a silent scream. Gritting my teeth so I didn't scream out, I leaned forward and ground myself on him until I came hard, gushing on his cock. He caught the bottom of my thighs and pumped hard into me until his cock swelled even more and he exploded inside me. I looked at him, panting and triumphant. I had taken all of him.

CHAPTER 24

Tawny Maxwell

Lying on my stomach, I licked the vinegar of a pickled okra while Ivan looked sideways at me. He had already dismissed this Southern delicacy as inedible. I nibbled the tip.

'Hey, you know when we first started to, you know, do it, you left me and went to your room because you had something important to do.' I turned my face towards him. 'What was so important?'

He popped a cheese ball into his mouth. 'I had to jerk off.'

'What? You left me waiting on my hands and knees and went to jerk off?' I spluttered in disbelief.

'You obviously have no comprehension at all of the male body. I couldn't have lasted a few seconds inside you the way I was. I wanted your first time to be a bit more memorable than a premature ejaculation experience.'

I looked at him startled. 'Well, in that case … thank you?'

'You're welcome. So you and Robert didn't have sex, huh?' he asked casually. Too casually. He made a point of not even looking at me.

I felt my body contract. We were travelling into dangerous territory here. I felt the relaxed lazy atmosphere change. A stillness fell over us. I bit my lip.

'Uh, no, he … um … couldn't,' I said.

I didn't think I had sounded convincing, but to my surprise he grinned suddenly and said, 'Don't get me wrong. I'm not complaining. It was fun being the first one inside you.'

I looked at him long and hard. His mouth was smiling but his eyes were deliberately expressionless. His reaction was not at all what I expected, but it was much better for me if we dropped the subject.

'By the way, my mother wants to meet you.'

I shot up. 'What?'

'Fraid so,' he said.

I put the half eaten okra back on the plate. 'When does she want to meet?'

'Tomorrow. She's invited you to tea at Foxgrove.'

'But you said she wouldn't be caught dead in England during winter.'

'Ordinarily yes, but she wants to meet the woman her son's chosen to be the next Lady Greystoke.'

'But I don't have anything suitable to wear,' I wailed.

'That's why you're going shopping tomorrow. Something for tea with my mother on Sunday and something for our wedding on Monday.'

I worried my lower lip with my teeth. 'What time is she expecting us?'

'Actually,' he said, 'it's only you who's invited.'

'Oh no! She's not going to give me the third degree, is she?'

'Nah. My mother's cool. She doesn't suffer fools gladly so she'll be right up your street.'

'How should I address her?' I asked nervously.

He grinned. 'Call her Bobo.'

I scowled. 'What?'

'Bobo,' he said slowly, as if I had said what because I had not heard him properly, and not because it was the most ridiculous thing you could call someone's mother.

'I can't call her that,' I protested.

'Why not? That's what her inner-circle call her.'

'To start with I'm not part of her inner circle and I'd feel really silly calling your mother Bobo.'

'You can't call her by her official title either,' he said reasonably.

'You're really serious. You want me to call your mother Bobo.'

He shrugged. 'It sounds funny to you because you're not used to it, but we all have nicknames. It's what we aristocrats do. We give each other silly names that no one outside our circle would dare to use.'

I grinned. 'So what's yours?'

He looked at me playfully. 'Should be BigDick, but in truth I don't have one. From the time I was three years old I refused to answer to anything except Ivan.'

I screwed my face playfully. 'Hmmm ... so why do I remember Robert mentioning something about Ivan the Terrible.'

He frowned. 'Robert mentioned that?

'Mmm ... so are you Ivan the Terrible or aren't you?' I asked.

He sighed. 'Yeah, that's me.'

'So why did you say you didn't have a nickname?'

'That's not a nickname, Tawny. That's a title I earned while I was at Oxford.'

I lay back down and leaned my head on my temple. 'You earned it?'

He looked embarrassed and I stared at him in surprise. 'You're not having a shy moment, are you?'

He looked down at his flat stomach, his eyelashes as extravagant as fans on his cheeks. 'It's hard for me to explain to you.'

'Why?'

'Because you're so real and down-to-earth and this story will only fly with the over-privileged, the shallow, and the utterly self-obsessed, narcissistic dip-shits that I, being one myself, ran around with in my youth.'

I touched his shoulder. 'Try me. I'm not afraid of getting a little mud on my boots.'

He looked me in the eye. 'You think you want to know, but you don't, Tawny.'

I lean closer and whisper in his ear, 'Do you know, they say in my neck of the woods, that if the dirt ain't flying, you ain't trying.'

He jerked back and looked at me, an odd glint in his eye. 'All right. Let's see how much dirt you can stomach.'

I stared transfixed at him.

'I used to belong to a super elitist secret club. A gathering of the sons of the crème de la crème of society. All those who were in it with me now hold high political posts or are respected captains of industry, but back then we wore purple waistcoats tailored at Ede & Ravenscroft with pompous, swaggering conceit, and held grand banquets full of boisterous ritual. We drank heavily and reveled in vulgar and ostentatious displays of wealth and power.'

He sighed heavily.

'We mocked the poor and the downtrodden, we destroyed purely for the pleasure of destroying. We'd go to restaurants and clubs and completely vandalize them. I mean tear them apart, cause tens of thousands of pounds worth of damage. At the end of the night we'd pay for the damages in cash, and just walk away.'

I gasped and he looked uncomfortable, but he carried on.

'Our goal was to be as profligate as possible. We did anything we wanted, took anything we wanted, because we could. Because there were no consequences for us. We could buy our way out of everything. As horrible as it may sound to you, our parents took the attitude that it was a good place where we could unleash potent, pent-up aristocratic testosterone. Boys will be boys.'

I inhaled sharply, disgusted that such a society could even exist, and shocked that Ivan had been a member of it. How was it possible that the very people I always held as more refined and civilized than the rest of society, should be members of such a horrible club?

Ivan ignored my shocked expression.

'There was another aspect to the club. It was very competitive. One time the club held a contest. Up for grabs were the words "The Terrible" affixed behind the winner's name. The rules. The member who impaled the most women in a one-hour period would be the winner and forever after carry that title. No using prostitutes. Of course, I couldn't let anyone else win. It would have been a slap in the face if someone else got the title that was so obviously meant to be behind my name. What was going to sound better than Ivan the Terrible. I wanted the title.'

He shrugged.

'While everyone else was running around trying to get drunk women to lie low with, I got twenty women—some I'd already fucked before, some whom I knew wanted me but I had no interest in, and some that I promised to go out with even though I had zero interest in doing so—to stand in a row and I literally fucked my way down the line. At the end of

less than an hour, my cock had dipped into every one of those women. I was crowned Ivan the Terrible during a drink until you vomit ceremony. So there, that's my dirty little secret.'

I have to admit the story sickened me. 'Awww ... bless your little pea pickin' heart,' I said softly.

'Don't think I don't know that Southerners say that when they think someone is an idiot?'

'I don't know what to think,' I confessed truthfully.

'We were just a bunch of schoolboys, frauds, parading around pretending to be men. We didn't feel like frauds because everyone else in our little club was just as fraudulent. Some of us grew up, Tawny. I did.'

'Would you still do anything to win?' I asked softly.

He looked me in the eye. 'Yeah.'

'That's terrible.'

'I can't help it. It's just in me. Once I set my mind on something I have to win at all costs.'

I stared at him. I definitely would not want to be in competition for something he wanted.

'By the way,' he said, and reached down to the floor for his pants. He put his hand into the side pocket and brought out a small box. He opened it and dislodged a ring from its velvet base. Then he pulled my hand towards him and slipped the ring on my finger.

'That's your engagement ring,' he said flatly.

I looked at the ring. It was a baguette cut diamond ring, the biggest, showiest one I had ever seen.

I looked up at him. 'It's ... big,' I murmured.

He shrugged. 'The bigger it is, the easier they will believe the lie.'

'It feels so strange to be marrying you.'

'It's just an arrangement, Tawny.'

'I know, I know,' I said quickly.

'Is there anyone from America you want to invite to our wedding? I can fly them over.'

I shook my head.

He frowned. 'Your grandparents?'

I looked down at the huge ring on my finger. 'They died in a car crash when I was fourteen.'

'I'm sorry.'

'It's all right. It was a long time ago. It actually feels like another lifetime.'

'No cousins, uncles or aunties?' he asked.

I looked him right in the eye. 'No, they all dropped away when my mother became a stripper.'

Then he said the most beautiful thing. 'How I wish I could have met your mother,' he said softly and sincerely.

My eyes welled up with tears. When I blinked to clear them away they rolled down my cheeks.

He wiped them away with his thumbs. 'Do you have a photograph of her?'

Unable to speak, I nodded.

'Can I see it?'

I nodded again and, uncrossing my legs, got off the bed and went to my phone. I came back to the bed and showed her to him.

He looked at her photograph carefully before raising his eyes to me. 'You look just like her.'

I sniffed. 'You really think so?'

He smiled. 'Yeah. Like an angel. When angels take their clothes off they make rainbows in men's hearts.'

I stared at him. 'Why Ivan, I didn't think you had it in you. You're a poet.'

He laughed and, imitating my accent, said, 'Honey, I am many things, but I ain't no poet.'

CHAPTER 25

Tawny Maxwell

Nothing suited Ivan's mother less than the nickname Bobo. She had straight black hair like him and the same sensual lips, but her eyes were dark chocolate and her skin was carefully preserved and tended to, and despite her penchant for sun and heat, kept a delicate share of pale. She was wearing a grey turtle-neck jumper, a knee-length pencil line black skirt, and a pair of black kitten-heeled court shoes.

She stood up to receive me and it was immediately obvious that she must have been a great beauty once. Even now she was attractive, elegant and as narrow-hipped as a snake. Robert once told me that when he met her she was a drop-dead beauty. He called her a free spirit who could never be tamed by a mere man.

Her marvelously painted eyes watched me with vivid interest.

'Hello, Tawny,' she greeted. As I had expected, her voice was cultured and clear.

'Hello Ma'am.' I realized that I had unconsciously scrubbed the Southern twang out of my voice.

She smiled charmingly. 'Do sit down,' she invited, and vaguely gestured towards the sofa next to the one she had been sitting on.

'Thank you,' I said in my normal voice and perched at the end of the sofa.

She rang a bell and a woman in a black dress with a white apron appeared at the door.

'You may serve tea now, Betty,' she said.

The woman nodded and disappeared.

She sat on the sofa diagonal to me and crossed her smooth legs. 'So you are about to marry my son.'

I smiled. 'It would seem so.

'Yes, I can see how my son would adore you, but you don't seem to be Robert's type,' she observed shrewdly.

'Well, I must have been. He married me,' I said coolly. *You were right Robert.* Still she ain't gettin' no secrets from me.

'Well,' she exhaled. 'He must have changed a great deal since I knew him.'

'He always said wonderful things about you.'

'Did he? He was a sly devil.'

I smiled. 'Yes Ma'am, he was that, but he changed a lot in the last years of his life.'

'I didn't go to his funeral,' she admitted softly.

I gave a little shrug. Looking out of the window at the rolling green landscape I remembered Robert. 'I know. We played him Gustav Mahler's Adagietto, 5th symphony.'

'Yes, I remember now he told me he wanted me to play it for him at his funeral.'

An awkward silence descended on us. I brought my gaze back to her. 'It doesn't matter that you didn't go. He knew you wouldn't.'

She tried to frown but the Botox wouldn't allow it. 'Really?'

'In fact, he said, if you came he would be disappointed.'

Her eyes were alive with curiosity. 'Why?'

'Because it would mean life had finally beaten you into doing things you did not want to do. He admired you for being, in his words, wildly and fiercely independent.'

She took a deep breath. 'Are you in love with my son?' she asked archly.

I bit my lower lip. She was far too intelligent for me to lie to her. 'I hope you won't think me rude if I don't answer that question. I find it almost impossible to talk about my private life with someone I have just met.'

She leaned back and regarded me with a frown. 'So you're not in love with Ivan and yet you are marrying him. My son is no fool. Why would he marry you? Is it to protect you?'

'You'll just have to ask him that. I'm afraid I'm not at liberty to say.'

'I wondered about you. Everybody said you were a gold digger, but you're not, are you?'

'What makes you say that?'

She smiled. 'Because, my dear, I'm a gold digger and you're nothing like me.'

My mouth dropped open.

She lifted one elegant shoulder and dropped it. 'It's not a secret. I married Ivan's father for his title, but he was an impoverished Lord other than this place, which had been heavily mortgaged. He was, what is that charming saying you Americans have for a person who has nothing?'

'Doesn't have a pot to piss in?' I said.

She smiled. 'No, I was thinking of something else, but that will do. I left him shortly after I conceived Ivan. I always wanted my child to have a title. They're so useful. Then I married Robert for his money, but he was ... too headstrong and too selfish. Too much like me, I guess. I divorced him and married my current husband who is perfect.'

I stared at her, stupefied by her honesty. She was an awe-inspiring woman. The way she totally owned all her actions was impressive and empowering. She knew what she wanted and went out and got it, and in return for her unflinching honesty she seemed well adjusted and totally at ease with all her decisions.

Betty came in with another girl carrying silver trays filled with a teapot, cups, and a three tier cake stand loaded with finger sandwiches and cakes.

Ivan's mother picked up the pot of tea and began to pour it into two cups. Then she looked at me inquiringly.

'Milk and two cubes,' I told her.

She added the milk and sugar and passed the cup and saucer to me. Her hands were rock steady.

'Thank you,' I said, and took them with a smile of thanks.

She helped herself to a finger sandwich. 'Cucumber. My favorite,' she said.

I reached out, took one, and bit into it.

She put the plate down. 'It's nothing like Southern food, is it?'

'No. If we see something we like we immediately smother it in cheese and fry it.'

She makes a comical face. 'I had Country ham once with a gravy made of black coffee called red eye gravy, cat-head biscuits and melon. It was rather delicious, but very filling.'

'My granddaddy used to say that Southern food always got him so full he felt like he was fifteen months pregnant. He swore he even got contractions.'

She laughed and so did I. I liked her.

She raised her cup, took a dainty sip, and put it back on the saucer. Then she regarded me, her smile quite genuine and totally harmless. 'So,' she said softly. 'You're in love with my son.'

The cucumber sandwich in my mouth felt like a lump of clay. Heat rushed up my throat and into my cheeks. I swallowed and looked

at her pleadingly. 'Yes, but please don't tell him.'

She laughed. 'I won't. He is perfectly capable of running his own life.'

'Thank you,' I said gratefully.

She smiled mischievously. 'You will be good for my son. It's about time he had a real woman in his bed instead of one those vapid creatures he is so fond of picking up in all those strange clubs he frequents.'

After our tea, I asked her if she wouldn't mind if I wandered around the grounds. Her eyes crinkled at the corners.

'My dear, you don't need permission to walk these grounds. Tomorrow you will be the mistress of Foxgrove Hall.'

'Thank you,' I said.

'I am returning to London in the next half hour to catch up with some old friends, so I will see you at the registry office tomorrow.'

I nodded. 'Thank you. I'm glad I met you,' I said sincerely.

'By the way, while it's true that it is not often my son comes up with a good idea, you really should start calling me Bobo.'

'It doesn't suit you.'

She smiled warmly. 'That's where you're wrong, dear child. It's the perfect camouflage. Ivan's father came up with it. Bobo. Doesn't it make you immediately think of a brainless Duchess or a soft toy?'

I grinned at her, liking her even more. 'See you tomorrow, Bobo.'

'Until then,' she said.

I knew Ivan was busy working in the library and I didn't want to disturb him, so I went out through the conservatory and walked out past the formal gardens towards a wooded area. I took a narrow path until I came upon a breathtaking landscape. It was filled with tall straight pine trees. Their barks were covered with dark green ivy. I had never seen such a thing before. It was an amazing sight. Like being in a fairytale.

For a long time, I stood staring at the enchanted scene until a couple of rabbits caught my attention. They were brown with white on the undersides of their tails and they chased each other until they disappeared in some undergrowth. Still smiling, I moved on and followed a little stream. A couple of ducks were sitting on the bank and I was struck by the unspoilt beauty and wonderful silence around me. I sat on a rock and stared into the water. I heard a sound and turned. Ivan was a few feet away.

'Hey,' he drawled.

'Hey yourself,' I said, my heartbeat quickening at the sight of him. How on earth did he manage to look sexy in rubber galoshes? I wished I had worn a pair too, seeing that I had completely ruined my shoes in the mud on the pathway.

He walked towards me. 'Peaceful here, isn't it?'

'Beautiful,' I said quietly.

He stood a foot away from me and looked deeply into my eyes.

I blushed. 'Has your mother gone?' I asked to cover my awkwardness.

'Yes,' he said shortly.

I licked my lips nervously. 'I like her.'

'Apparently the feeling is mutual.'

His closeness and that intense look in his eyes were doing strange things to me.

'She was nothing like I thought,' I prattled on.

'She's like no one else.'

'You're a bit like her, aren't you?'

'Maybe. It's getting cold. We should be getting back,' he said, taking my hand. Holding hands, we began to walk back to the house. I stole a glance at him and there was a slight frown on his closed, preoccupied face.

'If it wasn't love, it was an addiction ... never a pair of lips made me come back so many times for a kiss.'

-

German Renko

CHAPTER 26

Lord Greystoke

I walked into the drawing room and halted when I saw her lying on the sofa. I stopped to drink in the moment. She lay perfectly still, anticipation swimming in her eyes. In the soft light she looked every bit the peach that I was going to consume and devour. It was going to be another long, long night and I was in no hurry to show her just how bad a bad boy could be!

'Got a present for you,' I said softly and walked towards her.

Her eyes shifted down to the box in my hand. A slow smile lit up her gorgeous face. She sat up and carefully put her knees together. She was a sweet thing, after all. Imagine trying to keep her knees together while I was around.

I held the box out to her.

'Thank you,' she said formally and took it from me.

'My pleasure.'

She lifted the lid. 'You bought me shoes,' she exclaimed, pulling a hot-pink, six-inch-heel shoe from the tissue in the box.

'They're not just any shoes. They're for fucking in,' I told her.

She blushed a pretty rose. 'As long as I don't have to walk anywhere in them.'

'Only as far as my dick, darlin.'

She swallowed hard and squeaked, 'I'm sure I'll be able to manage that.'

I made it over to the drinks trolley and poured myself a very large shot from the whiskey decanter. I turned around and took a sip. The burn was good. It was going to be a good night. I could feel it in my throbbing cock.

'Go on. Let's see what they look like on,' I urged.

She raised her eyebrows. Saying nothing, she put the box on the floor and took the shoes out. They were gaudy things. The way shoes for fucking in should be.

I walked over to the big old armchair, where my great uncle used to sit reading his morning paper. I sat down and watched her put them on. She had to bend to fix the strap. She looked up at me. 'There you go. I hope your Lordship likes what he sees,' she says provocatively.

'Come to me.'

She started walking towards me. Her walk was tentative and I'm afraid very unsexy, but fucking hell, it turned me on. Six feet away from me, I said. 'Easy, baby.'

She stopped, a small curious smile playing on her lips.

'Lose your T-shirt,' I instructed.

'Anybody could come in,' she protested, panic in her voice.

'Nobody will come in. My staff know better than to come in when I'm in here with a woman.'

With a small smile she pulled off her T-shirt.

I took a sip of my whiskey. 'Jeans.

She unzipped and wriggled out of her jeans.

I put the glass back on the table. 'Bra.'

She unhooked it and flicked it off. Her beautiful perky breasts made me so fucking hard I had to shift around in my chair.

'Take your panties off.'

'Are you sure?' she asked cheekily.

That'll cost her. She was way too at ease for my liking. I took a sip of my drink. 'Tawny,' I warned.

She obeyed the instruction instantly.

Fucking beautiful she was, in her new it's-time-to-fuck-shoes. 'Now go and sit on that chair.'

She walked towards the old antique chair I was pointing to. I noticed that she was braver. She had deliberately put extra sway and bounce into her hips.

'This one?' she asked in an insolent voice that just made me want to fuck her mouth. It would be interesting to see how long the impertinence prevailed. I nodded and she sat deep into it, crossed her legs languidly, and regarded me with cool eyes. Very pretty but not quite what I had in mind.

'Drape one leg over the armrest.'

Her eyes widened. She bit her lip and hesitated.

I raised a haughty eyebrow. That never failed to work.

She took a deep breath and complied.

I downed the rest of the whiskey and looked with satisfaction at her pussy, all opened up and put there just for my pleasure. It felt good to see how wet and swollen she was for me. I put the glass down and walked up to her. My greedy eyes honed in on her spread pussy. Nectar welling up along her slit. I put my hands on either side of her, hunched over her and licked the outer edge of her ear.

'Do you know what I see?' I purred.

'What?' she asked, wide-eyed, beautiful, and eager.

I already knew that look so well. It was burned into my brain. She was fucking throbbing for a deep, relentless, never-ending, mind-blowing fuck.

'A cunt I can't get enough of,' I whispered.

Her breath hitched.

I reached into my trouser pocket and pulled out two neckties. I got onto my haunches and securely tied both her legs to the chair in their spread position. I stopped and looked up into her flushed face.

'What now?' she breathed, her gaze riveted on my mouth.

I leaned forward and let my teeth sink into the tender spot between her shoulder and neck. Immediately she froze and waited. In the end we are all animals. We don't have to be taught the raw language of our bodies. She understood that it was a hold that conveyed primal possession. I released the flesh and sucked it slowly, knowing I was leaving my brand. She didn't move or protest. I nibbled her earlobe casually.

She moaned as I licked the skin along her jaw line and she turned her head, craving my mouth. I caught her bottom lip between my teeth and pulled. Her hand slipped into my shirt and slid up my abdomen, the nails catching on the ridges. Her thumb rubbed over the disk of my nipple. A shiver of need went through me. I caught her hand in mine.

'That's not how this game is played,' I told her.

She looked at me, her eyes full of desire. 'How is it played?'

'You have to be shameless.'

She smiled suddenly. 'I'm as naked as a boiled chicken and tied with my legs spread open to a chair. How much more shameless do you want me to be?'

'Let's see what depravity you can urge me to do,' I said.

I knelt on the floor in front of her and buried my head between her legs. Her scent made my cock jerk so hard it hurt. I kissed that open flower and she shuddered. My tongue parted her, delving into the wet heat.

Ah, the taste of Tawny, honey.

I could feel her sex swell, the valleys and ridges becoming more pronounced. With slow licks and kisses I explored every nook and cranny of her, teasing out more and more juice, letting it coat my mouth and chin. She pressed her sex into my face desperately and the rest of the world fell away. There was only my mouth drowning in her sweet pussy. I strummed her clit and she drove her sex harder and harder against my mouth.

I lifted my eyes and watched the way she began to glow from the inside. Low, feral sounds came from her mouth. Tremors rolled through her body and her legs quaked as she climaxed, her juices gushing into my mouth. Her face was flushed, her lips parted and her eyes half closed, her body arched and trembling.

She's mine, I thought triumphantly.

My fucking woman.

She placed her hands on either side of my head. 'That was awesome,' she whispered, thinking it was over, but it wasn't. Not by a long way.

I returned my face between her thighs. My tongue was relentless, darting, and flicking. She pushed her fingers through my hair. I sucked her until she gushed again. Orgasm chased orgasm.

'No more,' she begged, grabbing my head and trying to push me away, but I wouldn't stop sucking her clit. In the end her hands dropped away. I made her come again and enjoyed watching her go over the edge once more.

'I can't. I'm too sensitive. It's enough,' she begged almost in tears, but she was mine and I would decide how much was enough for my pussy. I bathed her with long licks from the bottom of her sweet cunt to the shivering tip of her hard nub until she trembled through another climax.

Half an hour later I wiped my face.

Her eyes moved down to my stiff cock. She smiled tiredly.

'Masturbate and cum on me,' she said, tipping her head back and opening that deliciously filthy mouth of hers. Her voice was barely a whisper, and eyes were heavy-lidded. All her strength had been stolen away.

Sure I wanted to jerk off and spray my seed all over her face. Which man wouldn't? That was what this game was about. To see how she'd return the favor. How lascivious she could be. She had turned out to be extremely generous. Extremely shameless.

I looked down at her flushed face. She looked like a woman who had had too many climaxes. Her body sagged. Her eyelashes were wet. Her legs held wide open with ties must be stiff by now. Her clit was so swollen it protruded out of its hood, and there was a puddle underneath her pussy.

All in all, she was an intriguing mixture of obscene, vulnerable, and innocent, so it was a shock to realize that what I really felt for her was pity.

I felt sorry for her.

For what I was going to do to her. It had to be done, but I didn't want to hurt her. Not for a moment. It broke my heart to even think of what I was planning. She would be so hurt, so shocked. She would not be expecting it. Not a betrayal of such proportions.

'Go on,' she urged. 'Don't waste it. It's good for my skin. Come on my face,' she urged.

I hesitated.

She opened her delectable mouth wider in invitation and her hands moved. One hand pinched and teased her nipples and the other went down to her reddened, swollen pussy. I watched her very deliberately plunge her finger deep into her cunt and gasp with the sensation.

She stopped playing with her nipple and brought her hand to me. Leaning slightly forward, she placed her hand under my sac and caressed it gently. Her skin was like warm silk. My dick was stone hard and pointing towards her. Gently she pulled me closer towards her mouth until it was resting on her bottom lip.

'Your cock is so thick and big I can barely wrap my mouth around it,' she complained softly. With a devious smile, she widened her mouth and started suckling the helmet head for a few moments.

I felt myself tense.

She looked up at me with saucer eyes and said. 'Go on then.'

My eyes moved from her half-open, waiting mouth to her finger jammed into her pussy.

I curled my palm around the base of my shaft and started to jack my cock with brutal speed and violence. Occasionally, the tip would brush against her lips sending jolts of electricity up my shaft and right up my spine. The only sound in the room was the sound of me frigging myself so hard my hand was a blur. The dam broke quickly, blood roared in my ears, and I felt the first, thick, hot burst of semen rush up my shaft. I watched it hit her face like a slap.

I saw her willingly open her mouth.

The first spray of white cream jetted onto her cheeks, the bridge of her nose, and sparked onto her long lashes. With both hands she pulled me into her open lips and sucked me hard while I came and came. Until she had emptied me and I was spent. I watched my semen spill from the corners of her mouth. She extended her tongue and lewdly licked her lips.

Then grinned wickedly.

I smeared the cream all over her face and neck, and worked until it was all absorbed and I was inside her skin. Then I untied her, gently lifted her into my arms and carried her up the grand staircase to my bedroom. I laid her down on the big four-poster where for centuries Greystokes' had been bringing their conquests.

She looked up into my eyes.

'I feel like a Princess in a Disney movie,' she said in a hushed tone.

'Princesses in Disney movies don't have sex,' I told her.

'This one does,' she said, taking my right hand and pushed the middle finger into her. God, she was slick and hot.

At that moment she was the most beautiful creature I'd ever seen.

'Do you really enjoy eating my pussy?' she whispered. She was not being sexy or seductive. She couldn't believe that anyone could be as crazy about her pussy as I appeared to be.

'Darlin', I could eat your pussy for hours.'

'Really?' Her voice was breathy. My finger was still buried inside her.

'Absolutely.'

'What's it like eating pussy?' I noticed the generalization and smiled.

'Some pussies taste and feel like oysters. No problems there, since I like oysters. Others taste salty and occasionally some taste sweet.'

I slowly slid my finger in and out of her pussy.

'Do you want to know what your pussy tastes like?'

She nodded.

'Eating your pussy is like sucking a peach. Not one of those plastic-covered, half-ripe ones you get on a Styrofoam tray at the supermarket, but one of those perfectly sun-ripened ones you pluck straight from the tree during the peak of summer in an orchard in a Mediterranean region. You bite into it and sweet juice pours down your chin so you have slurp and suck at it.'

Her eyes moved down.

I had another erection. My cock was pulsating. I exchanged my finger for my cock, and after she fell asleep from sheer exhaustion, I watched her sleep. I wished I could wrap her up in my arms and protect her from the hurt that was coming.

I slept very little that night and woke her up early on our wedding day with my tongue in her pussy and my cock in her mouth.

CHAPTER 27

Tawny Maxwell

'Tell me what time the wedding is and I'll pick a dress.'

-Chris Crocker

If my first marriage made me cry, my second filled me with such nerves that my whole body felt raw and jumpy. This would be the second time I was marrying for the wrong reasons. I had not wanted to marry Robert, but he begged me to. It was the only way, he said.

Of course, I would never tell anyone the real reason why I did it, but at least marrying him meant there was never any possibility of me getting hurt.

But marrying Ivan?

I could see nothing but confusing and painful problems ahead. I was also conscious that it was all moving too fast. Too intense. Too crazy. It was all right for him because his heart was not in it. I was just fun and sex to him. A temporary fling while he fulfilled a promise to his dying stepfather. I, on the other hand, was already hopelessly in love with him. To solve one problem, I had allowed myself to be persuaded into a solution that would almost undoubtedly cause me to end up heartbroken.

Ivan dropped me off at the apartment and went to a friend's house. He would get ready there and meet me at the registry office. Angela was going to come to the apartment and we were both supposed to be together at the registry. Ivan had planned it so I would only have ten minutes to myself before the hairdresser came around at twelve.

As soon as he arrived he did not even want a quick coffee. I offered him champagne.

'Well,' he said with a grin. So we opened a bottle. 'This is nice,' he said as we settled on an armchair by the window.

Sipping champagne, he set about putting my hair up into a complicated twist-plait hairstyle with delicate seed pearl pins in it. He was very chatty and a balm for my frayed nerves. Or maybe it was the champagne at midday.

When he finished we were both a little tipsy, and he seemed extraordinarily pleased with his creation. I had to admit it looked the business.

After he left I pulled on sheer nude tights and dressed in my new cream two-piece St. Laurent suit and matching cream shoes. I carefully applied my make-up and went to stand in front of the mirror. Well ...

I looked the part.

A widow marrying for the second time.

I was a believable gold digger striking it rich the second time around.

Hello magazine would be there because Ivan said he could think of no better way to spread the news. In return for exclusivity they promised that all the photos would belong to us, and Ivan would have the last say as to what they printed and which photos were used in their spread.

I looked at my reflection in the mirror and suddenly felt tearful. When I was a young girl I used to dream of a white wedding. A happy, giggly occasion. With my mother, my grandparents, my relatives, all my friends, bridesmaids in matching outfits, cute little flower girls, and a wonderful man who loved me with all his heart.

But here I was. In Ivan's flat getting ready on my own to marry a man who did not love me. The future stretched out strange and foreign.

I blinked hard.

It's OK, Tawny. Maybe one day he will come to care for you. Or most probably he never will, but you'll survive. You overcame everything else and you will again.

I walked to the middle of my room. So many things were up in the air. I didn't even know if after today I would be officially moving into Ivan's bedroom. The doorbell rang and I quickly went to the door. It was Angela.

'Oh, Tawny. You look beautiful,' she said with a catch in her voice as soon as I opened the door.

'Thank you,' I replied automatically. I felt quite light-headed as I closed the door and turned towards her. 'The driver should be here soon.'

'Good, because I wanted to say something to you before he comes,' Angela said quickly.

'OK.'

She took a deep breath. 'I just wanted to say that I realize it's really soon after Robert that you're marrying Ivan, but I think it's right.'

I gave a short surprised laugh. 'You've never even met Ivan.'

She bit her bottom lip. 'I know, but once Robert said to me that Ivan was the man he would have chosen for you.'

'What?' I exploded.

She put both her hands up, palms facing me. 'He didn't say it in a bad way. He just meant that in an ideal world Ivan would be the perfect husband for you.'

I walked to the wall and leaned against it. 'Why did he never tell me that?' I whispered.

'Look, I'm sorry. I should never have said anything. I feel as if I've ruined everything.'

I put my hand to my forehead. *Oh Robert. Have you done something behind my back?*

'I'm really sorry. I didn't mean to spoil your wedding day. I'm just stupid. I thought you'd want to know that Robert wouldn't mind,' Angela said.

I took a deep breath. 'It's OK, Angela. You haven't spoiled anything. I'm glad you told me. I'm just like a cat on a hot tin roof at the moment.'

The doorbell rang.

We both looked at each other.

'Robert was a good judge of character. He could see right through people and he liked Ivan,' she whispered.

'Thank you for telling me that,' I said and went to answer the door. The driver was downstairs. It was time to go.

I walked towards Ivan in a daze. Angela had brought a bouquet and I was conscious of my hands gripping its stem hard enough to snap it. There were only a handful of people. I could not even look at them. The photographers from Hello were there too. My legs felt shaky.

There he was! So straight and tall and ...

A thought popped into my head, would a day ever come when I could look at him and not fall all over myself at how hot he was? The answer was immediate and cruel. *Sure honey. When he leaves you.*

I looked into Ivan's face and my vision blurred. My eyes were filling with tears. What the hell? I wasn't going to cry in front of these people and Hello photographers for God's sake! I felt so stupid. I didn't even know why I was crying. I had no tissues, and tears started rolling down my cheeks.

When I reached his side someone had already passed him a scrap of tissue. He gently brushed my cheeks with it.

'Don't cry, babe. Marriage to me won't be that bad,' he teased, his eyes kind and warm.

I laughed shakily.

He took my hand. I clung to it like a life jacket in a swirling sea. His hand was warm and strong. He would never know how much strength I took from it. The ceremony began. I dutifully parroted everything I was told to repeat.

'I do solemnly declare that I know not of any lawful impediment why I, Tawny Maxwell may not be joined in matrimony to Ivan de Greystoke.'

The registrar asked. 'Are you, Ivan de Greystoke, free lawfully to marry Tawny Maxwell?

'I am,' he replied.

Then he smiled and made his vow.

'I, Ivan de Greystoke take you, Tawny Maxwell to be my lawful wedded wife.'

The registrar looked at me.

'I, Tawny Maxwell take you, Ivan de Greystoke to be my lawful wedded husband.'

That was the end of the statutory declarations. We slipped rings on each other's fingers and Ivan pressed his mouth on mine while flash-bulbs went off. He lifted his head and I looked dazedly into his face. He was like a stranger. Yet I loved him. He was my first love. He was my first for everything. At that moment I loved him so much I couldn't even imagine ever loving anyone else. He curved his hand around my waist and turned me towards the small group of people gathered there.

His mother was the first to congratulate us. She was immaculate in an apricot dress suit.

'Well done, darling,' she said to her son. Kissing me on my cheek, she whispered, 'You look absolutely beautiful, my dear. I wish you every happiness.'

There were more photos at the steps outside before we were driven to the Ritz. In the car, Ivan took my hand. 'Are you OK?'

'Yes,' I said.

'Good. We only have to down a couple of glasses of champagne and eat a few canapés then we can escape.'

'Where will we escape to?' I asked, not expecting the kind of answer that he gave me.

'It's a surprise.'

'Oh?'

'I'm giving you a wedding night you will never forget no matter how long you live.'

No matter how bad I felt, a few minutes in his presence always made me experience the truth of the saying, it is better to have loved and lost than never to have loved at all. No matter what happens I will never regret how he has made me feel. I smiled at him.

'Are you bigging up your cock again?' I mocked.

He laughed. 'No, I'm taking you to a very special place. It's a secret club and it's by invitation only.'

I raised my eyebrows. 'And they invited you?'

'Obviously.'

'Is it another sex club?'

'Sort of. It was set up by a reclusive, mysterious, billionaire Duke. It is not a sex club in the way you are thinking. People go there to have sex, yes, but you can't go there if you don't already have a partner to have sex with, and while you are there you will never see another patron of the club.'

'Hmmm. Where is it?'

'The Square Mile.'

'Where all the money is.'

He glanced at me and flashed a smile. 'Exactly.'

'What is it called?'

'The Blue Butterfly.'

'I like the name. Pretty.'

'The name comes from Puccini's opera adaptation of Madame Butterfly. Do you know the story of Madame Butterfly?'

I shook my head.

'It's based on a Japanese tragedy. In 1904, U.S. Naval Officer Pinkerton rents a house on a hill in Nagasaki, where he intends to live with a fifteen year old girl called Cio-cio san, which means butterfly in Japanese. He meant it only as a temporary marriage of convenience. His real intention was to leave her once he found himself a proper American bride but, of course, poor Butterfly falls deeply in love with him, and it all ends tragically with her slitting her own throat behind a curtain, and Pinkerton taking their small son back to the states.'

'And they based a sex club on that? I'll tell you now you better not be expecting me to slit my throat over you.'

He gave me a dry look. 'The club is structured on the premise of the many sexual arts Butterfly, if she had been older and more sexually savvy, could have employed to seduce and entice her American lover into staying with her.'

'That's quite clever for a sex club.'

He smiled. 'Yes, I thought so too.'

'Well, it sounds extremely expensive,' I said lightly.

'It's worth every penny.'

I looked sideways at him. 'Have you been to it many times?'

'Not often enough,' he said shortly.

CHAPTER 28

Tawny Greystoke

https://www.youtube.com/watch?v=mN9Dipgqdtw

We arrived in the City where Ivan found a parking space on a side street. It was nearly six in the evening. There was hardly anyone on that street. We got out and walked down it, side by side, but not touching.

'Here we are,' he said, stopping outside the faded entrance of an old-fashioned Japanese umbrella shop.

'Mysterious and intriguing,' I said looking at the disguised façade where the club was apparently hiding in plain sight.

'Ready?' he asked softly.

'Definitely,' I said, a swirl of excitement beginning to run up my spine.

To access the club, Ivan dropped his American Express black card into a metal container that had been painted to look like a letterbox. A whirling sound came from the box.

A few seconds later the lock on the door clicked. Ivan pressed open the door and we went in. He closed the door behind us as lights flickered on. We seemed to be in a small shop full of umbrellas. From speakers came orchestra music. A woman with a fierce and darkly hued timbre wailed hauntingly to it. Her voice had such power that it made me shiver. That would be exactly how I would have imagined the betrayed Butterfly would sound.

'That's Maria Callas,' Ivan said. 'A bit different from Dolly Parton, huh?'

'Completely,' I said softly. 'I've got goose bumps.'

'Some people say it is like having a Goddess look right into your soul.'

'I agree. It's emotionally devastating,' I said.

To be honest I couldn't imagine how this could be the entrance to a sex club. It was somber and dowdy, nothing like The Dirty Aristocrat. The last thing I wanted to do here was have sex.

He pressed a panel within an illuminated glass case, which activated a mechanical steel door that slid back to reveal a lift. As soon as we got in the doors closed and we started travelling down. The doors opened to reveal a small area with Japanese screen doors. The silhouette of a woman in a kimono appeared on the screen. She parted the screen and revealed a vibrant green room.

'Welcome, Pinkerson san and cio cio san,' she said.

Ivan nodded in greeting and I did the same. Right, we were role playing. He was the horrible officer and I was the betrayed Butterfly.

It was like peeking through a keyhole into someone else's life. It had memorabilia that made it seem like Butterfly's bedroom. Kimonos, a child's wooden toy, sandals, a waxed paper umbrella, beaded flower decorations and, inside a glass box, a dagger on a velvet bed. There was real pathos in the little shoes and the face paint we were meant to think Butterfly had used.

The woman who had opened the screen slid another screen open. We followed her down a corridor. She went through a door, ushering me in with her. It was a small room, more like an ante room.

'We will prepare Butterfly for you, Officer Pinkerton, while you have some hot sake in the Gentlemen's room,' she said, bowing her head.

'You're going to leave me here?' I asked, my eyes saying don't you dare and a small whine of panic in my voice.

'Relax and enjoy it. It's truly a treat,' he said coolly with a smile. With a quick kiss on my lips he casually strolled away.

'This way please, Butterfly,' the woman said opening another door. The place was like a maze. We entered another room with a long steel table that looked like one of those tables they have at the morgue.

She opened a plastic packet and took out a red silk bed sheet that she covered the metal table with. She made sure the amount of material falling over the metal table was exactly the same on both sides. Then she turned to me.

The lighting in this room was much better so I got a better look at her. She was at least fifty. Considering Asian people never looked their age, she must have been much older.

'Please take all your clothes off and put them in this box,' she said, indicating a plain cardboard box on the floor.

'You want me to undress here?' I asked, a little surprised by the whole set-up. Where was the velvet and the sumptuous furniture, the throbbing music? It was all so sterile. So unsexy.

She bowed her head again. 'Yes, please cio cio san.' I must admit I didn't too much like her calling me by the name of the woman who had slit her own throat. I began to silently curse Ivan. Where on earth had he brought me? This was easily the least sexy place I had ever been to in my life.

She patted one end of the metal table. 'Head up here, please. We have much to do.'

'We have?'

'Yes, Pinkerton san is waiting.'

I sighed inwardly. I suppose I was here now, and Ivan had obviously paid a great deal of money for this experience, so here goes. He did say it would not involve anyone else but me and him.

'Right,' I said, taking my clothes off and folding them before putting them into the box.

'I will go and get the fruit now,' she said as she slipped out of the room.

It was warm in the room so at least I was not cold. Gingerly, I climbed on the silk covered metal table and lay down. First I laid my hands on my stomach and then laid my hands down my sides. I wriggled around uncomfortably.

The door opened. I lifted my head nervously, but it was only the woman returning with a very large tray. I craned my neck to look at its contents. It was filled with an array of fruit sliced so thin the pieces were almost transparent.

'You're going to cover me in that fruit, aren't you?'

She smiled and followed it with that little bow she had going.

I lay back down. How sexy? I was going to be covered in cold fruit!

It was such an anticlimax that I almost giggled. If my grandma could see me now! Less sense than a wet bag of flour, she'd say. I considered hopping off the metal table and demanding that I be taken to the Gentlemen's room so I could just down a couple of sakes before going home with Ivan. We could have sex there instead of this crazy place, but some part of me thought, what the hell. I'm here now. If it's such a great fantasy of Ivan's to see me dressed up in fruit, so be it.

The woman set the tray on a folding metal stand. Then she opened a little drawer and took out a plastic shower cap that she carefully fitted around my hairdo.

She looked at me with a smile. 'Are you ready?'

'Yeah, sure,' I said, hoping I didn't look as big a fool as I felt.

'This will not hurt even a little bit. It is an ancient technique. Older than Buddha.'

I smiled at her tightly. Was she kidding me? Sticking fruit on a human body was older than Buddha?

'Ready?' she asked again.

I sighed. 'Yeah, go for it.'

She put the heels of her hands firmly on the mound above my sex and started moving them in small circles.

'Hey, hey, what are you doing?' I asked, sitting up.

'Be patient. This is the ancient way.'

'Look,' I said.

'No pain,' she insisted.

I opened my mouth to say thanks but no thanks, but she nodded, saying in quite a stern voice, 'Ancient way. Must do.'

Oh sweet Jesus!

'Try. Please. Always good to try new things. Ancient things.' Her face was like a closed door. I was not going to win this argument.

'Fine, fine, go on,' I mumbled lying back down.

She carried on doing the same action. It helped that there was no expression at all on her face. It was more like being at the gynecologist. Totally unerotic. I stared at the ceiling and hoped her ancient way would soon be over.

Then a strange thing began to happen.

A slow wave of heat began lapping at me, and I started getting hot. The heat did not come from her hands, but somewhere at the base of my spine. At first I thought it was the friction of my body against the table, and then I realized that it was almost like an electric current that was running up my spine.

'Is it OK that I'm feeling a bit … strange?' I asked her.

She nodded. 'Ancient way,' she said sagely.

I swallowed. The sensations were becoming stronger and stronger. I could feel my skin getting warmer. In fact, the air in the room suddenly seemed cool compared to the heat emanating from me. To my alarm, a tingling started inside my vagina. Jesus. What the hell? I was getting turned on! I pretended to clear my throat.

'OK. That's enough now. Can we get on with the fruit?' I asked with a strange tremor in my voice.

'Body not ready. Ancient way,' she said.

'No, no, I'm ready.'

'Nearly,' she said. It occurred to me that I might climax if she carried on much more and I really didn't want to. I thought I was here to have sex with Ivan not get into some lesbian shit.

'Listen, there might be some mistake here,' I said, as I felt my sex begin to contract and tighten.

'Ah, ready,' she pronounced.

Thank God. My skin was flushed. I could see how hard my nipples were and I could feel juices pouring out of me. She reached back into the drawer and took out a brush.

Yeah, that's right. She dipped the soft bristle brush into me and painted my slickness onto my body. She used that as the glue to stick a fruit slice on me. It was strangely hypnotic and addictive. The smell of the fruit as she carried it from the side of my head to its destination on my body. The extraordinarily erotic sensation of being painted on with my own juices. I began to wait for the soft brush to enter me.

When she painted my nipples I could feel my body wanting to arch and beg for more. I was so turned on.

She worked fast but meticulously. She did the sides of my body and the soles of my feet last. Finally, she put the brush down and covered the entrance into me with strips of fruit.

She straightened and rang a bell. Then she pushed the trolley with me on it through a door opposite the one we came in from. To my surprise it was the most sumptuous bedroom I had ever seen. It was decorated entirely in shades of red. Another woman was already waiting in there. They pushed the trolley to the bed and lowered it using some kind of cranking mechanism until it was flush with the bed.

It was only then I realized that under the red silk I was lying on was a thin sheet of metal. They slid it on the surface of the bed until I was positioned in the middle. Then they pulled it out from under me, sliding it out under the red silk effortlessly.

Quickly and efficiently they made the bed with the red sheet I was lying on. Then they began to attach thin silk ropes to my wrists and ankles. They tied me spread eagled to the bed's posts.

'Open your mouth,' the woman who had painted me said.

I immediately obeyed and before I realized what she was doing she had put an egg into it.

'Aggg,' I uttered with a frown.

'It is raw. Better not to break, cio cio san,' she advised emotionlessly.

Both women then bowed respectfully before leaving, their shoes making no sounds on the floor. There was a mirror above the bed, and I gasped to see what a work of art my body had become. All the different fruits, all the different colors, blending into each other.

Then I heard footfalls.

A man's.

CHAPTER 29

Lord Greystoke

I walked into the room and stood over her.

She was the beauty that was missing from my world. For so long I had been running from myself. But no more. This was it. I was running no more. Maybe, just maybe I could have it all.

She whimpered and looked at me with dazed, desperate eyes. I knew she wanted me to take the egg out of her mouth, but I put my finger across my lips.

Her eyes flashed with anger. She was a strong independent girl, and she didn't like giving up so much power and control over to me. I smiled. Oh Tawny, always the adorable pain in the ass. Couldn't she tell that it was all for her benefit? I shed my clothes without haste.

Anticipation was a good thing.

Naked, I climbed on the red silk to begin my meal. Tonight I was dining on my wife. I began with her toes. I sucked in pale, greenish-orange papaya. Not too ripe and drenched in vinegar. At first thought it may have seemed stupid to use vinegar since one couldn't taste the girl's own secret juices, which was the whole point of the exercise, but on second reflection: Brilliant. It whetted my appetite.

I worked my way up her leg, eating with abandon, using my lips, tongue and teeth. Licking, sucking, nibbling. She writhed and bucked under my mouth. Sometimes I deliberately halted and enjoyed the sensation of her straining against her bindings, trying to push herself back against my lips, her hoarse cries muffled by the egg in her mouth.

Her almost hysterical need was immensely pleasing.

Gloating lust rumbling in my throat I did all, her fingers, her hands, her shoulders, her chest, her breasts, her stomach. While she made muffled, feral sounds, I calmly sucked away the thin slices of apricot that had been arranged around her little pink hole to look like a flower.

Then I parted her with my fingers and drew my tongue along, lapping at the copious juices pouring out of her. She angled her hips to give me more access. I plunged two fingers inside her and, curving them, stroked her inner walls. Her panting became shallow. She was being massaged into an uncontrollable frenzy.

Her climax was building very nicely.

Her arousal had been twisted into such a tight knot of intensity that she was thrusting her hips desperately, and her eyes were wild.

'Open your mouth,' I said.

She opened her mouth and I took her egg out.

'You fucking asshole,' she swore furiously.

I dropped the egg into a blue bowl on the low table by the bed.

'You pompous, aristocratic jerk.'

I positioned myself over her slick body.

'How dare you let strangers fucking tie me up and—,'

I plunged my tongue into her open, swearing mouth and forced her own essences upon her. She moaned into my mouth. She was like a starving animal. I could feel her hunger for my cock.

'Please, please. I need to come,' she begged desperately.

In one deft movement I impaled her on my cock. Immediately she spread her thighs wider for me and stretched around my cock in acceptance. We moved together. Tawny, arching her back. Trying to take in as much of me as she could fit. Urging me to roughness. My thrusts grew harder and deeper.

Then something burst inside her. Her eyes flew open as she cried out into my mouth, tears ran down her temples, and her fingers clawed the sheets helplessly. Inside her something else was happening. The inner walls of her channel were vibrating with the intensity of her impending climax. As if with a mind of its own, her pussy began to clench powerfully around my shaft. Milking me.

Careful not to rub her clit, I fucked her. I was nearly there anyway. A few more strokes. So close. I allowed my groin to brush her clit to begin drawing out her climax.

'Oh God!' she gasped. Then it began to happen. Her entire body started to convulse and jerk wildly. The sight of her naked body bound and contorted broke me and, with a lusty roar, I followed her into a white-hot climax. Her orgasm lasted much longer than mine. Her body was still straining around my semi-hard cock almost a minute later. I remained inside her until every last contraction had subsided.

I raised myself on my elbows and, leaning forward, took her lips in a leisurely kiss. Our tongues moved against each other, sated and lazy. She seemed very tired, her eyes had a far-away look. I untied her bindings and lay next to her. She raised her head and put her cheek on my chest.

'I'm sorry I called you a fucking asshole,' she whispered.

'You were very restrained considering the circumstances.'

She rested her chin on my chest, her hair was totally messy and her face was bright red and shiny. 'I lost all control. I must have looked like an animal.'

'You are so beautiful when you come,' I said.

'You're such a liar.'

'I am many things, but I'm not a liar.'

She smiled softly. 'I really, really, really like this club,' she whispered.

I chuckled. 'Even the egg?'

'The egg made it frustrating which, in the end, gave it all a different edge.'
She ran her finger along my jaw then leaned forward to kiss my damp neck. 'Thank you, Ivan. It was an absolutely awesome experience.'

I felt replete. I had spoilt her for any other man. 'Don't thank me. I was just spoiling you for all other men.'

She giggled. 'You definitely did that tonight.'

Something tightened in my chest. I looked down at her and had an overwhelming urge to stroke her soft hair or kiss her cheek. The tender things people do when they care about each other.

I didn't. I couldn't.

I had to maintain some sort of distance. Otherwise I would lose all control of the situation. I rubbed my palm on her nipple. A purely sexual gesture. She reacted by pushing her breast into my hand.

'There is only one problem,' she said looking at me with lazy, sultry eyes.

'What is that?' I asked amused.

'It seems to me that Butterfly had all the fun and poor Pinkerton had hardly any.'

I realized my erection was back.

CHAPTER 30

Tawny Greystoke

We had sex on the plane ... and yes! It WAS amazing!!

When we were leaving, the air-hostess wished me a pleasant trip and winked. I knew she had heard us even though I had tried my utmost to be as quiet as possible. Ivan and I had taken a bet that he couldn't make me scream if I didn't want to. Obviously, I failed miserably if she heard me too.

I blushed bright red and scampered down the steps onto the tarmac. It was mid afternoon and it was boiling hot. I could feel myself start to sweat. Ivan had arranged for a limo to pick us up. I was glad to get into the air-conditioned interior of the car. I turned to Ivan.

'You glad you came?'

'Depends how welcome you make me feel,' he said.

'A good welcome is worth four dollars, but since you're a man who knows a bargain you can have it for two,' I said with a happy grin. The whole world seemed bright and wonderful. I was on holiday with Ivan, my body exploding with new sensations. I was learning things and I was in love. Rosalind, Dorian and Bianca were like ghosts in the background. They couldn't touch me here. Not on Penyu Island.

In two hours we were at the jetty. It was already five in the evening. There were other boats full of tourists coming back from their island holiday. We were the only ones going out to it. Penyu Island was a small and remote island 45 minutes by boat from the eastern coast of Malaysia. The ride was scenic, we passed other islands mostly built up and full of tourists. Finally, we came to Penyu, and my heart did a little skip of joy at the familiar sight.

The boat stopped at the jetty. The water was so crystal clear that you could see the grains of white sand at the bottom. I turned to Ivan and my breath caught. The wind had ruffled his hair and the sun was shining on his face. God, it was distracting to be with a man who was such a sight for sore eyes. I wanted to push my fingers through his hair.

I suddenly remembered seeing him at the cemetery for Robert's funeral. Then too, his hair had been ruffled by the wind, but he had seemed so distant, so unreachable. A cold, unknowable stranger in a cold, bleak landscape. So much had happened since then. That time seemed like part of an unhappy dream.

'Like it?' I asked.

He nodded. 'Yeah, it's phenomenal to find a place so unspoilt.'

'Come on. I'll take you to the house first. The sanctuary is on the other side of the island.'

I jumped into the water.

'What's the jetty for?' he asked with a laugh.

'It's more fun this way.'

So he dropped into the water with me and we waded to shore laughing.

Rosli, one of the four permanent staff on the island, picked up our bags and hauled them onto the wooden platform.

'I take the bags to the house,' he said with a wide grin.

'Thanks,' I said, and he jumped next to the bags with the agility of a monkey. He was soon nearly halfway up the beach. It was the most wonderful sensation to feel my feet sinking into wet sand again. For a moment I felt a pang of sadness. I will never come here with Robert again.

'What's the matter?' Ivan asked.

I shook my head. 'Nothing.'

He turned towards me and took my small hands in his large ones. 'You miss him don't you?'

I looked up at him, trying my best not to cry, but tears filled my eyes. 'All the time.'

'Hey,' he said gruffly and pulled me against his chest.

'I'm sorry,' I sniffed.

'It's OK. I know you loved him … in your own way.'

I smiled at him. 'Yes, I did. I really did.'

He used his thumbs to wipe away the tears from my cheek.

Then I took his hand and led him up the beach as we walked to the house.

We climbed the stone steps to the front door as Rosli was coming down.

'I'll be on the other side of the island if you need me,' he said.

'Thanks, Rosli,' I said again as he waved and went his way.

I looked at Ivan. He was gazing at the tall bamboo trees that surrounded the house and bent over it, their leaves leaning down to touch the roof and walls.

'Come on,' I said skipping up the steps. I stood at the threshold of a large rectangular living space nestled among the trees. There were no walls, just a sandstone floor and old ironwood posts to hold up a thatched roof. It had an open floor plan with low sofas, a coffee table, a dining area, and at the back end, a kitchen. I turned around to watch Ivan's reaction. He looked at his surroundings then back again at me.

'No walls?' he asked looking at balustrades made from matted coconut leaves that edged the space.

I shook my head. 'No walls,' I confirmed.

He raised his eyebrows. 'Interesting.'

'It's a great way to maximize the outdoor living experience. We wanted to be able to see the sea from wherever we stood inside the house.'

'Must be a job keeping the elements and the mosquitoes from the forest out? How do you do it?'

'You can say that again. It's a full time job getting rid of the leaves flying around. I'm afraid nature is constantly trying to regain its ground.' I grinned. 'There are ferns growing out of the wood in the kitchen, we have bee holes in some of the teak wood, and it is a nightmare with spiders.'

I pointed towards the rolled-up blinds.

'At night we pull down those white nets you see over there. When there is no one here, wood panels are fitted into those slots to weatherproof it.'

Ivan walked away from me and stood by one of the posts looking down. He turned around to look at me with surprise on his face. 'This house is hanging over a river-valley.'

'Do you like it?' I asked breathlessly. I don't know why it seemed so important that this powerfully contained, beautiful being should approve of my dream holiday home.

'It's fabulous,' he said.

 282

'Let me show you the best part of the house.'

'Lead the way.'

I walked to the far end of the room and turned around. 'Ready to see my bedroom?'

'I'm always ready to see your bedroom, babe.' His voice was rich and throaty.

I descended the stairs and stood on the platform below the floor we had come from. 'Here we are.'

'You're kidding,' he said with a laugh.

'Nope.'

'What do you do when you're drunk?'

'You sleep upstairs,' I said very seriously.

He came down the ladder-like steps and joined me on the platform. He looked down at the river rushing thirty feet below.

'I hope we get a windy night while we are here. It's simply fantastic,' I said.

He looked up at the iron moldings holding the massive swing bed. 'Are you sure it is safe?'

I grinned. 'Try it ... Tarzan.'

He gave me a very dirty look, grasped the thick ropes, then hopped onto the swing platform with the king size bed on it. It jerked violently and he had to widen his stance, bend his knees, and throw his arms up to regain his balance. 'Fuuuuck,' he said.

I tried not to giggle at that precious momentary look of panic on his normally cocky, arrogant face.

'We're actually going to have sex here?' he asked doubtfully.

'That would be completely acceptable.'

'What if these ropes break?'

'It is not just the ropes. The underlying suspension system was engineered to take the weight of a Boeing 747.'

His mouth curved into a slow, wicked smile. 'That's good to know because I have very sweaty, dirty nights planned for us.'

An electric tingle coursed through me. It would be a long time before I got used to the thought that Lord Greystoke, that mysterious, cold stranger who could barely bring himself to be polite to me, wanted me with the kind of intensity that Ivan showed.

'Where did Robert sleep?' he asked casually.

'Upstairs. He was a big coward. There's another bedroom on the side of the kitchen,' I said pointing up to my left. 'I tried to get him to come down here, but he always refused. On windy nights he used to keep waking up in the middle of the night and lean over the balustrade with a storm lantern to look down and check if I was still hanging on. I'm like a tick. No getting rid of me, I told him.'

He just laughed without making any comment.

'Come on, I'll show you the second best part of the house.'

He hopped off the platform and we went up the steps to solid ground again. I took him to the far end of the house out to the open air, heated pool made of old andesite stone from Java. Rosli had already filled it up with fresh water. It looked beautiful with the afternoon sun hitting the large dragon waterspout sculpture.

'Just what we need tonight,' he said.

Strange that after everything we had done I was suddenly shy. 'Now we really should hit the shower then make our way over to the other side of the island. I want you to meet everybody and I've got chocolates to distribute.'

We bathed outside in the custom-made rainforest shower. I arched my neck back, the water pounding on my face, my forearms pressed into the sweaty copper walls, and reveled in the sensation of Ivan's cock thrusting deep inside me. He bent his head over my face, his eyes glittering hotly as he kissed my mouth.

CHAPTER 31

Tawny Greystoke

I slipped into a T-shirt, boy-shorts and flip-flops, let down all the net blinds, and went to look for Ivan. He was standing at the edge of the water.

'Hey,' I said.

He turned to look at me and for a moment there was such a sad look in his eyes that I took a step back.

'What's the matter?' I asked.

He shook his head. 'I was thinking of Robert,' he said. I think part of me knew that he was not really thinking of Robert, but something connected to Robert.

A wave lapped at my feet. I squeezed my toes. 'Why were you thinking about him?'

He shrugged. 'Just how little I knew him. How he had this whole other life that I knew nothing about.'

'Yeah. Robert was special.'

'You still miss Robert very much, don't you?'

'Yes.'

'Wasn't it awkward with your age difference?'

'No.' I smiled thinking about Robert. 'Neither of us cared what anybody else thought. We used to go places where people would mistake us for father and daughter and we'd just laugh and tell them we were husband and wife.'

He nodded. 'Hmmm ...'

'We should get going. They've probably prepared a barbeque for us. They always have a lovely bonfire.'

'Ah, bonfire,' he said mildly.

'I'm from the South. It's in my nature to *love* a bonfire.'

'Let's go to this bonfire then.'

We walked to the back of the house and took the narrow path that cut across the island. Once I nearly tripped on some roots and Ivan caught me. 'Be careful,' he warned with a scowl on his face. 'I'd hate to see even a scratch on you.'

As we neared the beach on the opposite side of the island, we could hear the sound of laughter and music and smell the food they were cooking. When we arrived in the clearing where the volunteers all lived they gathered around us, and I introduced Ivan to everyone. It was not breeding season for the sea turtles so it was a smaller crew, but they were a young, lively and idealistic group. Two Australians, a French boy, three British lads, a couple of German girls and some students from the local universities.

We distributed the chocolates, drank ice-cold beer, and ate fish grilled with curry and rice. Then they turned the music up loud and some of them danced around the fire. Ivan and I didn't dance. We sat close to each other and just listened to the others. Their stories.

All I knew was that I was happy. Ecstatically so.

By nine the bonfire was put out and everybody left. Part of the group went to bed to prepare for the second shift of the night. The others went to the different locations on the island to guard the nest eggs. They made nightly patrols around the island to check for evidence of sea turtles. If they found any nests they collected the eggs and took them to the incubation center.

Ivan and I walked back. I was feeling pleasantly tipsy, happier than I had ever felt in my life. I looked up at him hardly able to hide the way I felt about him.

As we walked into our house all the lights suddenly went out and all the big fans stopped blowing.

'What the hell?' Ivan said.

'Oh, darn it,' I said. 'The generator has stopped working and it gets hotter than hell at night around here.'

'Where is it? Let me have a look.'

'Let me get a torch,' I said. It was a moonlit night so I quickly found my way to the kitchen drawer, fumbling around before I found one.

Carrying it we went out behind the house to have a look, but there is nothing to see.

Just a massive, ominously still, silent, locked, grey container.

'We can go back to the volunteers' hall and sleep with them tonight. Rosli will call someone to come and repair it tomorrow,' I suggested unhappily.

'Er ... no.'

I bit my lip and thought of what else we could do. 'There is another generator that keeps the fridge working. Maybe we can keep the fridge door open and sleep in front of it.'

He grinned, his teeth gleaming whitely in the dark. 'Sure, I can have sex in front of an open fridge.'

'You want to have sex in this heat? I don't think you know how hot it can get without the giant fans.'

'I haven't given up on the idea yet.'

We went back into the house and lit some storm lanterns. The white nets surrounding us billowed in the gentle breeze giving the scene a hazy, unreal atmosphere.

'God, it's so damn hot. I'm having a cold beer. You want one?' I asked.

'Sure,' he said.

I opened the fridge door, took one out and rolled it along my neck. The bottle was wonderfully cold and I sighed with pleasure. I turned around to find Ivan looking at me.

'Mmmm ...' I gave him a sultry look. I reached for the bottle opener that was hanging by a string next to the fridge and removed the top. It clattered on the stone.

He said nothing, just stared at me.

Then I knew what I wanted to do. I'd seen this in a Tarantino movie once. She had given the killer a lap dance. I would improvise and use my bottle instead.

I arched my neck and dragged the bottle down to my chest. I pulled the neckline of my T-shirt and stroked the heated skin on my shoulder with the bottle. I let the cool glass travel slowly down to my cleavage.

The dark lust in his eyes made my breath come in short gasps.

I grasped the edge of my T-shirt, lifted it as I rubbed the bottle on my stomach. It was no longer ice-cold, but since I was not actually doing it to cool myself ... Slowly gyrating my hips I threw my head back and poured the cold frothy liquid onto my chest.

That did it. He began to peel the clothes off his spectacular body. He walked over to one of the low sofas and sat with his knees spread wide apart and his cock pointing up.

'Come here,' he said, his voice thick and full of wanting.

I put the bottle on the table before walking up to him and, putting my bare foot between his legs, almost touch his balls.

'Talk dirty to me,' he invited, his eyes half-hooded.

I had never talked dirty with anyone, but I didn't want to spoil the mood. In the sexiest voice I could manage, I said, 'Mmm ... when you say talk dirty what do you actually mean?'

Something flickered in his eyes as if he had expected a totally different reaction from me. 'Do you like my cock? Tell me what you see. Talk about it. Describe it. Go a little over the top,' he encouraged.

'OK,' I said slowly. Describe his cock. I decoded that as praise my cock. Mama used to say all men are in love with their own cocks. That should be easy enough. In fact, I could be great at going over the top.

He fisted his beloved cock and waited expectantly.

I took a deep breath. 'Your cock,' I said in a grandiose voice, 'is an exquisite work of art. It is so beautiful and so distinctive it should be hung in the portrait gallery.'

An odd expression crossed his face and was quickly gone. He was definitely ... surprised, or probably even disappointed. Obviously, I needed to up the ante.

'They should pen poems and songs about the fabulousness of your cock. Why, it should be considered one of the wonders of the world. They should name universities after it and ... and ... build, yes,' I said warming to my theme, 'they should build a monument to it.' I raised my hand and flashed it in the air on top of my head. 'Greystoke's Amazing Cock.'

He blinked.

'People should come to pay homage to this cock that can stay titanium hard for hours. It's like a Special Ops soldier: sleek, dangerous, and as strong as a charging bull.

As a matter of fact, it is so lethal it should be given a medal. Or an award of excellence. Wars should be fought over it.'

I looked at him. He did not look too happy. 'What's the matter?'

'Are you fucking taking the piss?'

'No.' I frowned. 'You said to talk about your cock. Obviously you didn't mean for me to say bad things.'

He gave me a slow motion assed stare. 'That's not how you talk dirty to a man.'

'No? All right, give me an example.'

'Fill me up, daddy, fuck my tight cunt! Make me scream with that big dick of yours.'

I grinned. 'Where I come from you got your mouth washed out with soap for using words like that.'

'What's going to win, upbringing or me?'

'Fuck me,' I breathed almost inaudibly, watching the excitement on his face as he waited to hear me talk dirty. I let the words fall out of my mouth. 'Fuck my cunt hard with that dirty big cock of yours.'

'That'll do,' he said. Reaching forward, he grabbed me around my waist, then set me on my hands and knees on the big sofa. He yanked my shorts down, tore my little bikini bottoms from my body and flung them into the darkness.

His hands were on my hips and, snarling like a wolf, he slammed his full length deep into me. I let out a sharp gasp and arched back and up. He grabbed my hair, forcing me to keep that impossibly twisted position as he pounded me mercilessly. With every thrust, my juices spurted around his cock and ran down my thighs. His grip hurt and his cock was too deep for comfort, but that didn't matter, the only thing that mattered was the way my slick, hungry pussy welcomed his bull-like thrusts.

'You're mine,' he snarled.

'Yes,' I gasped eagerly. I cannot explain what it felt like to be called his while being possessed and fucked in that primal way. It was indescribable. I was as God made me. I was his cunt.

Underneath us the river rushed.

CHAPTER 32

Tawny Greystoke

"It is the hardest thing in the world – to do
what we want.
And it takes the greatest kind of courage"
– Ayn Rand

One of the activities the Foundation undertook was to rebuild the reefs destroyed by illegal cyanide fishing, so there were three or four dives per day by the volunteers who were helping to rebuild them by transplanting prepared samples from the ocean nursery to the reef. There were unlimited snorkeling opportunities so we spent our entire morning snorkeling and viewing the new reefs. Some of the newly transferred coral was already the size of dinner plates.

Later I took Ivan to watch the volunteers mix the concrete to produce the bases for the hard and soft coral plantings that would later be attached to the reefs. It was interesting, and I knew that Ivan was impressed with the conservation center's efforts to return the reef to its natural glory.

We shared a simple lunch of rice, chicken and vegetables with the volunteers. By the time we got back Rosli had already sorted out the generator so Ivan immediately opened his laptop and started work. I spent the afternoon on the beach. As I was about to go back for a shower, Rosli arrived on the beach with a durian. He had knocked it off a tree in the jungle.

'Want to share?' he asked, tapping the thorny fruit with his knife. He knew I couldn't bear the smell and he took great pleasure in tormenting me with it.

'Nooooo,' I said, crinkling my nose and pulling a face.

'Hello,' Ivan called out from the steps.

I grinned at Rosli. 'You know what, open the fruit. Let Ivan smell it.'

'You sure?'

'Absolutely.'

Immediately Rosli squatted down and started hacking away at the fruit. Slipping his fingers into the cut at the top of the fruit. he pulled it apart until it separated into two pieces. Instantly the disgusting reek hit me. He picked up a golden bit of flesh and started eating it.

When Ivan came to us he gave me a strange look. He then looked at Rosli.

'Want some fruit, Ivan?' I asked innocently.

'Jesus, what the fuck is that smell? It smells like something's crawled up in here and died.'

I laughed. 'It's that fruit there.'

'It's a durian, isn't it?' he said, making a disgusted face.

'You like fruit, don't you? Try it,' I urged with a cheeky grin.

'No thanks.'

'Chicken shit,' I taunted.

He crossed his arms. 'Have you tried it?'

'No she hasn't,' Rosli piped up. He was sucking the flesh off the fruit and grinning from ear to ear at the same time.

I shot Rosli an ugly glance.

'Right,' Ivan said in a voice slower than a bread wagon with biscuit wheels.

I squirmed uncomfortably.

'I'll have it if you have it too,' he challenged with a devilish look.

I took a deep breath. Oh shit. I pretended to be unconcerned. 'Sure.'

He bent down to pick up one of the fruit halves and held it up to me. Immediately, the pungent smell of something in the late stages of rotting mixed with smelly socks filled my nostrils making me want to gag. I tried hard not to jerk back. 'Well, we have to do it together,' I said.

'All right, but you have to swallow.'

'Ha, ha,' I said.

He took one piece and I took another. I held my nose with the fingers of my left hand and prepared to put it into my mouth.

'At the count of three,' he said.

'I'm ready.'

Rosli was happily chewing and watching us curiously.

'One, two, three ...'

I stuffed it into my mouth and my eyes bulged. It was like eating rotten mushroom. Slimy and disintegrating on my tongue. Horrible. Just horrible. Both of us looked at each and then both of us spat it out at the exact same time.

Rosli was rolling on the sand with laughter as we raced to the water's edge and rinsed out our mouths with saltwater.

'Oh my God! That was vile,' I cried as we both erupted into laughter. While he laughed I looked at him. The sun had already browned him. His eyes were full of warmth and he looked so relaxed and happy. If only he could always be like that.

That evening we went to watch a nest of turtle eggs hatching. If at all possible I never missed one of those. I had seen twenty-five so far, and every single time I saw those tiny little turtles scramble out of their nest and start running out to sea, I felt as if I had received a blessing. The other volunteers had also turned up. It was the culmination of all their work, seeing those babies hatch, and watching their mad dash to the sea.

Rosli gently caught a baby turtle and put it into Ivan's cupped palms. I saw him look in wonder at the little thing squirming in his hands for all it was worth.

I knew exactly how he felt. The first time I held one in my palm I almost cried because I knew it would probably not make it to adulthood, but I prayed it would anyway. That it would come back to Penyu Island and carry on the cycle of its evolution. I felt such a great love and sense of responsibility for it. Its little legs were hard and covered in sand and they thrashed on my palm. It kept craning its little neck towards the sea as if it could hear it or smell it.

Ivan looked up at me, his face and eyes shining.

'He's gorgeous,' isn't he?' I said.

'Gorgeous,' he repeated.

Very gently, Ivan held his palm close to the sand and the little creature raced out.

'Good luck little fellow,' I called out watching them race towards the sea. To my surprise Ivan took my hand.

'So you liked him,' he said softly.

'I'm more fond of him than I am of you,' I replied.

His eyes sparkled with laughter. 'You're in so much trouble,' he warned.

'You best know that we're going to have matching caskets,' I promised.

He bent his head to my ear and whispered, 'I'd love to put you into one of those pregnancy stirrups, your cunt open, wet and ready for me. I'd shove my tongue into you and lick you for hours.'

'Trust you to think that pregnancy stirrups could be even remotely sexy.'

'Even mud is sexy if you're in the equation.'

'I think I prefer Jell-O,' I said.

He laughed and his face softened. 'I'm proud of you, Tawny Greystoke,' he said suddenly and squeezed my hand.

I was so surprised by his remark that I looked up at him, grinning stupidly. At that moment I was the happiest woman alive.

It was beautiful on the beach. The moon was full, the air was filled with the soothing sound of the waves, the wind in the leaves, and the wet slapping of flesh against flesh as Ivan pumped into me. Oh and of course, my own moans and whimpers of pleasure. I drew my knees back as far as I could to open myself up more for him and then experimentally squeezed him tight. He began to move harder, faster, more urgently.

My climax was beginning to build when his palm suddenly closed over my mouth.

I froze.

'Shhh ...' he warned, his eyes narrowed.

I grasped his ribs, slippery with our intermingled sweat, and listened to whatever it was he was listening to. Still with his hand around my mouth, he turned his head very slowly. I didn't dare move. He turned back to me, his eyes shining.

'You won't believe this,' he whispered, 'but a turtle has come ashore and is about four or five feet away from us.' My eyes widened with shock. To the best of my knowledge turtles didn't often come to this side of the island. Mostly they went to the other side, and even if they did come to this side it was always during the breeding months of May to September. I listened and I heard her: the heavy, rasping sounds of her dragging herself on the sand.

To my surprise I suddenly felt loose sand being flung in our direction by her flippers. She was digging her nest chamber next to us! Slowly, Ivan removed his hand from my mouth.

I opened my mouth. 'Oh my God,' I mouthed silently. It's a Hawksbill.'

As gently as possible, Ivan lifted himself out of me and lay next to me. Together, lying side by side, we watched her. Grunting, bellowing and hissing as she laid over one hundred eggs, two sometimes three at a time. We saw her shed the tears that had so moved Robert.

She never acknowledged our presence. Perhaps we were just rocks or shadows to her. Rosli once told me that the locals believe that while laying her eggs a sea turtle goes into a trance from which she cannot be disturbed.

When she had finished she used her rear flippers to cover her nest with sand. Gradually, she packed the sand down over her pit, then used her front flippers to disguise her nest from predators by throwing sand in all directions. Exhausted, she slowly made her way back to sea.

Neither of us spoke. It was so special we couldn't speak.

I felt humbled and in awe of the amount of trust that the mother turtle had entrusted her children to nature. I wanted to be brave like her. I turned to Ivan. He was still staring at the spot where she had slipped into the sea.

'I love you,' I said.

His entire body stilled.

'I know you don't love me back and I didn't tell you to make you feel awkward. I'm sorry if I spoiled this moment for you, but I just wanted you to know. If I die tomorrow, I don't want it to be a thing unsaid.'

He sighed heavily, like a man burdened and tortured with inner demons. 'We have to go back tomorrow,' he said, his voice throbbing with some deep emotion.

For a moment I felt a flash of anger. How dare he dictate when I went back? Let him go back if he wanted to. I would stay on. And then my fury deflated. What would be the point? I would be miserable here without him. I would have to return to England to face the reality of my pretend marriage.

There was something wrong, very wrong with my marriage, and the sooner I got to the bottom of it the better.

CHAPTER 33

Tawny Greystoke

"Love doesn't just sit there like a stone, it has to be made, like bread."
- Ursula Le Guin, *The Lathe of Heaven.*

I woke up because I heard a sound. I turned my head and saw that the pillow beside me was empty. Pushing hair out of my face I sat up and looked around. There was no light coming from under the en-suite bathroom door and the bedroom door was closed. How strange.

I got out of bed, walked in my bare feet to the door, and opened it. I could see the light in Ivan's study was on and I could hear his voice. It was quite loud. He must be on the phone with someone. I walked towards the sound.

Something made me hold back in the corridor.

'No, she doesn't know and I want to keep it that way. For this plan to work she must be kept totally in the dark.'

There was a silence, then he was speaking again.

'Absolutely. More than a hundred million is at stake. You have to come up with a foolproof plan to eliminate her. A way that cannot be traced back to anybody. Especially not me.'

Of their own volition my hands flew up and covered my gaping mouth as if to stop myself from screaming, but it was not me that was screaming it was my very soul. I just stood there in the dark frozen with shock and horror.

There was another pause and then his voice came back, urgent and hopeful.

'Are you sure?'

Another long pause while the person on the other end probably explained something. Then came Ivan's voice, ghoulishly excited.

'Yes, yes, that might work. Run it by them and see if they are happy to go ahead with it. The sooner the better. I can't stand this waiting anymore. I need to know it is done.'

'Right. I got to go, but thanks for all your help.'

Very quietly, I tip-toed back to the bedroom and got under the covers. I was trembling. I knew without a doubt that he was talking about me. Who was he talking to? He must be in cohorts with my stepchildren. There could be no other explanation. What was it he wanted me to be kept in the dark about? Was the foolproof plan to eliminate me? Was this my worst fear? Was Ivan plotting to kill me and share my money with my stepchildren?

It seemed impossible. He didn't need my money. He was a billionaire. It made less sense than a bull with tits, but no other explanation would fit.

There was a sound in the corridor.

I turned on my side, closed my eyes, made my breathing deep and slow and pretended to sleep.

Ivan came in, got into bed, kissed my forehead and lay beside me. After a few seconds his hand came to rest lightly on my hip.

'Mmm,' I said sleepily and curled further into myself.

His hand slipped away. For a long time he did not sleep. Finally, his breathing became deep and even. I turned over and watched him. He looked peaceful and prettier than a Tennessee Bluetick Coonhound. I felt confused and scared. I couldn't understand what was happening. Nothing was as it seemed. Even now how I longed to reach out and stroke his thick, silky hair, but I did not. I simply watched him in wonder until dawn lit the sky.

How did it come about that unnoticed I had slipped into my enemy's bed.

Very carefully, with my eyes fixed on Ivan's sleeping face, I inched out of bed. Once out I stood looking down at him. I was still shell-shocked. It was incredible how completely he had fooled me.

With cat-like quiet, I lifted my tracksuit and running shoes out of the wardrobe and dressed quickly in the living room. Without making any noise I let myself out of the apartment. While I ran I tried to think. I really, really did. For a whole hour I tried, but my mind wouldn't function properly. I kept wanting desperately to believe that I had made a mistake. There was no motive. He didn't need my money.

He had a private plane for God's sake.

Besides, I trusted Robert and he told me again and again that Ivan was the only one I could trust. Another voice in my head said, Robert constructed a will that left me open to Ivan's total control. If he had not made me Ivan's ward I would never be here and married to Ivan.

By the time I returned I was no less bewildered or shocked. Ivan was already out of the shower.

'Good run?' he asked, and for the first time I saw him without my rose tinted glasses. He was hiding something big. He had been for a long time, but I was so caught up with him not finding out my secrets. I never took the time to examine the things that didn't sit right about him. It was always there, in the background and almost undetectable, but there all the same. Even now I saw it. The only time it was not there was when we were in bed having sex.

'Yes, thank you.' I even managed a smile. 'Want some coffee and some toast?'

'Yes, please.'

I nodded and went to the kitchen. I was arranging the slices of toast in the toast rack when he appeared, knotting his tie in the doorway.

'I've got to run. Something's come up,' he said.

'No breakfast?'

'I'll just take that coffee.'

I carried the mug and held it out to him.

He took a sip. 'What will you do today?'

I shrugged. 'I don't know yet. I might go into work.'

'Good. So I'll see you tonight. Maybe we can go out to dinner or something.'

'Yes. That'll be nice,' I said. I knew my voice sounded wooden, but I couldn't help myself. I never was good at pretending. What you see is what you get with me.

He took another sip and put the coffee mug down. 'Right. I'm off.'

After a quick, hard peck on my lips he was gone. I touched my lips. God! I *still* wanted him. What was wrong with me? What an awful mess I was in.

I took the mug and poured the remaining coffee into the sink. Almost on autopilot I opened the dishwasher and placed it inside. Still on autopilot I crossed the living room and went towards his study. I opened the door and stood for moment at the threshold.

There was hardly anything on his table, just a few papers. I approached it and glanced at them. A report about some Chinese town, a development of some kind. I went around the desk, sat on his chair and opened the drawers. The first one had odds and ends. The second had files. The middle drawer had stationery.

The first drawer on the left-hand side made me pause. It was locked. I knew where the key was. I'd seen where he hid it. I ran out into the hallway and checked a small decorative bowl. It was at the bottom. I took the key and ran back to open the drawer.

There was a crumpled letter in it. I put it on the desk and straightened it out. It was a letter from the bank. I stared at it in disbelief. It cannot be. It just cannot be. I blinked and re-read it.

Jesus Christ.

The bank was recalling one of their loans for twenty million pounds. There were other letters too. Some had been torn open and other remained unopened but they all carried the same return address. With shaking hands I slipped out the ones that had been opened. They were just more letters warning that his accounts were going to be closed, warnings about bankruptcy proceedings, and warnings of late payments.

Sick to my stomach I sat back on the swivel chair.

He was broke. It was all a lie. The black American Express. The brand new Lamborghini. The champagne worth thousands of pounds. The boast that he was a billionaire. Everything. Everything was a lie. My breath came out in short, sharp gasps. I never expected this. Never. Not in a million years. What a lying bastard.

Oh God!

Oh my God!

I never did sign that pre-nup agreement. My heart was racing. *Wow, Tawny!*

I closed my eyes. *Calm down. Calm down.* Carefully I thought about everything that had happened. He had taken me away from Barrington Manor, where I found security for the first time in years, and brought me here. Married me in a rush as if he was doing me a favor. I had been so naïve and stupid, so blinded by lust I had even forgotten to ask for the prenup.

I frowned.

What about Foxgrove? That still belonged to him. Perhaps, he had mortgaged that as well. And his mother. She seemed so sincere. It was obvious she didn't know the state of Ivan's finances either.

What was he planning? Who had he been talking to last night? I needed to see my solicitor and I needed to get out of this house. My head was throbbing. He betrayed me! I couldn't believe how completely he had fooled me.

I put all the letters back into their envelopes and placed them exactly where I found them. I scrunched up the first letter into a ball and put it back on the top of the pile. I closed the drawer, locked it, and made sure the file on the table was back in its original position. Then I walked out of the room, closed the door and returned the key to the bottom of the bowl.

I needed time. I needed a strategy. My heart was broken and I was badly, very badly wounded by this new development, but I was not beaten. I survived being a hungry, homeless orphan, hiding from the authorities. I could survive this too.

I took a shower and tried to think. I needed one day, just one day, to get myself together. I got out of the shower, called my solicitor, and made an appointment for the next day. Then I deleted traces of the call from my phone.

I couldn't possibly go to work today, but I had to get out of this house. I put on my coat, took my handbag, and left the apartment. As I was closing the door, Ralph appeared in his doorway. He was about to go out.

With a cold stare he closed his door and went back into his apartment.

Whatever, Ralph. And everybody thought I was the gold digger!

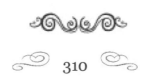

I took a taxi to Harrods where I wandered around listlessly. I had no plan. I needed a plan, but my mind was blank. I felt so depressed and numb. I could not believe that Ivan could betray me for money. All he had to do was tell me the truth. I would have given him the money. Robert would turn in his grave to know he had been so spectacularly wrong about Ivan.

Ivan was as bad as the rest of them.

All I wanted to do was run away and hide for just a little while. Until it didn't hurt so much, but there was nowhere to run or hide. I had to stay and face the music. I was married to a psychopath who could have incredible sex with me all night, then plot with my stepchildren to have me eliminated. I turned a corner, still in a daze, and bumped into someone.

'I'm sorry,' I said, my voice dying in my throat when I saw who it was.

My old butler, James.

'Oh, Mrs. Maxwell! Well, it's Lady Greystoke now, isn't it?' he said with a happy smile. 'I can't believe it. You look very well. How are you these days?' He seemed so happy to see me that I felt myself go red with embarrassment. I had asked him to stay on, but then Ivan had fired him, yet he seemed to bear me no ill will.

As I stood there I understood Ivan's game. James had been loyal to Robert and me, so Ivan removed him from the picture. As a strategy it was brilliant. He removed my entire support system. The butler that Robert had trusted for twenty years, the housekeeper, my home, my horses. Everything had been taken away from me.

I suddenly felt like crying.

'Oh Mrs. Maxwell, I mean, Lady Greystoke, what's the matter? You look so pale. Are you all right?'

'I'm fine. I'm just glad to see you James. How have you been?'

'Not good. I've haven't been able to find new employment. I'm too old. And the missus is sick so most of my inheritance is gone.'

'Oh no. You must let me help you,' I cried, horrified to know what had happened to him.

'That's very kind of you.'

'Yes, you must tell me everything.'

'Will you allow me to buy you a coffee?' he asked.

'Of course. But you must let me buy it.'

'No, please. For once let me treat you.'

I smiled. 'All right.'

We walked together to the coffee house on the third floor. I sat down. 'Do you mind if I call the missus and tell her I'll be a bit late?' he asked, taking his phone out of his pocket and holding it respectfully in his hand.

'Of course not,' I said with a smile.

He called and told her that we had met in Harrods, and that he would be a bit late. He listened, then looking at me apologetically, said, 'No, Martha. It wouldn't be appropriate.'

'What wouldn't be appropriate?' I asked.

He took the phone away from his ear. 'Martha wants me to bring you home for tea. She's always been dying to meet you.'

'Oh,' I said. I remembered then that James had mentioned her before. Not only that, once she had even baked some cookies for me, and I had gone out and bought her a beautiful designer handbag as a gift.

He put the phone back to his ear. 'Maybe another time, Martha. Lady Greystoke is busy.'

'Wait,' I said. 'Where do you live?'

'We live in West Kensington. It's just up the road. We'd love you to come, but I realize you're probably too busy. Just say no if you can't. You can come another time.'

'No, no,' I said with a smile. 'I'll come today. I'd love to meet your wife.'

'Are you sure?' James asked, his eyes bright.

'Of course, I'm sure.' The truth was, bumping into him couldn't have come at a better time. I needed to not be alone. I needed to talk to people from my old life, from before Ivan came into it.

James ended his call and beamed at me. 'My car is parked one street away from here. I can bring it around or we can walk. I know you enjoy a good walk.'

It was good to be with someone who knew me so well. 'Let's walk, James. As you said, I've always enjoyed a good walk.'

We walked to his car. Like a true gentleman, he held open the passenger door while I got in. He closed the door before going around to the driver's side. He started the ignition and was about to drive away when the back door opened suddenly. I twisted my head around in surprise and stared into Dr. Spencer's pale blue eyes.

Oh, dear God!

'Hello, Lady Greystoke,' he said, and slipped a needle into my arm.

I barely heard him. I looked at my arm in frozen shock. In a flash all the missing pieces of the jigsaw puzzle fell into place. James had spiked my drink. They were all in this together. The picture was now complete. Ivan was talking to the doctor yesterday. Of course, the good doctor always hated me. Oh no, I was beginning to feel disorientated. I was going to black out.

Then everything went black.

CHAPTER 34

Tawny Greystoke

"I can't carry it for you, but I can carry you!"
- Samwise Gamgee
(A Hobbit &
the real hero)

Dr. Spencer was holding smelling salts under my nose when I came to. My head lolled about but my seated body was totally immobile. I tried to speak and realized that my mouth taped shut.

I coughed and blearily tried to make sense of my surroundings. I was immobile because from my shoulder to my ankles I was tightly mummified in Clingfilm.

One look at the ceiling and I knew that I was in Barrington Manor. I swiveled my eyes around and saw there were other people in the room. My vision was still fuzzy and they appeared as blurred shapes. I blinked to clear my vision.

'Can you hear me Mrs. Maxwell?' Dr. Spencer asked calmly.

I pulled my eyes back to him and focused on his face. There was no expression at all on his thin, sallow face, but he was wearing what appeared to be a white boiler suit.

I nodded.

'She's fine. She's was always as fit as a horse,' a woman's voice dismissed rudely, and Rosalind came into my sight. She was wearing a similar white boiler suit. 'Anyway, it doesn't matter if she's not. She'll be dead soon.'

My blood ran cold at her words.

'I can't have any chemicals found in her system,' Dr. Spencer explained patiently. 'It *has* to look like an accident or we'll all be going to prison.'

'Look, can we get this over with. This place is giving me the creeps. All these fucking sheets over the furniture look like ghosts, Bianca said with a shudder. She too was dressed the same way.

'Don't be such baby. We have to wait for Ivan,' Rosalind scolded her sister.

'And me,' an amused man's voice said.

Dorian came into view. He was not wearing a white suit.

'For heaven's sake. I thought I told you stay away. What are you doing here? And why are you not wearing one of these.'

'Ivan asked me to come and why should I wear those ridiculous things. It's not like I'll be the one who's going to do the deed.'

The mention of Ivan's name hurt me more than I cared to admit.

'Why did Ivan ask you to come' Rosalind asked suspiciously.

'I think he didn't want to leave any loose lips and, figured correctly, I might add, that I might have loose lips. All who benefit must be implicated was what he said.'

Dorian strolled over and stood in front of me.

'Why on earth is she covered in plastic?'

'We didn't want to leave tie marks on her wrists or ankles,' Dr Spencer explained. It has to look like an accident.'

'What kind of an accident?' he asked almost childishly.

'An accidental drowning in the lake. I've already prepared a large pail of lake water that her face will be submerged in until she drowns and then she will be put in the lake so it looks like she fell into the cold water and drowned.'

'A pail of lake water?'

'Yes, if she downs in the bathtub the type of water inside her will be different than the lake's.'

'Fan of CSI, are you?' Dorian asked sarcastically.

'No,' Dr Spencer denied stiffly. 'Unlike you I thought it out.'

I listened incredulously. They had thought of everything and I had been led here like a lamb to slaughter.

'I'm far too squeamish for details like that.' He turned to look at me. 'Goodness is it kinky that all this plastic is giving me a hard on.'

'Shut up,' Bianca said nervously. 'None of this is funny.'

Dorian ignored his sister and turned to Dr. Spencer. Can I fuck her very quickly?'

'You're drunk, aren't you?' Rosalind fumed. 'Just once you couldn't come sober.'

'Chill out, sis. I had half a glass of Merlot at lunch. It isn't like I was going in bareback. I've got condoms.' He comes closer to me. 'I've always wanted to give her one. Ivan got to, I don't see why not me too.'

'God, you are such an idiot. Do you want to leave your calling card inside her,' Rosalind sneered.

Dr Spencer cleared his throat. 'Yes, you definitely don't want to leave your DNA on her. Even the smallest particles can incriminate you.' He lifted up his hands to show that he was wearing surgeon's gloves.

Dorian shook his head regretfully at me. 'All you had to do was fucking share.'

In his weak jaw I saw my chance. The weak link in the chain. I made a muffled sound and begged him with my eyes.

He stared at me for a moment as if considering my request then suddenly reached his hand out and viciously ripped the tape off my mouth. I gritted my teeth to stop myself from crying out with the pain.

'What the hell are you doing?' both Rosalind and Bianca screamed.

'Relax, what's she going to do? Scream and alert the neighbors. There's nobody for miles in this godforsaken part of the world. Let her have a few last words. Besides I like hearing her talk. I like her lips.' He leered as he said that.

'I can give you money,' I cried.

He sighed exaggeratedly in a pretend sad way, the way Mafia killers in movies do. He was really enjoying this. 'I allow you to talk and this is what you say. Disappointing. Truly disappointing.'

Tears burned the backs of my eyes. I knew my last hope was my secret. I had vowed never to tell, but there was no point in keeping it any more. In fact, I no longer knew why Robert had put me through this whole charade. In the end I still ended up their prey. I wanted to live and I would do what it took to survive.

'I'm not who you think I am,' I cried out.

Dorian smiled, the sick twisted, smile of a nasty boy pulling the legs off insects just because he could. 'Go on then. Who are you?' he taunted. The others said nothing.

'I'm not your stepmother. I'm your half-sister. I'm Robert's daughter.'

Dorian's eyes bulged with shock. 'Bollocks' he shouted.

'No, it's not. I can prove it. I have the results of the paternity test. It's with my solicitor. We're flesh and blood.'

Rosalind stalked towards me. 'You're telling me, you're my sister?'

'Yes,' I said.

'And why are you telling us this now? Do you think that we will take pity on you because one microscopic sperm from my father, one that should have been flushed down the toilet, instead impregnated a whore's egg and produced you?'

'My mother was not a whore,' I said through gritted teeth.

'Yes, she was.'

'She wasn't. She was a dancer.'

'Oh well, here's something you didn't know. Your mother sold her body to pay for her treatments.'

I felt angry tears flood my eyes and start dribbling down my face. 'I don't believe you,' I shouted angrily. My mother was the one pure thing in my life.

'Believe what you want. As if I care either way. You're not my sister. I hate you and I've always hated you. If anything this makes me even happier to get rid of you. How could Robert favor you over us? If we didn't have to preserve your face, I would love to punch it in.'

'Don't even think about,' Dr. Spencer interjected. 'Keep the emotions out. Or we'll all be rotting in prison.'

I concentrated all my attention on Rosalind. 'The money was not for me. It is supposed to be used for the charity.'

She frowned. 'That ridiculous turtle nonsense?'

'Yes. It is not for me. I'm just supposed to administer it. Make sure the foundation carries on in the way Robert wanted.' Then an idea occurred to me. 'But I can sign it all over to you.'

She stiffened suddenly. 'Thank you, but that won't be necessary. I'll just do it the old fashioned way. Murder.'

'That's just stupid. Why take such a big risk? Don't you think the police would find it very suspicious that I came here for no reason at all and drowned in a shallow lake?'

'Maybe, but if there is no proof of foul play...'

'Are you sure you covered all your tracks Rosalind. In this day and age there are many way to trip up a murderer? How did you get here? How many CCTV cameras caught your face, or Dorian's, or Bianca's?'

Then I saw a tiny glimpse of hope. A look crossed her face. Uncertainty.

I pressed home my point. 'My marriage is not legal. You have the proof sitting in my solicitor's safe. You can contest the will.'

'You must think I was born yesterday. And while I'm doing all this, you're not going to tell anyone that we kidnapped you and brought you here intending to kill you.'

'Who would believe me?'

She shook her head. 'Nope. I'll take my chances with murder. It's worked for millennia. It's how all my ancestors got rid of their enemies.'

I could feel the adrenaline pumping in my blood. I could take her. Even bound up I could whoop her ass. She was not as clever as she thought. I stared at her fiercely. 'You don't get it. I've already transferred all my money into the trust. None, of you can touch it without me.'

Dorian and Bianca froze.

'You're lying,' Rosalind shouted, but I could see that I had unsettled her for the first time. For the first time I had the upper-hand. I could do this.

'How do you know?' I challenged, my voice strong and sure.

'Because you haven't,' Ivan's voice reverberated around the room.

At the sound of his voice my body sagged. The betrayal was complete. He came into the room.

'You made a phone call yesterday to his office and you have an appointment for tomorrow, but even so, without my say so you cannot make any such decision. So my darling, as it stands, the Maxwell fortune is still all in your name.'

He stood in front of me in his black leather jacket, a total stranger. Did I dance goofily with this man in a sex club called The Dirty Aristocrat?

'Are you all right?' he asked me, his eyes quickly and impersonally pouring over my body. Where had all the passion gone?

I wanted to spit in his face. I knew there was no point in trying to ask him for mercy. He knew I was in love with him and he could do this to me. I glared at him with murderous hatred, and he smiled. 'That's my girl,' he whispered softly and turned away.

'Are we all agreed that we do this?'

Without the silence of hesitation every single person in the room spoke up and offered their agreement.'

'Right. Let's get on with it, but first there's something I've wanted to do for a very fucking long time. Faster than I could blink, he swung his fist out and crashed it slap bang into the middle of Dorian's face. The thud was rather delightful. I thought I heard bone crunch.

'Fuck,' Dorian screamed in pain, clutching his nose with both his hands. Blood rushed out between his fingers like a bubbling brook. 'What the fuck? You broke my fucking nose.'

Ivan grinned. 'I did you a favor. Now you won't be the prettiest bitch on your prison block.'

'What?' Rosalind screeched. 'You asshole you.' She went flying towards him in a fury.

'We're done,' Ivan shouts and all of a sudden the place was crawling with policemen and other people. I was in such a state I couldn't make sense of the scene before me. Men were grabbing Rosalind and she was screaming wild abuse at me and them. Bianca was sobbing and telling everyone that she was innocent. She had been forced to cooperate, and Dorian, with blood pouring down his face, looking stunned and stupid.

CHAPTER 35

Tawny Greystoke

As soon as our eyes locked, everyone else and everything else in the room melted away, my mouth opened and I started howling like some demented animal. I seemed to have no control over my actions. My whole body was shaking uncontrollably. In an instant he was there next to me. He wrapped his strong arms around me and held me like he had never done since Robert gave me to him.

'You conspired with them,' I sobbed loudly. 'You made me hate you.'

He stroked my hair, his face pained. 'I know. I know, darling. I'm so sorry, but there was no other way to do it.'

I looked at him with accusing eyes. 'I was so frightened. I thought they were going to kill me, but what hurt even more was that you betrayed me.'

'I'm sorry, sweetheart. I really am. Please try to understand. I had no choice,' he murmured in my ear.

'You could have told me,' I whimpered.

'You are the worst actress I've ever met in my life, Tawny Greystoke. You'd have given the game away straight away. It was too important. I couldn't take the chance, my darling.'

'They could have hurt me, and then what would you have done,' I said.

His jaw hardened suddenly and his eyes were like chips of slate. 'You were never in any danger. Not for one tiny second.'

I sniffed pitifully, and he took an army knife from his leather jacket and started to cut through the Clingfilm.

'I was always there, sweet Tawny. I had to do it this way. I had to flush them out. I can't be looking over my shoulder for the rest of our lives. That bunch of airheads would never give up, and they are stupid enough for me to actually fear them.'

As soon as I felt my limbs become free, the dam I had been holding back broke, I hid my face in his chest and sobbed my eyes out. He held me and let me stay there. He knew it was just pent up emotion and it was better out than in.

When the tears subsided and I raised my head, Dr. Spencer was standing in front of us. The whole world was upside down. Dr. Spencer who I'd always thought hated me was working behind the scenes to save me.

'I'm sorry I frightened you,' he said softly.

I shook my head to signify that it didn't matter. 'What about James?' I asked.

He shook his head.

'Right,' I said sadly. How blind I had been. Everyone had managed to fool me. 'Does he have a sick wife?'

'I believe he has a wife, but she is not sick.'

'Well. Never mind.'

He leaned forward and gently patted my shoulder. 'You'll be all right, Lady Greystoke.'

'Please call me Tawny.'

'Then you must call me Harry,' he said with a smile.

'I will. I always wanted to be close to you because Robert loved you so much, but you were always so cold and horrible to me.'

'I'm sorry. It was necessary.' He put his hand into his jacket and held out an envelope.

'For me?' I whispered.

He nodded.

'What is it?' I asked looking at it.

'It's from Robert.'

'Robert?' I repeated with a frown.

'Yes. He knew this day would come. He planned very carefully, Tawny. He loved you so much. You changed him. He said until you came into his life, he was a cold, unfeeling creature. He always thought of you as the golden child that changed Silas Marner's life.'

I took the envelope in my hand. It had my name across the front in Robert's scrawly handwriting. I looked up at Harry, confused and disturbed. 'But he never left you anything in the will?'

'No, if he had then Rosalind would not have trusted me.'

'But you lost out,' I said.

He smiled. 'Everything I wanted I already received while Robert was alive.'

'No,' I decided firmly. 'I'm going to give you the inheritance you deserve. I'm going to see that you're all right, Harry. I'm going to make you rich.'

He smiled sadly.

'Why does that make you sad?' I asked, surprised by his reaction.

'I was just thinking of Robert. How well he knew us all.'

'What do you mean?'

'He told me that the day I gave you this envelope you would give me more than anything he would have. He used the exact words you used. "She'll make you rich," he said.' He sighed. 'Anyway, I should be going.'

'Goodbye Harry and thank you so much for everything you have done. You'll be hearing from my solicitor very soon.'

He smiled. 'Thank you.'

As he walked away Ivan turned to me. 'Come on,' he said. 'I'll take you somewhere you can sit and read that letter.'

There were still some policemen loitering about but almost everybody was gone. Carefully, Ivan lifted me up and carried me as if I was a baby to Robert's study. He took me to Robert's favorite chair and lowered me on to the dustsheet. 'Read your letter and we'll talk when I come back. There is so much I want to tell you,' he said.

I grabbed his hand. 'No, we'll read it together. No more secrets.'

He smiled. 'No more secrets,' he echoed. Hauling me out of the chair, he sat down and pulled me onto his lap.

I stroked the letter and suddenly felt like crying all over again.'

'It's OK, my darling,' Ivan said. Circling my wrist, he brought my hand to his lips and kissed my fingertips.

With great care I opened the envelope and was shocked by the faint fragrance of Robert's aftershave. I brought it to my nose and inhaled it before it was gone forever.

'I wanted to call him Daddy,' I told Ivan.

'I know. I know you loved him.'

I nodded. 'Yes, I did.'

My throat closed over and my eyes were blurred with tears. I pulled the letter out. It was only a short letter. Just like Robert. Writing me a letter from the grave and keeping it short.

I cleared my throat and read it aloud. 'My darling daughter, if you are reading this letter then everything has worked exactly as I planned. You have tipped your hat to the right angle and allowed the right man to seduce you. He's wonderful, my stepson, is he not? Have the wonderful life you so richly deserve, my sweet darling. I'll see you before you see me. Kiss the baby turtles for me. Love, Daddy. xx'

Tears were pouring down my face.

How much I had underestimated Robert. After his death I allowed myself to become convinced that his illness had made him careless. I believed he had miscalculated and misjudged, but he had not. He had laid his plans very carefully. He saw things far into the future that neither Ivan, or I had. I folded the letter and put it back into the envelope. Then I lifted my head and looked into Ivan's eyes.

'I can sell this house and you can have the money from the sale.'

To my shock his eyes filled with tears. 'Oh my darling,' he breathed. 'I don't need your money.'

'I know about the bank. I went into your drawer. I saw the letters,' I confessed.

He smiled. 'Oh, Tawny. I left them there for you to find. I knew you'd have to go looking. Those letters are not real.'

I frowned and shook my head. 'But they had letterheads and everything on them.'

'Yeah, you can have those made for nothing these days. I think Theresa still has about ten floating about somewhere.'

'Why did you do that?'

'Because without motive you would never have believed I could be involved. If you had not found those letters would you have gone with James?'

'Maybe not,' I admitted truthfully.

'When they made their move I needed you to be off balance and not the sharp little cookie you usually are. I needed you to follow them blindly because you were so confused. Even if you had called me to tell me where you were going it would have all fallen apart. I needed you to distrust me.'

So much thought had gone into his plan. My heart felt as if it was bursting with love for this man. I never truly understood him. There were still tears in my eyes, and he wiped them away tenderly.

'Oh Ivan. I really believed you were with them.'

'Shhh... I know. I wanted you to. It's OK. All is fair in love and war. I knew you heard my phone call. Hell, I threw a phone book against the wall to make a noise loud enough to wake you up.'

'But I suffered so. You don't have a clue how much it hurt me.'

'Not as much as me. It had to be done. There was no other way. It was agonizing to see your eyes turn wary. To see you look at me with such hurt that morning. I couldn't even stay in the apartment. I went straight to the office and I was like ... what's that thing you say I am in the mornings?'

'Madder than a wet hen?'

'Not that one.'

'When you fall out of the angry tree and hit every branch on the way down?'

'That's the one,' he said with a gorgeous smile. 'I could never betray you. I love you.'

'What?'

'I could never betray you.'

'The other part,' I prompted with a happy grin.

'I love you.'

'You really do?'

'Can't you tell? Fucking hell, for a smart cookie you sure are dumb. Don't you know when a man acts cold and disinterested in the presence of a drop dead beauty he is crazy about her?'

'This is so hard to take in. I really thought you didn't want me.'

There is only one word that comes into my head when I think of you. Mine. You were the one thing I couldn't walk away from, the one constant thing I desired more than anything else. No matter how hard I tried I couldn't get you out of my mind or my fantasies.' He winked. 'You don't know the things you've done in my fantasies. Besides I knew you secretly couldn't keep your hands off me.'

'You think the sun rises just to hear you crow, don't you?' I retorted.

'Doesn't it?'

I grinned. 'Well, I suppose I will keep you then. You'll be useful for picking up heavy stuff.'

'And licking your pussy.'

I licked my lips. 'By the way, I've got something to tell you.'

'That you're my stepsister?'

My mouth fell open. 'You knew? How?'

'It was the last piece of the puzzle for me. The moment I found out you were a virgin I knew. No matter how beautiful you are, Robert was not going to leave his entire inheritance to a random stranger he was not even fucking. The only thing I couldn't figure out was how it all came about.'

'All my life my mama never told me who my father was. I figure it was because he wounded her badly. I think he was the only one she ever loved and he left her after a month.'

I bent my head and looked at my fingers. They were twisted in my lap. It still hurt to think of that day my mama died.

'Then on the day it was clear to her that she was passing she whispered Robert's name in my ear and told me go and find him. She said he was a mean man, but I would melt his heart. I had no money at all. I went to the bank manger to beg for a little loan and he told me ... I could have the money if I got on my fine knees and sucked him off.'

Ivan's eyes flared and his large hands covered mine protectively.

'I didn't know what to do. I was in such a state. I sold a little chain my mama had given me to someone who gave me seventy dollars for it. Then I went into the café and did an Internet search for Robert Maxwell, the owner of Jetcorp. I made a long distance phone call to his office and told his secretary that my name was Tawny St. Clair who was the daughter of Tandy Sinclair and that I had something very, very important to tell him.'

Remembering that time still made a lump form in my throat and I swallowed it away.

'I said I would be calling again tomorrow at the same time and could she kindly tell him that. The next twenty-four hours were longest in my life. The next day I called and God answered my prayers. My palms were so sweaty the phone kept slipping out of my hand, but he only asked me two questions. Was mama still alive? When I said no, I heard him sigh, and there was so much regret in the sound I knew that somehow he was no longer the mean man that mama knew. Then he asked me when I could come. Straightaway, I said. So he sent me a ticket and I came to England.'

I smiled with the memory.

'I can still remember the first day I arrived at his doorstep. He looked at me with a smile in his eyes and said, "Well, I never would have thought it possible, but you're even more beautiful than your mama." I told him I thought he talked funny and he said, "That, young lady, is because you can't hear yourself." I laughed and so did he. And that was the beginning.'

'Why at that stage did he make you pretend that you were a nail technician he had hired?'

'I think he was afraid of what his children would do to me even then.'

'My poor darling. I've been so unfair to you.'

'No you haven't. I've had the best time in my life with you.'

'God, I love you so much,' he breathed.

'So you really, really do love me,' I asked, almost unable to believe that someone as grand as him could love me.

'I really, really do.'

'When did you find out though?' I wheedled.

'Oh, well. Wanting to kill Ralph that night might have been a good clue, but really, when you banged my head with the cake tin.'

'What?'

'Really. It knocked some sense into me,' he teased.

'Now you're just teasing me.'

'Tawny honey, I think I've been in love with you for years. I guess even Robert knew too. I remember he used to deliberately talk about you even when I pretended outright disinterest. I used to get so jealous. Tawny this. Tawny that. Fucking hell. I used leave his house in a terrible temper. I couldn't believe you were his and not mine. I used to out and get drunk, fuck a random blonde, and pretend it was you.'

I licked my lips and looked up from under my eyelashes. 'Don't you want those blondes anymore?'

'Did you not hear what I just said? They were substitutes for you. You know, like a sugar substitute. It doesn't taste as good and it leaves a bad aftertaste, but it helps soothe the craving. I never wanted any of them. I only ever wanted you.' He grinned. 'You were the mothership. The everything.' He nodded.

'Yup, my stepmother who turned out to be my stepsister.'

'Oh you kinky man you.'

'Ah, talking about that. We have an appointment at Blue Butterfly tomorrow.'

'We do?' I beamed up at him.

'Yes, we do.'

'Didn't you have enough fruit the last time?'

'Ah, fruit platters are not the only things they do.'

'Can't wait,' I said beaming happily.

'After that we are flying off to Penyu island to have a proper honeymoon. I still need to fuck you on that swing bed.'

'Yes, m'Lord,' I said meekly.

'Oh, while we're at it.' He reached into his pocket and brought out a little velvet box. He opened it and on a bed of midnight blue velvet sat the most beautiful ruby and diamond ring I had ever laid eyes on. I looked up at him with wide eyes. 'For me?' I gasped.

'Do you see anybody else?'

'Careful. You're spoiling the moment,' I scolded.

He pulled the gaudy ring off my finger and tossed it behind him.

'Hey?' I said.

'It was fake by the way.'

'What?'

'Yeah. Part of the plan. I was prepared for the eventuality that after you'd read the letters you might go and have it valued. A fake would have cemented my motive.'

'My God! You thought of everything.'

'You didn't really think I was going to let my wife walk about with that tasteless rock on her finger, did you?'

'Well, it was a bit Mariah Carey weds James Packer.'

'This,' he said, slipping the beautiful ring on my finger, 'has belonged in my family from the time we stole it from the Indian maharajas.'

I held my hand out and laughed.

'We're starting again, Tawny Greystoke, and this time we're going to make the stars come out just to watch us.'

I looked into his silver eyes. My heart felt as if it would burst with happiness. 'What will they see, these stars that come out to watch us?'

'They will see me loving you like no man has ever loved a woman before.'

I smiled happily. 'Who'd have thought I'd fall for a dirty aristocrat.'

'Who'd have thought I'd be a total sucker for a country girl,' he said with a twinkle in his eye.

EPILOGUE

Tawny Maxwell

https://www.youtube.com/watch?v=HQW7I62TNOw

'**T**alk dirty to me,' he said.

'How dirty?' I asked.

'Make it filthy.'

'I want to suck your dirty big cock until you cum in my throat.'

He grinned. 'Not bad.'

'I'm a shameless slut who loves to have a really, really big dick stuck deep inside her wet cunt.'

'Very good,' he approved and started to unbutton my blouse. 'Carry on,' he instructed in a pleased voice.

'And I love it when stretch me, and you fuck me hard in the ass.'

He stopped unbuttoning, his eyebrows rising. 'Really?'

'Well,' I said with a smile.

'Jesus, woman. You're always ruining my fantasy. Five years on and you still haven't learned to talk dirty. It's not just the words baby. You've got to say it like you mean it.

You can't be smiling and messing about like it was a joke.'

'OK, OK,' I placate.

He finished unbuttoning my blouse and slipped his hand up my skirt.

'Oh, Sir. What are you doing?'

'I'm just a sucker for a country girl.'

He allowed his hand to travel along the inside of my thigh and reached between my legs. 'Oh, you dirty, dirty girl. Where are your panties? Look how wet you are. Look at you. You dirty thing you.' A sexy smile lights his face. God, I am married to such a hot man!

I spread my thighs further apart and looked at him coyly. 'I am such a dirty thing. Sitting here with my creamy cunt being really dirty all over the table. All dirty and filthy and ready to be fucked.'

'I love it when you talk dirty,' he muttered, and freeing his big beautiful cock plunged into me so hard and deep I cried out and thought how amazing it was that after all these years he still managed to make me scream. How the love had just grown and grown.

From downstairs came the sounds of two children, Parker and Isobel, both little devils, whooping with joy. There were also the sounds of two crazy dogs barking madly, and an exasperated woman shouting at the top of her voice for the little thieves to bring back them muffins right away.

'I really should go down and stop them,' I mumbled distractedly. It's hard to think when such a big cock is deep inside you.

Thank God that dirty aristocrat totally ignored me and didn't stop.

The End

Hello,

Thank you for taking the time to read the Dirty Aristocrat. I hope you enjoyed my take on the stepbrother craze. :)

Next up will be Zane's story. Zane is the Russian Mafia boss from Beautiful Beast.

Until then ... have fun. Lots of fun.

xx *Georgia*

Want To Do An Author a SUPER HUGE favor?

Then, please consider leaving a review. Reviews help other readers find an author's work. No matter how short it may be, it is very *precious*.

Here are your respective links:

US Store: http://www.amazon.com/Dirty-Aristocrat-British-Billionaire-Romance-ebook/dp/B01BF6EVS4

UK Store: http://www.amazon.co.uk/Dirty-Aristocrat-British-Billionaire-Romance-ebook/dp/B01BF6EVS4

Au Store: http://www.amazon.com.au/gp/product/B01BF6EVS4

Ca Store: http://www.amazon.ca/gp/product/B01BF6EVS4

Coming soon...

'YOU DON'T OWN ME'
'Yes, I fucking do!'

Georgia Le Carre

I'll tell you just how much a dollar costs
The price of having a spot in Heaven,
                    -To pimp a butterfly

Chapter One

Dahlia Fury

'**O**h, my God, Dahlia, you have to help me,' Stella, my best friend and roomie cries. She has burst open my bedroom door and is standing at the threshold theatrically wringing her hands.

Stella is a well-known drama queen so I don't panic. I mute my video and turn towards her. 'Calm down and tell me what's wrong.'

'I have a massage client in less than an hour and I've just realized that I've also got another client coming here.'

See what I mean about drama. 'Just cancel one of them,' I suggest reasonably.

'I can't do that. The one who is coming here is that crazy rich bitch from Richmond who told me she is going to recommend me to all her crazy assed rich friends in Richmond. She's probably already on the train. And the other is a Russian Mafia boss.'

I frown. First of all I didn't know she had a Russian mafia boss as one of her client. Must address that one later, but for now. 'So what do you want me to do?'

'Can you stand in for me?'

I shake my head resolutely. 'Nope. Absolutely not. You'll just have to tell the Mafia boss that you can't make it.'

'I can't do that,' she wails. 'One of the clauses in the confidentiality agreement I signed was that I would never miss any of my appointments once I agreed it unless it was a life or death situation.'

'Huh?' I cock an eyebrow. 'He made you sign a confidentiality agreement?'

She makes an exasperated sound. 'Yes.'

'What kind of person puts an unreasonable clause like that into an agreement with their *masseuse*?' I ask, genuinely surprised.

'Dahlia,' she screams in frustration. 'Can you focus, please. I'm running out of time here.'

'It's simple. Go on to the Mafia boss, and I'll tell your other client when she arrives that she can have a free massage next week.'

'No, she can't come next week. She is away, and anyway, she's in pain and really needs me.'

'So tell the Mafia boss that you can't make it because you have a life and death scenario.'

'You want me to lie to Zane?' she asks incredulously.

'If that's what his name is,' I reply coolly.

She comes into the room and starts pacing the small space like a caged animal. 'I'm not going to lie to him. He'll know.' She stops and stares at me. 'He's got like the coldest most piercing eyes you ever saw. It's like they can see right through you.'

I laugh. 'I can't believe you said that.'

'I'm serious, Dahlia. Lying to him is out of the question.'

'Well, then you'll have to let the rich bitch down.'

'Did you not hear me. She's in pain. Oh, please, please, can you help me this time. I'll owe you big time.'

'No,' I say clearly. The solution to her problem seems obvious to me —she should cancel the Russian guy.

'I'll do the dishes for a whole month,' she declares suddenly.

I pause. Hmmm. Then I shake my head.

'I'll do the dishes and clean the apartment for a whole month.'

I hesitate. 'Even the bathroom?'

'Yes, even the bathroom,' she confirms immediately.

'I'd love to help but—'

'Two months,' she says with a determined glint in her eyes.

My eyebrows fly upwards. I open my mouth and she shouts out. 'Three fucking months.'

To say that I am not tempted would be a lie. I HATE cleaning the bathroom. I am very tempted, but I can't actually take her up on her offer even if she offered me a year's worth of bathroom cleaning.

'Jesus, Stella. Just stop. You know I'd love to take you up on your offer, but I simply can't massage like you. I just about know the basics and rich bitch's problem sounds complicated. For all I know, I'll just end up making her back worse and instead of giving you a glowing recommendation to all her rich friends she will do the opposite. '

Stella fixes her hazel eyes on me. 'I wasn't thinking of her.'

I look at her incredulously. 'What?'

'He just needs a simple basic Swedish. Just exactly what I've already taught you. You just need to put a bit more effort into it. He likes it really hard.'

'Like hell, I'm massaging your Mafia boss.'

She falls to her knees. 'Oh please, please, please.'

'If you're trying to make me feel guilty, it's not working,' I say.

She looks at me pleadingly. 'Pleeeeeeease. I promise you he's really easy to do.'

'Oh yeah. Is that why you're so terrified of him?'

She turns her mouth downwards. 'I'm not terrified of him.'

'Could have fooled me.'

She sighs. 'Actually, I'm a bit ... in lust with him,' she confesses with a wry smile.

'A bit? You?' I explode in disbelief. This is Stella, the woman who turns a spider sighting in her bedroom into a shrieking Victorian melodrama.

'Yeah,' she says softly.

'In lust?'

'Yeah.'

I shake my head in wonder. 'Since when?'

'Since,' she shrugs, 'forever. I've always had a thing for him, but of course, he's way out of my league. The women he dates are all like six feet tall and totally perfect. I only register on his radar as a pair of strong hands.'

I stare at her suspiciously. 'Are you just making all this up so I'll go and massage him?'

She shakes her head. 'No.'

'Why haven't you told me about this man crush before?'

She looks down at her right shoe. 'There seemed to be no point. I've come to terms with it. The truth is it is way stronger than a crush, and it could even be love, but there's nothing I can do about it.'

Suddenly I realize why every time we go out she freezes out every man, even the ones that look like serious contenders, who comes up to her. 'Oh, Stella!' I breathe. I had no idea she was suffering in silence.

She looks at me sadly. 'It doesn't matter. It'll pass. But right now I just need your help. I don't want to let him down or give him cause to fire me. Until I'm ready to let go of him I want to keep this job going.'

'But—'

She holds up her hand. 'Don't say it. I know. It's stupid and it's crazy, and I don't know where I'm going with this, but I can't let go. Not yet. One day I'll eventually leave, I know that, but just not quite yet, OK?'

'OK.'

One corner of her mouth lifts. 'So you'll do it?'

Now I am torn between feeling horribly sorry for her and not wanting to be manipulated into massaging her Russian. 'I do want to help, Stella, but I can't. I'm not qualified. I wouldn't know what to do or say to someone like that.'

'You don't even have to talk to him. He never says a word. Just comes in and lies there, and after I've finished, I turn down the lights and leave. He doesn't even lift up his head to say goodbye.'

Ugh, sounds like a horrible man. I have a sinking feeling in my stomach. 'I think this is a really bad idea,' I say, but my voice is weak. Both of us know that she has won.

'Yes, you can. It's a plain massage. Nothing fancy. Just basic moves. You could do it with your eyes closed. All you have to remember is that he likes it hard.'

I stare at her indecisively.

'Remember three months of no cleaning.'

'Stella,' I groan.

'Oh, thank you. Thank you. I promise you'll never regret it. I owe you one.'

I sigh. 'I'm already regretting it.'

'Come on. Let's get you into one of my uniforms.'

We go into her room and I take my T-shirt off and slip into her white uniform. It has a black collar and black buttons all the way down, but because my boobs are so much bigger than hers I cannot button all the way.

'Now what?' I ask.

Her head disappears into her closet. She comes out with a scarf, hooks it around the back of my neck tucks it into the front of her uniform.

I look at myself in the mirror.

'I really don't know about this, Stella,' I say doubtfully.

'Are you kidding? You absolutely look the part.'

'Are you mad. This uniform is too tight.'

'No, no, you look great,' she says quickly and bundles me out of her room. 'Look, you best get going or you'll be late. The car will be here anytime now.' She grabs my handbag from the dining table, presses it into my hands and practically pushes me out of the front door. Holding on to my elbow she rushes me down the corridor. We go into the lift together and as she said, there is a black Mercedes with tinted windows waiting outside. She opens the back door and manhandles me into it.

'See you later,' she calls cheerily as she closes the door with a thick click.

The driver glances at me in the mirror.

'You all right Miss.'

'Yeah, I'm all right?' I say with a sigh. Looks like I'm massaging the man Stella is in love with.'

Hey, I heard you are a wild one, wild one, wild one.

Chapter Two
Dahlia Fury

The Mafia boss's house is in Park Lane. A dour, deeply tanned man in a black suit and a white shirt opens the door and raises his eyebrows. He is wearing an earpiece.

'Stella can't make it. I'm taking her place,' I explain shortly

'We do body searches on people we don't know,' he says, his eyes travelling down my body.

'The fuck you are,' I tell him rudely.

He grins suddenly. 'I like you. You've got balls.'

'Whatever,' I say in a bored voice.

His grin widens. He's got good strong teeth. 'If you've got a weapon hidden in that tight dress you deserve to kill him.'

'It's a uniform,' I say stiffly.

'No kidding,' he leers.

I look at him with raised eyebrows.

'Come with me.'

I step into the mansion, he closes the door, and I follow him into the Mafia Don's residence. What can I say? Wow? Crime really does pay? Yeah, must be nice to have so much. Polished granite, marble columns, fantastic lighting, touches of platinum, sleek black leather trimmings. Nope, not my thing, nevertheless very, very impressive in a cold, masculine sort of way. He takes me up a sprawling staircase to the massage room.

He flicks his wrist, looks at his watch, and says. 'He'll be with you in five minutes.'

Then he winks and disappears. I look around the dimly lit room. Opera music is being piped in through hidden speakers, and it is wonderfully warm. I walk towards the massage table. All the different oils are in a kind of bain-marie on a trolley next to it.

Shit. Suddenly I feel really nervous.

I've never massaged anyone other than Stella and my sister. I take a deep breath. No, I can do this. I will tell my grandchildren about the day I massaged a Russian Mafia boss. I smile to myself. I pick up a bottle of oil. I twist the cap and smell it. Oooo... lavender, musk and something else... Rosemary?

I pour some on my palm and rub my hands together. The smell surrounds me. Very nice. I adjust my clothes. I know exactly why the black suit had been staring at me. The uniform is way too tight. I hear a sound outside the door and quickly put my hands to my sides and look towards it.

The door opens and this huge hunk of a man with a small towel slung around his hips comes in. Whoa! I inhale in slow motion. Jesus! No wonder Stella is all tied up in knots. He excludes pure sexual energy. Let me describe him to you. The first thing that hits me after his height and breath are his incredible tattoos. They cover his body and they are not an untidy collection of random images, but each one subtly connected to the others. To give you an example, an angel smiles at a tiger tearing into an impala, above their heads are intricate images of stars, demons and other strange creatures. On his shoulder a cobra hisses dangerously its mouth and hood open.

The next thing that floors you are his eyes. You know those crazy drawings of Nordic aliens, their ice-blue eyes. That's what his are like. Piercing and magnetic. Shit. I couldn't stop staring. Those crazy eyes slide over me, lingering on my breasts, and then pulling back, and narrowing on my face.

I want to smile, but I am frozen.

'Where is...' he makes a rolling motion with his big, powerful hand. Stella was right, after six months, twice a week, she has not even registered enough for him to even remember her name.

'Stella,' I supply helpfully.

'Where is ... Stella,' he asks quietly. His voice is deep and the accent is strong and actually extremely sexy.

I clear my throat. 'She couldn't make it. I'm here to take her place.'

He nods. 'Ok,' and going to the massage table lies on it face down.

I gaze at the splendid body, the muscles, gleaming in the dim room and think of Stella. God, I'm not surprised she's all in love. I am vaguely aware of a kind of animal attraction. I want to touch him. The sexual desire is so strong, it is as unsettling as a fingernail on a blackboard. It sets my teeth on edge. It's almost like making love. I take a deep breath. Right. Swedish. Make it hard, Stella is saying in my head.

There is a strange feeling inside my belly. I feel hot and excited. A light sheen of sweat starts on my body. I wipe my brow with the back of my forearm. I flex my fingers and move forward.

I pick up the oil that has been warming in the hot water. Jesus, suddenly the smell of oil feels too musky and erotic. I gaze at his sinewy neck and feel the hair at the back of my own rise. He is like an animal, a big cat. Sleek and dangerous. I put musky oil back down and pick up a random bottle.

I pour the warm, lemon scented oil on the plateau at the base of his spine. I watch it pool. Then I take a deep breath and open the massage with a long, slow stroke. He doesn't react. I shift my hands down to the two mounds of the gluteal muscles. They are firm strong and tight ... and bulging insolently.

Make it hard. He likes it hard.

I dig down and get to work, careful not to make the mistakes that amateurs make – work too fast. My breathing rate increases, but the man does nothing. Just lies there silently. I move to the front of him, grab his shoulders and push down his back with my thumbs and finger pads..

Smooth and sensuous.

My hands roll back. It is almost hypnotic to feel my palms sliding down the tatted skin, and feel the muscles underneath move. By now sweat is running down my back. I have been so caught up in the job I do not see his hands move, but they are without warning cupping my buttocks. For a few second I freeze, more in shock than anything else.

The inert body moved!

Then I jump back in horror. 'What the hell do you think you are doing?'

He lifts his head and looks at me with those wicked eyes. 'I figured since you are not a real masseuse you were a hooker.'

'What gave you that crazy impression?' I demand outraged. How dare he?

His eyes slide down to my breasts. I look down and the scarf is dislodged and my breasts are practically spilling out of my uniform. My ears burn as I pull the scarf upwards and clutch it against my chest.

'Well, I'm not a prostitute,' I deny hotly.

His reaction is swift and smooth. He rolls to his side and lands lightly on his feet like a cat or someone with some kind of stealth training. He straightens. Naked and utter unashamed of his body he takes a step towards me. Shocked and a little frightened I take a step back, but the wall pulls me up short. He stops a foot away from me. His palms land on either side of me.

I gaze at him with wide eyes.

'Then why did you massage me like that?' he asks hoarsely,

The breath escapes me in a rush. 'Like what?' I whisper.

'Like you want to taste my cock.'

'I didn't. I don't,' I stutter.

'Then why are you fucking wet?' he asks softly. His eyes drop to my mouth.

'I'm not,' I say clearly.

His hands leave the wall and grab my hips. 'Do you want me to make a liar of out of you?' he asks.

'Don't touch me,' I spit.

He pulls me towards his naked body until his rock hard cock twitches against my belly.

A strange languor overtakes me, and I am suddenly struck by the desire to submit. To let him have his way. To let him fuck me hard. Because I know it will be a hard fuck. Yes, I'd be just a nameless fuck, and yes, there will be the walk of shame afterwards, but I can live with all of that. The thing that stops me is the thought of facing Stella.

'How dare you?' I gasp, outraged.

He laughs, a humorless, cold laugh. 'Is that a challenge or a fucking invitation?'

'It's a fucking warning,' I say furiously.

Ignoring my fury, he runs his fingers along my inner thigh.

I draw in a sharp breath. 'Let go of me or I'll scream.'

His eyes light up. They are like the underside of certain fish, slivery blue. He lets go of my hips. One of his hands comes up to my face. He drags his thumb along my lower lip while I stare up at him, mesmerized by the naked lust in his eyes. The fingers of his other hand arrive at the apex of my thighs.

'Don't,' I whisper.

He brushes his fingers along the crotch of my panties. There is no expression at all in his face when he finds them soaking wet. Without a word he pushes the material aside and inserts a long finger into me.

Holy fuck. My body starts trembling.

'Don't. I don't want you to,' I order, but even I can hear how weak my voice sounds. My brain is already thinking of his thick girth pounding mercilessly into me.

He withdraws the finger and jams it back in. 'Don't?' he taunts.

Blood rushes to my head and pounds so hard I can't even think.

'I ... we ... oh ... ah ... shouldn't.'

He doesn't even bother to answer me. Just keeps up the steady finger fucking. I am so excited I feel as if I already at the point of no return. To my utter shame and humiliation I climax, and really hard too, all over his finger.

He smiles, a condescending, triumphant smile.

And suddenly I feel sick at what I have just allowed him to do to me. Jesus, I have behaved like a cheap slut. I swallow hard. I can't even look him in the eye. How could this have happened to me? He made me

come with one finger! And that digit is still inside me and my muscles are contracting helplessly around his finger.

'Take your finger out of me now,' I say in a cold, hard voice.

'Why? Are you ready for me to replace it with my cock?' he mocks insolently.

I am so inflamed that it seems natural that he should bear the brunt of my fury. My right hand flies up towards his cheek. It never connects. Instead a band of steel curls around my forearm.

'Don't ever do that again. I don't like it,' he says very softly.

I try to wrench my hand out of his grasp, but it like someone has poured concrete around it. His impassive eyes watch my puny struggles almost curiously. Like a child watching an insect it has caught before it pulls its wings off.

I take a deep breath. 'Let me go,' I cry.

He curls his finger and starts stroking my inside walls and I automatically feel my body begin to respond to his manipulation. Oh no. I can't allow him to take total control of my body again. I stare into his eyes.

'Please,' I beg. My voice sounds strange and strangled.

One corner of his mouth lifts. It makes him look at once beautiful and cruel. He pulls his finger out of me and releases my hand. 'Fly away little bird,' he says dismissively.

I feel so ashamed I am almost tearful. No man has even reduced me to a feeling of

such utter lack of worth. To him I am nothing but a sexual object. He thought I was offering myself, and he just helped himself even after I objected. And now he is just getting rid of me. My knees feel like jelly.

I press my lips together and take a sideways step. Some part of my brain tries to make sense of what has just happened. It's OK, you'll never see him again. No one will ever know what happened here today. It's just one of those inexplicable moments that you have never experienced before. A powerful man totally floors an inexperienced idiot!

I straighten my spine. You know what. I can do the walk of shame. So what. I take one step in the direction of the door and another step and then another step. I put my hand on the handle and his voice, like warm honey, pours into my ears.

'Hey, if you ever need help or anything, anything at all, call me.'

I shouldn't have responded. It would have been better, more dignified to walk out of the door without even an acknowledgement that he had spoken. Instead, I whirled around.

'If you think I need more of what you just dished out, you are much mistaken. You can take your arrogant offer and stuff it up your ass.'

'The world is a dangerous place, *rybka*. You don't know when you need a helping hand. It is better to have a friend than an enemy.'

I look at him scornfully. A man like him could never be a friend of mine. He's the exact opposite of me. This man has ice water flowing in his veins. I nearly fainted at a pearl farm when I found exactly how pearls are harvested. (The cut through the flesh of the poor oyster and dig around until they locate the pearl. Ugh.)

'I wouldn't come to you if you were the last fucking man on earth.'

He shrugs. 'One day you will come to me again and you will be eager for what I dish out.'

'You'll die believing that.'

'I made you come harder than you've ever come using just one finger. You'll be back for more,' he says confidently.

I feel heat start climbing up my neck. 'You're a real bastard, aren't you?'

'Like you wouldn't believe.'

I shake my head with disgust. There is no way to win an argument with someone who cannot be made to feel ashamed of their rude and arrogant ways. I open the door and walk out.

Chapter Three

Zane

I watch her leave the room and hear the muffled sound of her footsteps go down the best of Italy's pink marble. I hit the button on the intercom. Noah replies almost instantly.

'Get Corrine to come up,' I tell him, and remove my finger from the button.

I open a drawer and take out a condom. I tear it open and fit it on to my dick. The door opens and Corrine slinks in with a seductive smile. She is blonde with long legs and a great pair of tits. She is wearing a semi transparent white blouse, no bra, an extremely short black skirt and as I have stipulated, no panties.

I don't like wasting time.

I grab her by the wrist and throw her against the wall. She gasps as I rip her top open. Her pink-tipped breasts strain forward. I look at them without any feeling. I am dead inside.

'Suck my nipples, Zane, please' she pleads.

But I'm not in the mood for that. If my mouth gets anywhere near those breast I'll bite hard enough to leave marks. I feel that vicious.

I hold my hand out and she immediately hooks her leg over it giving me an uninterrupted view of her shaved, beautifully swollen and creaming sex. I never got to see the other one's pussy. It is her pussy I want to see open and dripping for me. I won't rest until I have her in this position of utter submission. Until the day I train her to hook her leg onto my hand and beg me to suck her nipples and slam hard into her I won't be satisfied.

I ram my cock directly into Corrine's little hole and she makes a grunting sound. Today the sound irritates me. I place my palm over her mouth and twist her face to the side so that I don't have to look into her eyes, carry on thrusting hard.

The room fills with the wet sound of my flesh slapping hers. I come in record time, so quickly, in fact, that Corrine moans and desperately rubs her unsatisfied sex against me in a submissive, almost animal like begging gesture. I stay still until with my palm covering her mouth and her leg hooked over my hand, she finds her own release.

Immediately, I pull out of her clinging body and turn away, but not before I glimpse into her half-hooded eyes. At the desire and need still shining in them.

'Zane, I—' she whispers.

'Get out,' I say coldly.

I hear the sound of her clothes rustling, a small sulky sniff. It's nearly time to get rid of her. She leaves and I feel like punching the wall.

'Damn you,' I grate. 'Damn you to hell.'

I just **LOVE** hearing from readers so by all means come and say hello here: https://www.facebook.com/georgia.lecarre

9 781910 575260